THE PAYBACK PLAN

AMY ANDREWS

First published in Great Britain in 2025 by Boldwood Books Ltd.

Copyright © Amy Andrews, 2025

Cover Design by Lisa Horton

Cover Images: Lisa Horton

The moral right of Amy Andrews to be identified as the author of this work has been asserted in accordance with the Copyright, Designs and Patents Act 1988.

All rights reserved. No part of this book may be reproduced in any form or by any electronic or mechanical means, including information storage and retrieval systems, without written permission from the author, except for the use of brief quotations in a book review. This book is a work of fiction and, except in the case of historical fact, any resemblance to actual persons, living or dead, is purely coincidental.

Every effort has been made to obtain the necessary permissions with reference to copyright material, both illustrative and quoted. We apologise for any omissions in this respect and will be pleased to make the appropriate acknowledgements in any future edition.

A CIP catalogue record for this book is available from the British Library.

Paperback ISBN 978-1-83617-962-7

Large Print ISBN 978-1-83617-963-4

Hardback ISBN 978-1-83617-961-0

Ebook ISBN 978-1-83617-964-1

Kindle ISBN 978-1-83617-965-8

Audio CD ISBN 978-1-83617-956-6

MP3 CD ISBN 978-1-83617-957-3

Digital audio download ISBN 978-1-83617-958-0

This book is printed on certified sustainable paper. Boldwood Books is dedicated to putting sustainability at the heart of our business. For more information please visit https://www.boldwoodbooks.com/about-us/sustainability/

Boldwood Books Ltd, 23 Bowerdean Street, London, SW6 3TN

www.boldwoodbooks.com

To Pippa, Rachael and Clare. What an adventure this has been! It's not only been the most enormous privilege to work with such incredible authors but also so much fun plotting wicked deeds with you all. Remind me to never get on your bad sides!

IN THE BEGINNING
CHICAGO, O'HARE AIRPORT, 21 DECEMBER

Paige Barker had been pissed off for four years. Getting snowed in at O'Hare with thousands of other disgruntled holiday travellers just before Christmas *and* on her birthday was the cherry on top of a life so derailed she might as well be the Fat Controller.

Happy freaking twenty-fifth.

She glared at the departure boards all stubbornly flashing *delayed* – no shit, Sherlock – and then through the large floor-to-ceiling windows festooned with garlands and red holly berries, to the runways. Or what she could see of them through the biblical-ass storm.

The irony of Dean Martin crooning 'Let It Snow' through the PA system right now almost made her laugh. But she was too damn mad for that. She was stuck here for who knew how long with the roads too hazardous to check into a nearby hotel and no taxis to be had anyway. Also, she wanted to be on site the second the runways opened to make sure she was on the first flight to London.

Or any UK destination really. Hell, she'd take Shetland if it was all she could get. She'd promised her mother she'd be home for Christmas.

And if that meant she had to aimlessly wander the halls for days existing on ridiculously expensive airport food and booze, then she would. And when that all ran out, which she supposed was entirely possible if the storm dragged on, she had three packets of Oreos stashed in her bag and plenty of pounds between her and starvation. She also had panty-liners and toothpaste.

Eat your heart out, Bear Grylls.

What she needed now was a drink. Or John McClane to burst in and kick Snowmaggedon's ass. Given that was unlikely, she'd settle for the drink. Although where in hell she'd find a table when every other person in O'Hare had the same idea, she had no clue.

'Ten per cent off at Just Desserts.'

Paige stopped glowering at the windows to find a stocky woman with pink cheeks, sparkly eyes and fluffy, flyaway magenta hair offering her a flyer. Her voice crackled like an old record but her accent was pure New York.

'Oh no, thank you,' Paige said, her accent becoming painfully British, as she warded off the proffered piece of paper. 'I doubt I'll be able to get a seat anywhere at the moment.'

The woman smiled beatifically. 'You could be lucky.'

Paige snorted. *Luck.* She swore she must have broken a mirror, walked under a ladder *and* crossed the path of a black cat several times in a previous life. 'I doubt it.'

Undeterred, the woman offered the flyer again. 'You never know.'

For reasons she couldn't explain, Paige took it, earning herself another beatific smile. 'It's just around the corner,' she said before turning away and disappearing into the crowds.

Paige glanced at the pretty pink flyer featuring pretty drinks with pretty umbrellas and pretty calorie-dense desserts. At ten in the morning it was way too early to be indulging in either but airports were like casinos – time was amorphous. And her mouth *was* watering.

Cocktails and cakes didn't make up for a lengthy delay or the pervasive inertia that had stalled her life for so long now but they *did* make her feel less stabby. And besides, if she *was* stuck here for days and all the food ran out, she should probably carb load.

* * *

It took Paige five minutes to reach Just Desserts which was as eye-wateringly pink as the leaflet. It was a huge place that spanned the width of the central aisle separating two parallel thoroughfares and had multiple entrances. It was also crowded but, right there, in the centre of the restaurant, was one spare, round table with four chairs.

A waiter was withdrawing after just having wiped it down and it shone under the bright lights like a Taylor Swift arena, beckoning her inside. She half expected to hear a choir of freaking angels.

Huh. Maybe her luck *was* turning.

Scurrying to the table, her eyes never leaving the prize, Paige reached her chair just as another woman skidded in to claim the opposite one, careening – crotch first – into the back.

Maybe *not*.

'Fuckity-fuck!'

Paige blinked as the woman – a fellow Brit – recovered from a landing that would have crippled a man. She was about to ask her if she was okay but was interrupted by a third woman claiming the chair to one side with a puffed little whoop. A fourth, coming in hot from a different direction, laid claim to the last spot at the table.

For a moment none of them said anything as they all eyed the table like a quartet of single bridesmaids might eye a tossed wedding bouquet, but then Paige noticed each woman was clutching a pink leaflet. *Just like her.*

'If none of you are with anyone else,' she said tentatively, 'we could share?'

There was an immediate round of relieved sighs and big smiles as chairs scraped and everyone settled in, hanging coats over chair backs and stashing bags on the floor.

A quick round of introductions was undertaken. Bella, to her right, was a poised American with a sleek blonde updo. Astrid, sitting opposite, was a somewhat less poised brunette with knockout locks which Paige, as a frizzy ginger, wanted to chop off and keep.

In a non-serial killer way.

Sienna, to her left, another American, was a honey-blonde with big blue eyes. Dressed in her usual monochrome palate her curls mostly still contained in a twist at her nape, Paige felt decidedly dowdy.

A waitress appeared at their side asking them if they were ready to order a drink. They all glanced around tentatively for long beats. 'Would you think me a terrible lush if I got a glass of prosecco?' Paige finally asked.

It shouldn't matter what three random strangers at an airport thought of her but the fact they'd all found the one free table in the entire café, possibly the entire concourse, and were all in possession of the same leaflet, made their meeting feel somehow more ordained.

'Oh God no,' Sienna said on a relieved sigh. 'I hate flying and waiting around in airports even more. Let's get a bottle. I'll help you.'

'I'll have a glass,' Bella told the waitress. 'And some water for the table, please.'

Astrid glanced at the wall of clocks mounted above the bar, each displaying times from different capital cities around the world. 'It's five o'clock in Berlin.' She smiled at the waitress. 'Make it four.'

And suddenly Paige didn't feel stabby at all.

* * *

Two hours, two bottles of prosecco, two cocktails and two desserts (each) later, the four of them had settled in, riding the buzz. People came and went around them but they chatted easily in the way of people who have known each other for a long time – not two hours. Nothing particularly personal. Just about where they were from and their jobs and their holiday plans. They talked about the best way to cook a turkey and the most exciting place they'd travelled and checked out each other's socials.

'I can't believe you have your own VA business,' Astrid mused as she scrolled Paige's business account on Instagram. 'That's awesome.'

Paige shrugged, being a virtual assistant wasn't what she'd planned for her life and it wasn't making her rich but it paid the bills. 'Thanks.'

'So, you don't have an office or anything?'

'Nope.' Paige shook her head. 'I actually house-sit for people so I move around a lot and the nature of my business means I can work from wherever I am. Have laptop, will travel.' She tapped her bag where the item in question was stashed, injecting a note of cheer she didn't feel about her nomadic lifestyle, which was more about living within her means and avoiding permanence and roots than choice.

'Is it why you're in the US? Work?'

'No. I was at a wedding in Chicago.'

'Oh, how lovely.' Sienna smiled softly, her voice a little dreamy. 'How was it?'

'You know. Pavlova dress. Drunken best man's speech. Smooshing cake into each other's faces. A handsy Uncle Chip.'

Bella downed the remainder of her glass before scraping up the last crumbs of her two slices of red velvet cake, which she'd pronounced to be the best cake in the history of cake. 'I'd rather not talk about weddings.'

Paige raised an eyebrow. 'Not a fan?'

'Absolutely not.'

'Don't believe in love?'

'I did. And then six months ago I stood up in front of 400 guests to let them know that my groom wasn't coming.'

Their combined gasp was enough to turn heads at nearby tables. 'Holy mother of...' Astrid spluttered as she clutched Bella's forearm. 'You were jilted?'

'Yup. By text. The morning of.'

'By *text*?' Astrid's mouth flattened. 'What kind of scumbag does that?'

Sienna, no longer dreamy and clearly affronted on Bella's behalf, demanded, 'Who is he? Tell me. I'll bring you his head.'

Everyone laughed but actually it felt very much like alcohol, carbs, a blizzard and that strange anonymity of a major international airport had heightened their fast friendship to this ride-or-die zenith. Sienna certainly seemed as if she was ready to go all crazy ex-girlfriend on Bella's wayward ex-fiancé.

'He's not a bad person really, he just did a bad thing. He's coasted through life with everything handed to him on a silver platter. He was a bit of a... Peter Pan. Commitment wasn't his strong suit and I made the classic mistake of thinking that it would be different with me. That I could change him.'

'Doesn't excuse him leaving you standing at the altar,' Sienna said much more gently, despite the murder in her eyes.

'Via *text*,' Astrid repeated, clearly still outraged.

'No, it doesn't. That was truly a low act.'

Sienna nodded. 'Yes, it was.'

'Well,' Astrid announced, 'you can string mine up.'

'Were you jilted as well?' Sienna's big blue eyes blazed white-hot indignation.

'No.' Astrid gulped down her fizz, her green eyes sparking. 'Unbeknownst to me, he'd already trotted up that aisle and merrily said "I do" to someone else.'

'So...' Bella's eyes widened. 'He turned you into the other woman?'

'Too right he did. Made me feel like a piece of shit.'

Sienna shook her head, her full, pink lips flattening into a line of sheer outrage. 'Are you freaking kidding me? He was already married?'

Astrid confirmed with a nod of her head. 'He's an artist too. All about creating the feels in people... Chase Miller can give you *the feels* alright. The kind you want F all to do with. Believe me.'

'Chase Miller?' Bella blinked, surprise in her voice as if she knew the name. And then, as if that piece of info had pushed her last button, she demanded, 'What is wrong with these men? Doesn't marriage mean anything any more?'

'I don't think men get the concept of commitment,' Sienna mused. 'Even the ones who seem to get it are just faking it.' The observation earned an enquiring look from all three. 'Sorry.' She laughed brittlely. 'That's a little dramatic, isn't it?'

Bella leaned closer. 'What happened?' she prompted, her tone solicitous, encouraging.

'My ex kind of just... discarded me. It wasn't like some big, dramatic break up. I didn't even get the chance to throw plates.' She waved a hand in the air, as if to dismiss it all but sadness cloaked her words. 'I mean, we were just kids but we were each other's firsts, you know? And I thought we were going to have a life together but he hightailed it out of town without a backward glance. Like nothing we had mattered.'

Bella reached across to squeeze Sienna's hand. 'I'm so sorry. That's terrible.'

'Sucks ass,' Astrid concurred into her glass.

After a few moments of silent enraged solidarity passed between them all, Sienna raised an eyebrow at Paige. 'Can I bring you anyone's head?'

Paige gave a half laugh and prepared to deflect but then surprised herself by how much she suddenly *wanted* to tell these women she barely knew her big ugly thing. Maybe they were misting the air in O'Hare with Valium to keep everyone calm or maybe it was precisely because they *were* strangers it made the telling easier.

'I broke up with my ex, Harvey, after a brief, intense relationship and then he... posted naked pictures and videos of me online. He'd taken them without my knowledge or consent.'

If the gasp for Bella had been loud, this gasp swivelled every head in the café. 'Revenge porn?' Sienna hissed in disgust.

Paige nodded. It was as shocking now as it had been back then, sucker punching her all over again. 'I've never felt so *degraded*.' Her gaze dropped to the table; she still found it difficult to meet people's eyes when thinking about those images.

'I met him at Oxford. He was studying IT and I was a third-year law student. It completely ruined my future career prospects. No prestigious law firm was going to take me on after that. Hell, not even a terrible law firm would. And I couldn't bear staying on at Oxford, where everyone had seen the pictures. So I...' She shrugged as she raised her eyes. 'Dropped out.'

'What a bastard,' Bella stated, stumbling slightly over the curse as if she didn't use it that often.

'Absolute *bastard*,' Sienna agreed with no stumbling, her lips a furious line. 'What's he doing now, do you know?'

'He's some kind of tech bro. Travels between London and Silicon Valley.'

Sienna rolled her eyes. 'Of course he is.'

For a moment everyone was quiet as they studied the clutter of glassware on the table. Paige wasn't sure if the others were considering their combined catastrophically awful taste in men, but she certainly was.

'They shouldn't be allowed to get away with it,' Sienna said eventually.

Astrid slapped her glass down, prosecco sloshing. 'Damn right they shouldn't.'

Sienna glanced around the circle and leaned in a little. Everyone followed suit. 'What if we... Look I know this sounds crazy and I may be a little drunk.' As if to underscore this, she hiccupped which caused a round of laughter before she got back on track. 'What if we... took it upon ourselves to exact some... revenge?'

Bella frowned. 'How do you mean?'

'I don't mean murdering them or anything.' She waved a dismissive hand. 'I mean... look, these guys have had everything go their way, right? They got to walk all over us. Or walk out on us,' she added with a grimace. 'Why should they just get to live their best lives while we're picking up the remnants of ours?'

'Yes.' Astrid's eyes were as effervescent as the fizz. 'I like where this is heading.'

'Why not have a little fun at their expense?' Sienna continued.

'What kind of fun?' Bella asked warily.

'Nothing serious,' Sienna assured. 'Stuff that would inconvenience them. That we could have a laugh over. Like...' She paused as if searching for a precise kind of punishment. 'Signing them up to hundreds of mailing lists. Or putting a dead fish in their wheel hubs. Buy them a cow and have it delivered. Switch out their clothes for a size or two smaller. Change all the names in their phone contacts to Dr Seuss. That kind of thing.'

Three sets of eyes blinked at Sienna. 'Wow,' Paige murmured, impressed. 'Remind me to never get on your bad side.'

Bella leaned in closer. 'Some of those things would require us to get close,' she said, almost at a whisper. 'They'll know it was us. There's no way we'd get away with it.'

Sienna smiled triumphantly. 'That's why we pick someone else's ex.'

The circle went quiet as they contemplated the idea and then Astrid murmured, 'It's an excellent plan. So good, I wish I'd thought of it.'

'Me too,' Bella admitted. 'Very Machiavellian.'

Paige was rather taken by the idea, as well. She knew she should just be drawing a line underneath the Harvey chapter in her life but screw that. Four years later she was still just treading water, stuck in a life she hadn't planned on, too scared to take any kind of risk.

And why should he get off scot-free?

'Okay.' She nodded cautiously, her law studies making her a little leery. 'Maybe.'

'Who would you pick?' Astrid asked Sienna.

Sienna snorted. 'Harvey the horrible. If he spends time regularly in the US I'm sure I'll be able to figure out something. You?'

Astrid didn't hesitate. 'I'd take your heartbreaker. Any guy who'd just walk out on a sweetheart like you deserves to be played a little.'

'And I'd take your cheating, married, *bastard* ex,' Bella declared, apparently finally comfortable with the word. 'Which leaves you with Olly.' She honed in on Paige. 'And that's perfect because he slunk back to England after the wedding. To his dad's place in Cornwall. How's your sitting schedule for the new year?'

'I have a few things lined up in Jan/Feb that aren't set in stone. I have a month-long gig in Edinburgh starting March.'

So she *could* go to Cornwall. Despite the inherent inadvisability of hatching a revenge plan with strangers while snowed in and tipsy at an international airport, Paige had the inklings of a plan.

'Is the place big enough for two?' she asked. Obviously the closer the proximity the easier it would be to mess with Olly.

'Yes!' Bella confirmed. 'It's very spacious and right on the beach.'

Now that sounded ideal. After all this freaking snow, sand appealed. Even if it did always manage to get into places not even a board-certified gynaecologist could access.

'How would he feel about a guest?'

A slow smile lit Bella's face. 'He's does like his privacy.'

'I know exactly how he feels,' Paige murmured.

Which was a sobering thought. Was this really a good decision to be making high on pink drinks and even pinker desserts?

Her boozy angels were screaming yes, her wiser angels were being more circumspect.

They could be a real freaking drag.

'I don't know...' Paige glanced around the group. 'Are we really going to do this? Maybe it's just the alcohol talking?'

'Good point,' Bella agreed, chewing on her bottom lip.

'Well, I sure as hell am,' Astrid confirmed. 'I don't know about you, but I'll sleep a little better knowing Horrible Harvey is getting his comeuppance.'

Yeah, Paige would, too.

'Look, this only works if we all agree,' Sienna said, suddenly serious. 'And nobody should feel pressured into doing it if it doesn't sit right.'

Bella placed her glass on the table. 'Definitely.'

'God, fuck yes.' Astrid appeared to gear down her enthusiasm. 'The last thing I want to do is browbeat my new co-conspirators. Sorry... *besties*.'

They all laughed but the idea was becoming more attractive. What was the harm in creating a little mischief for these men? For too long, too many men had been allowed to get away with stuff. Maybe they *owed* womankind a little cosmic rebalancing?

'I do love a cream tea,' Paige admitted. *And* a pasty. She glanced at Bella. 'I'd be safe there?'

'Definitely,' Bella hastened to assure. 'For all his commitment-phobe tendencies, he's a true gentleman. Painfully polite in that very English way. And I know he feels terribly guilty about the jilting. Which I'm perfectly okay exploiting to get you in there. I still have his number.'

'Oh yes,' Astrid enthused. 'That's a great plan. You could text him now.' She glanced at the clocks on the wall. 'It's six in the evening over there.'

An introduction would certainly help. And yet Paige still felt a little unsure.

'Look. How about this?' suggested Sienna who was clearly in tune with Paige's hesitancy. 'What if Bella texts and then we leave it up to the universe?'

Astrid frowned. 'The universe?'

'Yes, you know, fate. *Kismet*. If he texts back while we're all still sitting here at this table we randomly ended up at, then it's a go. If he doesn't? We've all had a laugh and filled in a few hours. No harm no foul.'

'Ooh.' Astrid nodded vigorously. 'I like that.'

'Me too,' Bella agreed.

So did Paige. 'Okay... yeah.' She nodded definitively. 'Okay.'

With everyone agreed, Bella took out her phone. 'Olly,' she read off as her fingers flew across the screen. 'A friend of mine needs a place to stay in Cornwall for a bit in the New Year.' Her fingers stopped as she considered her next words. 'She's very nice and won't bother you. You have room and you owe me.' Hitting send, she placed the phone on the table. 'Done.'

The die was now well and truly cast.

For the first time since their meeting, everyone was absolutely still as they stared at the device as if it was the Charlie's Angels' speakerphone. When an incoming text chimed almost immediately, they all startled.

Bella opened the text and read aloud, 'Is she a Roger Prendergast groupie?'

Paige frowned. 'The actor? That died a little while ago?'

'Yep.' Bella nodded. 'Roger was his dad.'

'Oh.' Roger Prendergast was a famed Shakespearian actor who had made the move from stage to screen seamlessly and won at least one Oscar that she could recall. She supposed she should be impressed and maybe she was, a little. But famous or not, it didn't change the fact his son was an asshole 'No. My movie tastes run more along the lines of campy superhero than Hamlet.'

Bella laughed but sent the reply. The response was lightning fast again and Paige watched as Bella's eyes moved across the screen. 'He says fine.'

Fine. *Just like that.* She was going to Cornwall to live in the house of a famous dead British actor to mess up his son's charmed life. She certainly hadn't had that on her bingo card for next year.

But, the universe had spoken.

Paige looked around the table at the expectant women. She hadn't trusted anyone in four years and yet she felt more connected to these women, these *spurned* women, than she'd felt to anyone in a very long time.

'Okay then.' She nodded. 'Looks like I'm off to Cornwall.'

Sienna whooped and held up four fingers to a passing waiter who promptly delivered four bubbling glasses of prosecco. The PA was playing 'Last Christmas' as they lifted their glasses in a toast. 'To just desserts,' Astrid declared and they tapped glasses.

'Now,' Paige said, 'tell me more about this Olly.'

1

John McClane had just dropped Hans Gruber off the side of the Nakatomi Plaza when the knock interrupted. Oliver Prendergast frowned and paused the action, Alan Rickman's face frozen in shock, his mouth open, his hands grasping nothing but air.

The interruption was seriously inconvenient.

He didn't care that he'd seen the movie approximately thirty times, that scene never got old. The next scenes provided the emotional pay off as John reunited with his wife but that right there was the Hollywood moment.

When the bad guy got his just desserts. And it was epic.

He assumed the knock was Bella's friend – Paige someone – who was supposed to be here *hours* ago. Thanks to parents who'd made an art out of late entrances, he abhorred tardiness at the best of times. But when it got in the way of watching Hans Gruber going *splat,* it really rankled.

As he climbed the stairs from the basement media room, Oliver couldn't shake the looming feeling of disaster he had about the whole set-up. Agreeing to let a stranger – one who clearly didn't value punctuality – into his house for an undefined period of time felt unwise. But, Bella had been right. He did owe her and, in the grand scheme of things she could have asked (and he would have granted), it was trifling.

Such was the depth of his guilt.

Hell, she could have asked him to never watch Hans Gruber go splat again. *That* would have been a real sacrifice.

The low moaning of the wind outside got louder as he approached the front door. Cornwall in summer was a thing of beauty. Cornwall in January, not so much. Rain, strong winds and chilly temperatures had been forecast for the next week.

He hoped she hadn't brought her bikini.

Unlocking the expensively sophisticated deadbolt locking system, Oliver yanked open the door to a face completely covered by a mop of curly red hair, a stack of mismatched suitcases, a skirt that looked like it had been made out of curtains, a thin-looking, unbuttoned hot pink cardigan that hung down past her knees and an ugly lime green T-shirt proclaiming:

I will put you in the boot and help people look for you. Don't test me.

He blinked as she shook her head, her wind-swept hair falling back to reveal what Peter Allen would have called an interesting face. Square with wideset hazel eyes, a little snub nose, a generous smattering of freckles, and despite her general dishevelment, a big smile showcasing an even more generous mouth.

Oliver hadn't known what to expect when he'd woken on yet another aimless Monday, but it wasn't this.

It was as if the north wind had dumped her on his doorstep like some kind of ginger Mary Poppins. Minus the hat, the coat, the umbrella and the carpet bag.

And, given her taste in T-shirts, any sense of decorum.

There was however, he noticed belatedly, a large cage

clutched in one hand. A cage containing what appeared to be some kind of... rat? A very *large* rat.

Bella hadn't said anything about a bloody rat.

'Hiya,' she said, smiling brightly, her accent bog standard, middle-class English. 'I'm Paige. You must be Oliver.'

'Ah, yeah...' Looking over her shoulder at the wet, deserted street, he asked, 'How'd you get here?'

'Uber?'

So, not the north wind then...

His gaze drifted to the words written across her chest. She also looked down before raising her eyes, their gazes meeting. 'Sorry, my brother and sister think it's hilarious to get me silly T-shirts.'

Oliver nodded like he understood but really, he didn't. 'Couldn't you just...' He shrugged. 'Not wear them?'

Frowning, she examined him like he was slightly dim. 'After they went to all the trouble to get them for me?'

Oliver was pretty sure zero trouble had gone into that particular purchase but he let it go. What did he know about sibling relationships? He was an only child.

'T-shirts are their love language,' she added defensively. Like that explained everything.

It didn't.

Oliver wasn't sure he *had* a love language, but if he did, it'd be more like classy monogrammed stationery than tacky T-shirts.

Good Christ. He gave himself a mental shake. He sounded like an eighty-eight-year-old Brexiteer lamenting the good old days not a twenty-eight-year-old foot-loose-and-fancy-free bachelor with a massive inheritance, oodles of charm, good looks and excellent contacts.

When had he become such a fucking *curmudgeon*?

'Could I...' She looked over his shoulder. 'Come in? It's freezing out here.'

Of course she was freezing. All that stood between her and the brutal January squall was a useless cardigan and a statement of murderous intent.

A little voice whispered, *Curmudgeon*, and Oliver suppressed a sigh.

'Of course... sorry.' He stood aside. 'Come in.' And then, ever the gentleman, he said, 'I'll bring your bags in.'

As he stepped outside, the biting wind caught his dirty blond hair and tossed it around. The ominous grey sky was already darkening as day began its descent into night, the lights illuminating St Nicholas's chapel on the headland already glowing. He stared at the three battered, ancient cases in dismay.

Just how long *was* she staying?

Dragging them in, he deposited each one next to the freestanding hat rack which his father had taken from some film set or other. The door banged shut after him as he set down the last bag.

She smiled as he straightened, the cage now on the floor at her feet. Her *leopard print, fur-trimmed, welly-clad* feet. 'Thanks.'

Oliver nodded and there was a moment's awkward silence as he took in his new house mate. His eyes shifted momentarily to the rodent – house *mates*.

They were both a sight, red hair and caramel fur tousled in such disarray it looked very much as if they'd been electrocuted. Catching sight of himself in the hallway mirror, Oliver grimaced at the state of his own hair. They all looked as if they'd been in a freak accident involving a three-for-the-price-of-one lightning strike.

He pointed. 'What is that?'

She followed the direction of his finger. 'A hamster.'

That was a hamster? 'I see...' Did it have a gland problem?

'He belongs to my nephew, Bunky.'

'Bunky?' It sounded like a nickname given to a posh kid by other posh kids at an even posher public school. And Oliver ought to know, his father had been an Etonian and all his *old chums* had incredibly infantile nicknames like Corky, Tuppy, Stiffy and Dumps.

'Short for Bunkleigh. It's a weird family name on my sister-in-law's side,' she said with a dismissive shake of her head. 'Anyway, Bunky loves him to death. Like *literally*. He's forever sneaking him treats. Caramel popcorn, Skittles, Peperami sticks. Dib Dabs.'

'Hamsters eat sherbet?'

'This one does. Devours the stuff. Thank God he doesn't know how to snort it. Can you imagine that sugar high?'

Oliver thought the question was rhetorical but her sudden raised eyebrow made it plain she was waiting for a response. 'Ah... no.'

Although now he'd probably think of nothing else.

'Anyway, the vet said that if Flower wasn't put on a diet, he'd die. To be fair, he was always on the chunkier side but well...' She glanced at the creature with affection. 'Things are getting critical.'

Yeah. Critical *mass*. But that wasn't really what Oliver was stuck on. 'Your nephew called his hamster *Flower*?'

'Yes.'

'Really?'

'What? You think he should call him something more manly? You think he should have called him Rambo? Or... Godzilla?'

Oliver flicked his gaze to the animal, his wind-frizzed fur not helping with his beefy silhouette. *Pavarotti* seemed more appropriate. 'It seems a little...' Delicate. 'Fanciful.'

She bugged her eyes at him. 'He's *four*.'

Checking the impulse to enquire about Bunky's vision, Oliver prepared to demur but she was off again.

'Anyway. I told my brother that I would take him with me and put him on a diet. Get him into shape. I even bought him a little wheel.'

They both looked at the object in question. It sat deathly still in one corner, brand spanking sparkly new, Flower situated as far away from it as was possible.

'It's the most expensive one on the market. It hooks up to an app to let you know how many revolutions per day have been logged and there's coloured LED lights embedded around the rim of the wheel that glow when it moves. It was the only way I could bribe Bunky into parting with him for a while. Let me tell you, that kid knows how to negotiate. But...' She shrugged. 'Favourite aunty status is not to be squandered.'

Oliver had to admit, it was the London Eye of hamster wheels.

'I hope you don't mind. He won't be a bother, quiet as a mouse. And I'll look after all his needs.' She lifted her gaze to lock with his. 'Bella said you wouldn't mind?'

And there was the magic word. The kicker.

Bella.

He still couldn't think of her or the way he'd acted without cringing. The guilt he felt over backing out of the wedding – *on the day of* – still ate at him. So much so that he'd holed himself away in Cornwall like some fucking recluse, ever since.

The media interest over Redondo's runaway groom had been no less intense in the UK but, six months had passed and the paps had lost interest. Mostly. He still occasionally felt the preternatural prickle at his nape alerting him to the presence of a telephoto lens but they'd stopped bashing on his door and going through his bins.

'Of course not,' Oliver responded, far more positively than he felt. 'Let me show you around.'

He gestured to her to lead the way and, leaving the cage behind, she headed in the indicated direction. Her wellies squeaked – of course they did – against the blonde birch floorboards as he followed her into the triple glazed quiet of the house. A light, Scandi-inspired open-plan living, kitchen and dining space unfolded in an understated elegance only achieved by a high-end interior decorator.

A bowl of shiny green apples on the dining table was the only pop of colour amidst all the white on white. Apart from the ocean, of course. A span of bifold glass doors dominated the far end, opening onto a deck and an absolutely spectacular view of the pounding surf.

'Oh wow,' she murmured on a breathy exhale as she squeaked to the doors and stared out transfixed.

Oliver couldn't blame her; there was something elemental about the sight of a wild, stormy sea. He'd lived on Redondo Beach in California since he'd been fifteen and that was breathtaking in a sunny, sparkly, Pacific kind of way. But, given his disposition these past months, the moody, changeable Atlantic was more his style.

Of course, that could just be his guilty conscience.

He was struck, as he watched her watch the ocean, by how colourful she was amid all the blinding Scandi pallor. Like some exotic bird silhouetted against the glass. Red hair, pink cardi, lime-green T-shirt. A splash of rainbow amidst the greyscale.

A bright orange lifebuoy floating atop the swirling background sea.

Jesus... Oliver rubbed the back of his neck. Pull yourself together, *knob head*. Now was not the time for a flight of fancy or to channel sodding Shakespeare.

'Help yourself to whatever's in the fridge or the cupboards,' he said, clearing his throat. 'It's a bit bare considering there's usually just me but I get a delivery from St Ives every week to restock. Let me know if there's anything in particular you need.'

'Oh, did Bella mention?' She turned from the window. 'I'm vegan. And gluten intolerant.'

Well, of course she was...

Not that it phased him. Nearly the entire population of LA were gluten intolerant and about 50 per cent of his friends were vegan.

'It's okay,' she assured. 'I'll go into town tomorrow and grab some things.'

Oliver nodded. 'The bedrooms are on the second floor.' He gestured to the stairs. 'If you want to follow me?'

He led the way, the carpeted stairs providing sweet relief from the incessant squeak of her shoes. 'That's your bedroom there,' he said when they'd reached the next floor, pointing to the right, down the thirty feet of hallway that separated the two rooms on this level. 'No sea view, I'm afraid.'

'I'm sure it's lovely,' she demurred. She glanced at the door to his bedroom. 'Yours? Or are you' – she tipped her chin at the staircase ascending another level – 'up there?'

Oliver shook his head. 'That was my dad's room.'

All the bedrooms were luxuriously appointed with their own bathrooms but the one at top was the pick of the bunch. It took up the entire floor, the windows taking in the grand arc of Porthmeor Beach from the artisan cafés and restaurants of St Ives at the south end to St Nicholas's chapel on the headland to the north, a 180-degree view of ocean in between.

It was criminal that it was being unused. But Oliver couldn't bring himself to go there. His father's clothes still hung in the closet. His towel still hung on the towel rack. His cufflinks still lay on the night stand. And his aftershave still scented the air.

'I was sorry to hear about his passing.'

Her commiserations were gentle but walloped him nonetheless. Since his father's death two years ago, condolences had long dried up. It seemed the rest of the world had moved on — why hadn't he?

Oliver hoped his tight smile wasn't as pained as it felt. 'Thank you.' He gestured back down the stairs. 'There's a media room in the basement.'

He didn't wait around to see if she was interested in a tour of that as well, he just hit the stairs and led the way down. He was conscious she was following though, a dazzling kaleidoscope of colour in his peripheral vision confirming her presence a few steps behind.

Hans Gruber's face was still frozen on the screen when they entered. The TV took up half the wall and below it, flush with the plaster, a long, sleek, artificial fireplace aglow with the dance of orange LED flames kept the room toasty warm.

Outside it was Vladivostok. Inside it was Margaritaville.

In warmer climes, the doors situated behind a dark, remote-controlled blind, opened straight onto the beach but Oliver hadn't opened them since the beginning of November.

The room was expensively furnished with three couches — one triple, two singles — grouped in front of the fireplace. Large, black bookshelves containing an impressive library of CDs, lined the walls either side. On top of the shelves sat his father's awards, subtle ceiling downlights positioned to illuminate them just so.

Five Oliviers, four BAFTAs, three Golden Globes, two Tonys, one Oscar. And a partridge in a pear tree.

'Aren't you a month too late for *Die Hard*?'

Oliver dragged his gaze from the intimidating ranks of his father's success. 'What?'

'It's a Christmas movie,' she said, once again regarding him like he wasn't the sharpest tool in the shed. 'And you're watching it in January.'

Oh hell no. She was one of *them*. 'Just because a movie happens to be set during Christmas does not make it a Christmas movie.'

For a moment he thought he saw her lips twitch before they pulled into an irritated little moue. 'It's set on Christmas Eve. There's a Christmas party going on. There's a massive Christmas tree right there in the foyer of Nakatomi Plaza. It has Christmas music. His wife is called *Holly*!'

'Right. Which merely makes it... Christmas adjacent.' Seriously, he shouldn't need to explain this. 'A classic Christmas movie has to have a certain vibe.'

She frowned. 'Like what?'

'Warmth, joy, hopefulness. *Jesus*. Peace, love, goodwill to all men. A Christmas message.'

'I think "*Don't mess with John McClane on Christmas Eve*" is a pretty clear message.'

'Exactly. The levels of action and violence absolutely rule it out of the Christmas movie canon.'

She shot him an incredulous look. 'Have you never watched *Home Alone*?'

Oliver grimaced. She'd been in his home for ten minutes and he was already regretting it. He certainly didn't want to have this argument with someone who didn't appreciate the nuance of cinematic mores. 'It looks like we're going to have to agree to disagree.'

'Okay.' She shrugged and Oliver almost sighed out loud that she'd dropped it so easily. 'I'll tell you what else it is, though. It's a romance.'

Had Oliver been consuming some kind of food or drink right now, he'd have probably choked to death. *No. Nope. Abso-fucking-lutely no way.* 'Um, no. It's an *action* film.'

She sighed with an exaggerated kind of patience he imagined she used when catching Bunky feeding Flower rodent crack. 'It's a romance.'

'He blows up the Nakatomi Plaza.'

'Yeah, but he's not doing it for shits and giggles, is he?'

'No, he's doing it because he's a cop. To get the baddies. It's instinct. And he's that kind of guy.'

Another sigh. 'Yes, you're right, he is that kind of guy. But he's not doing it for law enforcement or to save all those bearer bonds or for the Nakatomi organisation. He's doing it for her. For his *wife*. The stakes would be nowhere near as high for him if it was just random people. He's doing it for the woman he loves.' She crossed her arms as if resting her case. 'Romance.'

Until a few minutes ago, Oliver would have disagreed vehemently that the film could be classified as a romance and he was still of that opinion. But Paige had definitely made him look at it from a different angle.

And, on top of everything else, that was seriously fucking maddening.

'Let me guess,' she said, 'this is your favourite scene?'

'It is actually,' Oliver confirmed, annoyed at the defensiveness in his tone. 'I take it it's not yours?'

'No, it's mine too. Ever since Alan Rickman gave that office tart a necklace at Christmas and broke Emma Thompson's heart, anyway.'

She smiled at him then like she hadn't just conflated a character's deserved comeuppance in one film with their actions in another. From fifteen years later.

Who even did that?

'Would you mind if I went and settled in? I've got some unpacking to do and some work to catch up on and I shouldn't leave Flower too long in unfamiliar surroundings.'

Oliver shook his head. Frankly he needed a stiff drink and a good lie down.

'Thanks so much for this, Oliver.' She crossed to him then and, without a second's hesitation, wrapped her arms around him in a quick, hard hug. 'I promise, you won't even know I'm here,' she said as she pulled out of his stiff embrace and headed for the stairs, a living, breathing rainbow.

Somehow, Oliver entirely doubted it.

* * *

The next morning, Oliver stirred slowly through the layers of sleep. Something was warm and heavy on his chest and there were four little pin pricks of pain. His hand lifted to soothe them at the same time his lashes fluttered open to find two little black eyes, a twitching nose and a wild mop of fur staring right at him.

'Jesus Christ!' he hissed, startling himself out of bed.

Belatedly, he remembered from his midnight googling session that hamsters were exceptionally sensitive to being startled. Like, they could literally just drop dead from a sudden fright. Thankfully the displaced hamster staring up at him *calm-as-you-please*, appeared to be made of sterner stuff.

The same could not be said for Oliver. He pressed his hand

to his thundering heart. 'Bloody hell, Pavarotti.' He refused to call the animal, *Flower*. 'I could have had a heart attack.'

The hamster seemed unconcerned by the news and irritation bloomed as the digital numbers on his bedside clock told him it had only just gone six. The darkened room seemed to concur. *Not* a morning person, Oliver hadn't seen 6 a.m. in a very long time.

He frowned at the rodent currently sniffing his pillow. How did the little fucker not only manage to escape his cage but get in here? He'd shut the door, hadn't he? Glancing across, he could see it stood slightly ajar. Enough space for a small animal to squeeze through.

Although quite how Pavarotti had managed it, he had no idea.

Well... this wouldn't do. If he had to suffer a rodent-related animal in his house, it was through the bars of a cage only!

Without giving it much thought or even stopping to put on a shirt, he scooped the animal up, yanked the door fully open and stormed down the hallway in his boxers. He did knock but he didn't give her time to answer, barging in, determined to lay down some rules.

'Your damn hamster was in my bed,' he accused.

It was less dark in her room, her blinds not all the way down, giving him a very good view as she sat, one hand pushing her mop of hair off her face, the other clutching the sheet to her chest revealing bare shoulders.

Oh Jesus. Was she naked under there?

'What?' she asked, blinking at him blearily, her voice sleep husky.

She had freckles on her shoulders he absently noticed. And down her bare arms. It made him wonder where else she might have them.

Christ alive. Stop thinking about her freckles, *you fucking perv*.

'The hamster.' Oliver dropped the animal who landed with a soft thud onto the cloud-like layers of the feather duvet, arms and legs akimbo like some kind of coiffed flying squirrel. 'It got out of its cage.'

'I'm so sorry.' She sat forward a little, reaching for the animal, which made things shift very nicely beneath the sheet. 'He is a bit of an escape artist. I should have mentioned.'

Oliver suppressed the urge to say, *Ya think*? as she brought the fluff ball to her chest, rubbing her face against the manic spring of fur covering his head. It looked soft and pillowy where he was nestled and Pavarotti shut his eyes, clearly in a state of bliss.

And damn if Oliver wasn't insanely jealous of a hamster.

Annoyed at just about everything right now, he grouched, 'Don't let it happen again,' before turning quickly on his heel and getting the hell out of Dodge.

* * *

JUST DESSERTS WHATSAPP GROUP. 06.15 GMT.

PAIGE

> OMG lovelies! I've not even been here for 24 hours and it's working out better than I could ever have planned.

Realising it was after midnight in the US and she was unlikely to get an answer just yet, Paige went to put the phone down but three little dots appeared.

ASTRID

> Tell us everyyyyyything!!!!

Ah, okay, Astrid was up.

PAIGE
> That Die Hard info from Bella was golden! I thought he was going to have apoplexy when I told him it was a romance.

Bella's name appeared on the screen with three little dots. She was up, too?

BELLA
> So pleased you could use it.

PAIGE
> That's not even the cherry on top.

Dots next to Sienna's name also now joined the party.

SIENNA
> Okay, all the pinging woke me. What? Whaaaaat????

PAIGE
> Sorry, crappy timing, I didn't think. Too excited not to share. I let the hamster loose in his bedroom last night and it crawled into bed with him. He's just stormed into my room, grumpy AF.

BELLA
> Oh I'd have loved to be a fly on the wall for that!

ASTRID
> What's the agenda for today?

PAIGE

Operation kitchen chaos. Seriously, I could take somebody's appendix out in there! I mean, don't get me wrong, I like order as well but this is next level. I wouldn't be surprised if just standing in it makes a person sterile. It has to go...

BELLA

He'll hate that. I love it! 🤍

ASTRID

Ha! You've so got this 😏 💪 💣

SIENNA

Bwahhahahahahahaha 😼😼

2

Two hours later, Paige had made herself at home in the kitchen and was cooking up a storm. As best she could, anyway, considering Oliver's pantry was as sparse as the interior design. Old Mother Hubbard had definitely had more in her cupboard! But she loved to *make art with food* as her father called her rather freewheeling culinary style and with Instagram folders full of recipes and the entire purpose of the exercise to make as much mess as possible, she was improvising her ass off.

Today's T-shirt loudly announced *culinary ninja* and Paige was working that vibe.

She'd scraped together enough ingredients to make a rudimentary flourless chocolate cake which turned into cupcakes because there wasn't a normal cake pan to be had. They were currently in the oven and the Rice Krispie slice which she'd added melted mini marshmallows to – because they were apparently deemed necessary pantry items but flour was not? – was setting in the fridge.

A bowl with some beaten eggs, sugar and cinnamon stood at

the ready to transform slices of frozen white bread into delicious French toast as soon as Oliver decided to get his ass out of bed.

The debris from her endeavours littered every white marbled surface from the sink to the oven and on to the breakfast bar. Bowls, cups, saucepans and trays of varying sizes competed for space with used cutlery and discarded utensils. Plastic wrappers and ingredients she hadn't yet put away vied for space with various spills she hadn't bothered to clean.

A splodge of milk, a streak of egg yolk, a couple of big old coffee rings. A light dusting of gourmet cocoa powder on both bench and floor joined a scattering of Rice Krispies. For that satisfying crunch underfoot.

Had it been her parents' or anyone else's home she'd have been mortified to have plunged their kitchen into such a state but it wasn't and the mess in front of her just represented a job well done. Quickly, she snapped a pic of the detritus and admired the utter chaos of it all as she flicked it to the group with a before snap she'd taken prior.

JUST DESSERTS WHATSAPP GROUP. 08.30 GMT.

PAIGE

Now that's more like it 👿

Considering it was the middle of the night in the US, Paige wasn't expecting any replies just yet so she slipped the phone into the back of her charity flares that were so intensely fluorescent yellow they should have come with a pair of those solar eclipse sunglasses.

'I reckon it's time we kicked this up a notch, don't you, Flower?'

Surveying the scene from his cage placed in front of the massive window on the kitchen bench, the hamster didn't seem to have an opinion. In fact, he seemed much more interested in the view on the other side, not that Paige could blame him. The dark green thrash of the ocean and the heavy blanket of storm clouds hanging above were ominously immersive. It must surely seem like some kind of climate change documentary playing out on an IMAX screen from Flower's point of view. The animal may have been large but it was utterly dwarfed by the roiling seascape.

Paige's phone pinged a notification and she pulled it out of her pocket to discover that at least one of her new friends was still awake.

BELLA
OMG! Has he seen it yet?

PAIGE
No. Think he must still be sleeping.

BELLA
Yeah... he's so not an early riser.

PAIGE
Well, do I have a surprise for him 😉

BELLA
lol, what??

PAIGE
I feel a musical awakening coming on!

BELLA
Yes! Do it!!

PAIGE
Celine Dion or rock?

BELLA
Rock!

Paige needed no further encouragement as she Bluetoothed

her Spotify account to her portable mini speaker and tapped on a playlist. There was nothing like the dulcet tones of AC/DC in the morning to get up and at 'em.

She grinned to herself as 'Highway to Hell' belted out and she increased the volume loud enough possibly to be *heard* in hell. To that she added the harsh motorised clatter of the high-end electric mixer which looked in pristine condition, like it had never been used.

Which was so very sad.

To rectify that, Paige had spied some local gourmet cream cheese in the fridge which she was currently combining with a seriously amazing artisan chocolate stash she'd found to elevate the basic cupcakes into a mouthwatering divinity. Sadly, there were no sprinkles to add to the top of the final product because hello, *sprinkles*. Clearly, they weren't posh enough for the likes of Oliver Prendergast.

It took about two minutes to rouse the sleeping beast.

'What in God's name,' he shouted above the mayhem, 'is happening right now?'

Paige, who was singing into the spatula as she'd strutted and shimmied in front of the window/IMAX screen, startled. 'Bloody hell.' Paige, also shouting, whipped around, clutching her chest. 'You scared the living daylights out of me.'

'Consider us even.' He pointed at the speaker. 'Can you turn that racket off?'

Now she was recovering from the initial shock, Paige absently noticed he was still in his boxers from earlier when he'd stormed into her room looking as inconveniently hot as he did now. He had a T-shirt on this time though, one that looked old and soft and faded like he'd worn it a thousand times and she wondered how it might feel against her cheek as he cuddled her, warm from his skin and infused with laundry detergent and his deodorant.

The thought made her blink. *What the hell?*

She knew Oliver Prendergast was a good-looking guy, she'd googled him a lot since that day at the airport and, being a minor celebrity, there were plenty of online images to pore over. But, this very *weird* thought hadn't come about from his physical attributes and nor had she thought about a man in such warm, snuggly terms for a long time.

Harvey had seen to that.

He'd ruined her ability to let down her guard – to trust – and with that, any chance of feeling attraction. To Paige, the two had always been inextricably entwined.

Ignoring his ruffled, yanked-from-his-bed-by-the-roots-of-his-hair appearance and his piercing blue eyes that were apparently what Roger Prendergast had been known for according to her *research*, Paige quickly killed both the speaker and the beaters. The sudden cessation of noise was almost preternatural against the stormy backdrop.

'I'm pretty sure you just insulted the musical tastes of several million Australians,' she murmured, fixing a smile to cover her consternation. 'Considering they learn how to wrestle snakes and crocodiles before they can walk, it makes you a braver person than I am.'

He seemed unperturbed by her observation as he winced in her direction. 'Christ.' He squinted as he took in her retinal frying flares. 'Those pants should come with a public health warning. You could have someone's eye out with those.'

Paige supposed she should be insulted but it was hard to be pissed off at a guy who had a blanket crease on his face. And she'd bought them hoping for a reaction, right? Because no way would she normally wear anything this outlandish. Ever since Harvey had violated her privacy and shared those intimate, non-consensual images of her, she'd done everything she could to *blend in*.

But if her deliberately curated wardrobe was causing Oliver some discomfort then good. *Maybe you shouldn't have jilted a perfectly nice woman at the aisle, you psychopath!*

Giving a little twirl, she beamed with every ounce of enthusiasm she could muster. 'Aren't they great?'

He looked genuinely puzzled by the question as his gaze drifted north to her T-shirt then further north to her hair which she hadn't bothered to brush. By the look on his face she figured it was the usual bonkers morning flurry of ginger curls. When his gaze returned to hers, he gestured in her direction.

'You have a... smudge of cocoa on your cheek.'

Given the level of abandon she'd used when making the cupcakes, Paige was hardly surprised but she feigned it anyway. Rubbing both cheeks with her palms, she dusted her hand down the side seams of her pants. 'Better?'

As if the word *better* was far too euphemistic to describe her appearance, Oliver's gaze shifted to the war zone that was the kitchen. His wince intensified as he surveyed his formerly pristine space.

Excellent.

'What the hell?' he spluttered as he glanced at Paige, his face a picture as he clearly tried to control the rising horror. 'What on *earth* are you making?'

'Snacks.'

He blinked at her in disbelief as if something that embodied an entire kitchen's worth of mess could be boiled down to one tiny word. 'For an army?'

'Ha!' She grinned. 'Funny. Just a little something for us for during the week.'

'Snacks,' he repeated, as though computing the word had caused his mainframe to glitch.

And what a mainframe it was...

'Yes. Snacks.' Crossing to the oven, she opened the door to inspect the progress of the cupcakes. Another few minutes ought to do it. 'You know those things you consume in between established meal times to get you through and give you joy? Or do you only consume Rice Krispies, green apples – which are, by the way, the boring-est apples to ever apple – and Waitrose frozen meals for one?'

Yeah, she'd snooped in his freezer.

'They're tart,' he said defensively. 'And locally sourced.'

Paige would probably have found his defence of green apples – of which she was also fond despite their inherent boringness – endearing at another time but Oliver Prendergast didn't get brownie points from her just because his shirt looked soft and snuggly and he bought British.

'And anyway,' he continued, distracted by his continued perusal of the messy benchtops, as if glaring at them would cower them into some kind of self-cleaning mode. 'Food is just fuel for the body.'

Oh, dear lord. He was one of *them*. What in the hell had Bella red-velvet-cake-is-life seen in this guy? Yes, he was a hot, posh Brit and there was no doubt he and Bella made a striking couple but he acted like he was eighty years old living from one bowel motion to the next. She was amazed there'd been no Fybogel in his pantry.

'Well, that's very sad.'

'I like food.' His brows knitted together in a serious V as he dragged his attention from the kitchen havoc. 'Just not... obsessively.'

Spoken like someone who'd never had to think about a

single thing he put in his mouth unlike someone with hips and thighs and ass that so generously made a home for extra calories in case they ever found themselves in a series of *Survivor*.

'Hmm, okay. I bet I can change your mind about that. How about we start with some French toast?'

'Oh.' He shook his head. 'I usually just have…'

'Rice Krispies?' Paige cocked an eyebrow. 'Yeah, they're all gone. The milk's pretty low too. I'll buy some more when I hit the supermarket later. Take a seat, it won't take me a jiffy to cook up a batch.'

Clearly caught between his manners and the mayhem, Oliver hesitated slightly before giving into the chaos. 'You want some juice?'

He turned to the fridge and Paige watched him as he noticed she'd done a little redecoration. 'What the…?'

Paige pressed her lips together to stop the laughter rising in her throat from spilling out. Oliver was staring at her handiwork aghast. A magnetised *Get Shit Done* pad was the least horrifying thing attached to the previously pristine surface. Four crayon drawings belonging to her niece and Bunky's older sister by three years – Lulu – sat pride of place attached by fridge magnets.

Lulu was as cute as her name implied but slightly obsessed with witches from fairy tales. The drawings were very good, if a little *dramatic*. Thankfully her parents – Paige's brother Wilf and his wife Marissa – were unfazed by their daughter's artistic expression and gave her carte blanche to explore her talents.

Although Wilf did often joke that one day Lulu would come into her higher power and then they'd both be frogs.

'I hope you don't mind,' Paige said on a little laugh as Oliver turned startled, questioning eyes on her. 'Lulu – that's my niece, she's the artist – did them for me for Christmas and made me promise I'd take them with me.'

Given Paige was also a little leery of being turned into a frog one day, she had no qualms about currying favour with Lulu.

'And I didn't know,' she continued, 'if you'd have any fridge magnets so I brought some of my own.'

Oliver glanced at the magnets as if seeing them for the first time which was fair enough – the art was scarily dominant.

They were a collection of the gaudiest, tackiest fridge magnets she could find at the charity shop. One from Blackpool featuring the pier circa 1970s, a Lady Di button magnet from the eighties, an Alton Towers Christmas offering from the nineties and, the pièce de résistance, a retro Arsenal fridge magnet from the noughties that she'd sourced online because Bella had described in great detail how very, *very* much Oliver Prendergast despised Arsenal.

He stiffened the second he saw it, his jaw clenching, and Paige suppressed a grin as he adjusted the drawings so he could pluck it off the fridge. Turning to her, he shook his head. 'Absolutely *no* way. This stays here over my dead body.'

The clench of his jaw told her he was seeing red. Arsenal red, no doubt.

Paige lifted an eyebrow. 'You're not a Gunners fan?' She couldn't give a fig about football but this reaction had definitely been worth it.

'Man U all the way.'

'So... I shouldn't wear my jersey around the house?'

His eyes dropped to her chest and he grimaced at the culinary ninja proclamation. 'I'd rather read a thousand stupid T-shirts.'

'Oh goody.' She brightened. 'I have plenty.'

Clearly not deeming *that* worthy of a response, Oliver

opened the fridge and Paige turned back to the kitchen to get started on the breakfast. Without being asked, he set the table and, after clearing some space near the coffee maker, made them both a cup as Paige heated the pan and dipped the bread.

When the bread hit the pan with a sizzle, Oliver opened the sliding door to the deck and stepped out, possibly to toss the magnet into the sea. He shut it behind him but not before it allowed a gust of wind to swirl into the room. It ruffled plastic wrapping, blew cocoa dust into the air, tousled Paige's curls and split Flower's mad blond bangs right down the middle so he looked like a Machiavellian orchestra conductor.

By the time he stepped back inside with another flurry of wind, the French toast was cooked and Paige was placing their plates on the table. She moved the setting so they were sitting next to each other instead of opposite. Mostly because she figured it would irritate the crap out of him but also, why would anyone want to sit with their back to that view?

He frowned at the change but seemed less steamed than when he'd headed out and took the seat next to her without a complaint. 'Looks good,' he said, clearly surprised as he eyed the thin slices of apple she'd pan-fried and caramelised with a bit of sugar and added to the top of their toast along with a dollop of whipped cream cheese.

What could she say, she was quite partial to a tart green apple too…

Weirdly, Paige felt a tiny little glow flare to life in the centre of her chest at the compliment no matter how grudgingly it had been delivered. Unfortunately, it didn't last long.

As she opened her mouth to take her first bite, her mouth already watering from the waft of sugar and cinnamon, Oliver said, 'Wait.' He shot her a querying look. 'Aren't you a vegan? And gluten intolerant.'

Paige paused, her forkful of delicious poised midway between the plate and her mouth. Well... *shit*. She'd pulled that out of her ass at the last moment to try and irk Oliver. She hadn't thought about the fact that she was going to have to live with that little deception.

For the next couple of months.

When Paige had run her drip torture ideas for Oliver past Bella she'd concurred that two months of daily inconveniences would be more than sufficient. Paige's payback plan was all about death by a thousand paper cuts rather than one big climatic event. Unlike Sienna, for example, who was cooking up something way more epic for Harvey.

Which suited her just fine. That son of a bitch deserved everything he had coming. She didn't feel one ounce of guilt over it. Fuck. Harvey.

'Um yes.' She placed her loaded fork on her plate. 'But it's kind of a new thing. A new year's resolution so I'm still getting used to it. But I... get out of bed and I try every day.'

Oh Jesus, what bullshit Pollyanna crap had just escaped her mouth? But she plastered a smile on her face, picked up a fork and shoved the food in.

'And the gluten intolerance?' he asked sardonically. 'That new too?'

She smiled weakly around her mouthful, her tastebuds alive with the joys of sugar and fruit and gluten-laden carbs. 'Oh no. But it's mild so I can get away with the occasional slip up. I'll grab some gluten-free bread and other ingredients when I do a shop later.'

Thankfully Oliver let the topic drop in favour of eating and his little hum of appreciation after his first mouthful was satisfying in ways Paige had forgotten. She'd loved cooking for Harvey. Had felt immense satisfaction when he'd complimented her on whatever dish she'd made and complained good-naturedly that she was trying to make him fat.

The guy beside her was far less effusive but somehow even the slightest sound of appreciation from Mr Food-Is-Just-Fuel felt more genuine than dozens of moments of what now felt like performative praise.

Harvey had played her but good.

'How long have you and Bella known each other?' Oliver asked as he finished his last mouthful. 'I don't recall her ever mentioning a Paige?'

Stalling for time, Paige picked up their plates and delivered them to the kitchen, piling them into the sink that was already full of dirty dishes. 'Not long.'

But how long was acceptable to have known someone before a person felt comfortable enough to invite them to their bastard ex-fiancé's house?

'A week or two after the *not* wedding,' she added, her gaze trained on his. He blanched a little at her directness.

Yeah, you might have put that behind you, Oliver freaking Prendergast, but actions have consequences.

'Ah.'

Yes. *Ah*. To give him his due, he didn't shy away from her gaze. In fact, for a moment, Paige thought he was contemplating explaining or maybe even justifying what had led him to do something so horrifically damaging to a woman he had purported to love, but then he appeared to change his mind.

He stood, breaking eye contact. 'What are your plans for the day?'

'I want to go into St Ives and check it out,' Paige said as she fussed about decluttering the sink. 'I'll grab some groceries from the shop too so if you want anything just write in on the pad on the fridge.'

Oliver glanced at said pad and grimaced. It was clearly an affront to his minimalist tendencies but hey, at least the offensive Arsenal merch was no more.

'I already have Rice Krispies on my mental list,' she added with a smile. 'And Hobnobs because I cannot live without them and then I'll come back here and get stuck into some work. Do you mind if I set up my laptop at the dining table?'

Paige had never had such a picturesque work view and had to admit that while committing acts of karma wasn't her usual jam, the amazing vista before her would help soothe her conscience.

'Not at all,' he confirmed. 'What do you do?'

'I'm a VA.'

'Virtual assistant?'

'Yes.' Paige nodded. A lot of people had never heard the term but she supposed he'd grown up in a world where personal assistants were common. 'I've been running my own business for almost four years.'

A quick scan of his kitchen and a once-over of her very un-put-together appearance led to two raised eyebrows which left Paige in no doubt that Oliver had probably expected her to say she ran a clown-hire business.

'There's a lot of call for that, then?'

'I have several dozen clients on my list, yes.'

Oliver's eyes widened this time. 'Really?'

'Uh huh. Some only have occasional needs, others are more active but I have plenty to keep me busy and solvent.'

Of course, busy and solvent were hardly #girlpower goals. She'd certainly had loftier ones when she'd been accepted into Oxford to study law. But it was better than the deep dark pit of despair she'd found herself in after Harvey's betrayal.

'How'd you get into that?'

It was on the tip of Paige's tongue to say, *Because another bastard man whose ego couldn't handle rejection decided to wake up one day and ruin my life.* But she didn't. She just shrugged. 'I did a job for one of my father's clients a few years back when I was… in between things and it kind of snowballed from there.'

Paige had never expected the online collating of old electronic files to blossom into a business but before she knew it word had spread and she'd been juggling a dozen clients.

'Does it have a name?'

Unsure that she actually wanted to tell him, Paige hesitated. The name was polarising. Some people thought it was funny, others thought it wasn't *serious* enough. Not that Paige gave a rat's ass what anyone thought, least of all the son of a dead British actor who'd never, according to what she'd read, done a hard day's work in his entire life.

People's judgement was just so damn tiresome.

She plastered a smile on her face. 'What A Peach.'

Much to her surprise, Oliver just nodded as if he approved. 'Is there some kind of story behind it?'

'My first client called my dad and said what a peach I was and it just kinda stuck.'

'Fair enough. And what sort of things do you do for a client? I mean, you can't get them a coffee or anything right?'

'Nope, but pretty much anything I can do remotely, I do. It's what I love about it actually. The variety. Some clients just want some basic diary management, others want audio transcripts turned to text and don't trust tech to do it for them. I help some clients with social media or run their newsletter campaigns. I've done market research or background information for a variety of different people from company CEOs to doctoral students to a couple of small publishing houses. Turns out I'm exceptionally good at organising.'

He glanced at the disorganised mess of the kitchen but didn't say anything other than, 'Sounds interesting.'

'It is.'

Despite the reason behind the business existing, Paige was proud of what she'd created. What A Peach had been her silver lining in a very dark time and, bonus – the virtual world had allowed her to be anonymous after such humiliating exposure. Her logo and social media avatar was a peach emoji which she'd hidden behind ever since its inception.

But, thinking about the business genesis always raked over the not-quite-extinguished coals of her past life which was never easy and she was done talking about it as she delved under the sink for some washing up liquid.

'Why don't you head into town now?' he suggested. 'I'll do the kitchen.'

Paige hadn't expected that. Given the unholy mess she'd created, she'd expected to be on clean-up duties on her own. Was he afraid her cleaning skills were nowhere near as impressive as her ability to make an unholy mess? Or had her mentioning the wedding guilted him into it? If so she'd be sure to use it to her advantage over the next two months.

'Oh, are you sure?' She stopped short of batting her eyelashes as she said, 'I did make the mess...'

'Absolutely.' He made a shooing motion. 'You can take my car if you want. It's only a ten-minute walk but it's easier when you have bags to carry and more rain is forecast.'

Taken aback by his offer, she said, 'Oh... thanks.' Oliver kept surprising her and she hadn't even been here twenty-four hours yet.

Bella had said he wasn't a bad person but Paige's internal narrative had billed him as an entitled twat because that made it easier for her to carry out this little scheme. The fact he'd been nothing but polite and accommodating, despite being supremely irritated, was exceptionally irksome.

'Ten minutes is a long time to be dripping wet.'

Belatedly, Paige realised the connotations of what she'd said and so had he if that lip twitch was any indication. She hoped like crazy he didn't think she was *flirting* with him.

Because she was here to wreak havoc not make goo-goo eyes with Bella's exceptionally hot, bastard ex-fiancé.

3

It was good to get out of the house. The way Oliver's mouth had twitched at her verbal faux pas was still playing over in her mind. Actually, the way she'd felt to see those lips twitch was still playing in her mind. The fact she could make him smile made her feel warm inside and that was twice today. Two times too many for someone who had felt cold and numb inside for what felt like forever.

So, some distance was a good idea and having to travel it in Oliver's latest model Mini Cooper S in British racing green was no hardship. It was a sleek piece of machinery, perfect for a movie star's son. Perfect for Oliver. Too many men, in her opinion, liked to drive around in grunt cars to prove their masculinity.

Horrible Harvey being a classic example.

Give her a man who was secure enough in his own masculinity to drive a small, iconic, quintessentially British motor any day.

Paige was excited to get into town so she could get the lay of the land and investigate what was available locally to make Oliver's life as temporarily uncomfortable as she could. Thankfully, she discovered something almost immediately as she spied a battered-looking violin in an even more battered case for sale in an antique shop window. Smiling gleefully, Paige bought the instrument without blinking at the hundred-quid price tag.

She'd played violin for several years when she was a kid, eventually giving it up due to the clash in all her extracurricular activities. So, it'd been a while and might take her a while to get good again but, that wasn't the plan.

She knew from the pained expressions on her parents' faces when she'd first started out, that novice violin playing was a particular kind of hell. Her father's right eye had always developed a very specific twitch any time he'd had to sit through yet another painful rendition of 'Twinkle Twinkle Little Star'.

And it didn't matter that by the time Paige had given up she could play the violin with a depth and clarity that could make her father weep, it still hadn't stopped the family jokes about those dreadful *strangled cat years* as her sister had coined them.

So, death by strangled cat it would be.

With that purchase under her belt, she set out to find her next, buying a cheap burner phone and a dozen SIM cards before finding a café on the sea front to escape the chill. It had a large outdoor area that Paige could only imagine would be crowded on a summer day but that was *not* today. There were very few people out on the streets and only one on the beach rugged up in a puffer jacket, beanie and scarf to ward off the cold and wind.

'I'll have a pot of English Breakfast,' Paige asked the woman behind the counter who introduced herself as Jiya, the owner.

The broad Cornish accent was not what Paige had expected, which would teach her for making assumptions. Jiya might look South Asian but within a minute of her acquaintance, she'd proudly boasted about her family's three-generation – about to be four with the arrival of her first grandchild in a few months – history in the West Country.

Paige took a seat by the big plate glass window and got to work immediately. She'd already trawled the internet for harmless pranks and had settled on playing a bot. She slid a SIM into the burner and sent her first text to Oliver, whose number Bella had shared.

> Thank you for subscribing to HAMSTER FACTS! We'll be sending you regular updates about hamsters from around the world. To STOP, reply with STOP. Standard messaging rates may apply.

Paige smiled to herself as she sat the phone down then shifted it out of the way as Jiya delivered her steaming pot of tea. The phone vibrated on the table and Paige picked it up.

> STOP.

Grinning now, she consulted her list of facts she'd collated.

> Thank you for continuing HAMSTER FACTS! Did you know that all hamsters belong to the family Cricetidae? To OPT OUT of these messages reply OPT OUT! Standard messaging rates may apply.

She hit send and set the phone aside as she poured herself a cup of tea. The phone vibrated against the table almost immediately and Paige grinned. She didn't bother to look at it or reply just yet – it was important not to overplay her hand.

Taking a sip of her tea, she turned her attention back to the front to discover a skinny-looking dog sitting on the pavement outside the window looking at her with big brown eyes. It was some kind of Border Collie maybe, with brown and white colouring instead of black and white. Its nose was white with brown patches over his eyes that looked like a mask.

Well, they *would* have been brown back in the dog's heyday but now they were liberally streaked with grey. It looked at her longingly and Paige wondered who he or she belonged to. It was freezing out there and the dog appeared cold and miserable.

She looked across to ask Jiya if she knew the dog but she must have disappeared into the kitchen and, when Paige turned back to the window, the dog was gone. Sitting forward, Paige craned her neck in both directions to see if she could see the animal but it had vanished.

Maybe he'd been out for a walk with his owner and they'd called?

Pulling out the Get Shit Done list she'd torn from the fridge, Paige did some research on the Marks and Spencer site trawling for gluten free/vegan items and jotted down some things she could grab and cross-referenced them with her Instagram recipe folder.

This was her usual MO. She was neat and ordered and *got shit done* in a very neat and orderly way. She didn't create mess and chaos. She fitted in, she flew under the radar.

But she had to admit that playing the flibbertigibbet was fun.

Picking up the phone, Paige looked at Oliver's reply.

OPT OUT!!!

She laughed out loud this time. Whoever thought tone couldn't be conveyed through text was wrong.

Wondering how far she could push him before he blocked her ass, she was interrupted mid-thought by the bell over the door dinging and a group of about a dozen women entered chattering away. There were older, sporting varying shades of grey hair – from hip grandma to light purple – and were all in active wear and joggers, some even holding hand weights.

Collectively, they checked their smart watches and compared stats. Had they all been out for a walk together? If so, go them. The only place on a shitty day like today as far as Paige was concerned was inside with something warm to drink.

Tea. Or whisky.

One of the women wandered over to the window, standing the other side of Paige's table to look over at the view as she unzipped her puffer vest. 'I never get tired of this sight,' she murmured as she stared at the vista.

As there was no one else around, Paige assumed she was talking to her. Or possibly herself. Who knew? 'It's very special,' Paige acknowledged. 'Do you live in the area?'

'Oh yes.' The older woman turned sparkling eyes on Paige. 'For the past sixty years.'

Her accent wasn't West Country so she wasn't a Cornish native. 'How wonderful.'

And it was. Paige wasn't trying to be facetious. As someone who'd been relatively rootless for the past four years, staying in one place appealed to her in ways she'd only just realised she'd been ignoring.

'You're not from around here?'

'No.'

'Tourist?'

'Not really. I'm staying with a... friend of a friend. I'm here til March.'

'January's not the best time to come to Cornwall.'

Paige laughed as she looked out over the shifting menace of the Atlantic and the low skittering grey cloud. 'No.'

'Still, you get to know the real Cornwall in off season. When the town's not flooded with tourists.'

'Dorry, you want your usual?' someone called from the counter and the woman replied, 'Yes please,' before returning her attention to the window.

'You in some kind of walking club?'

'That's right. Every Tuesday without fail.'

'Even on days like this?'

'We're the local WI. Our mothers and grandmothers were WI. They kept this country fed through two world wars. WI women aren't scared of a bit of weather.'

Paige didn't think it had been Dorry's – Doris's? – intention to make her feel so very millennial, but she had. She looked over at the group of nattering, happy women. Even from across the café their spirits seemed indomitable.

None of them would have driven the ten minutes into town. None of them would have been cowed by a bastard ex. They'd have probably hatched a plan to do away with him and bury his body where nobody would ever find him. But then they hadn't had phones with cameras back in the day.

Or PornHub.

'Always come here for a coffee afterwards. In winter anyway. Gotta support local especially when the tourists leave and Jiya gives us a discount. In summer we usually go to Sheila's for a nice cool Pimm's.'

Paige laughed. Oh, to be an age where indulging in a morning drinking sesh didn't require a snowed-in airport. 'Do you have other regular meetings?'

'Oh yes, duck. We meet on the first Thursday morning of the month except January. We usually do some kind of craft or cooking or a fundraising activity. Sometimes we have guest speakers like next month. We've got Geraldine's' – she tipped her head in the direction of a woman with frizzy poodle curls and giant hoop earrings – 'great-niece, Pippa, who used to work for ITV in London in production. She's done all kinds of behind-the-scenes stuff for so many television shows including' – she lowered her voice to a hushed, reverent tone – '*Coronation Street*. She even wrote a couple of the episodes!'

Partial to a bit of *Corrie* herself, Paige was impressed. 'She sounds interesting.'

'Indeed.' Dorry nodded briskly. 'We always try to have some relevant kind of theme and as the BAFTAs are two days after the meeting we thought she'd be a good fit.'

'Perfect I'd say.'

'If you're at a loose end, you should come along. You don't have to be a member to attend and all are welcome. Plus' – she dropped her voice again – 'Myrtle over there makes the best scones you're ever likely to eat. Worth it for that alone.'

Paige got the impression that *Dorry* was a WI recruiting wet dream. Always on. Always ready to push her product like any good drug dealer. Or Scientologist. 'Thanks.'

Paige smiled. 'I'll think about it.'

'Doris.' A woman with steel-grey hair and an even steelier spine if her almost military erectness was any indication, shot an impatient look in their direction. 'Leave the poor girl alone and come pay Jiya for your damn order.'

Dorry rolled her eyes. 'That's Elizabeth, our dear leader,' she said in a low amused voice, clearly not cowed by the command. 'Better go before she has an apoplexy. But it would be lovely to see you at the next meeting. Just drop in. We meet at St Agnes's church hall at 10 a.m.'

Paige got the impression it was an order, not a suggestion.

And there was no doubt in her mind that this bunch of spritely women could hunt her down and kick her ass. After all, they *were* the daughters and granddaughters of women who had fed the country.

She turned to go just as Paige was struck by an idea. 'Are men welcome?'

'Of course. Eighty-five per cent of us are widows.' Dorrie winked. 'A man is always appreciated.'

And then she was gone, leaving Paige to tuck that morsel of information away as she pondered the possibilities.

* * *

Oliver wasn't upstairs when Paige got home but the kitchen was once again pristine. Even the cupcakes she'd taken out of the oven and left on a cooling rack amid all the debris had been set on a wooden cutting board and draped with a clean tea towel. The bowl with the frosting had been covered in cling film and placed in the fridge.

Paige smiled. Mr Neat Freak was making her job far too easy.

After unpacking the groceries into the pantry and fridge with zero care and attention, Paige tackled the frosting of the cupcakes. She generously slathered on the chocolate cream cheese, eating the first one as she finished the others. There were crumbs everywhere when she was done. She didn't bother with cleaning them up and left the rack, the frosting bowl and the utensils in the sink unwashed.

Wandering over to Flower's cage, she noticed his water dish had been filled and she smiled again. Plucking the rodent out of the cage, she cuddled him close to her chest and stroked him.

'Methinks he secretly likes you, Flower,' she whispered.

Flower had no opinion so she kissed his furry little head, placed him back in the cage and decided it was time to work.

Real work. That paid the bills. Not this karma stuff that she was doing to redress the cosmic imbalance. And was, thus far proving to be super fun.

As she mounted the stairs to her bedroom, she heard what she assumed was the television coming from the media room below. Was that what he did all day? Just sat on his ass and watched the idiot box?

Oh, how the other half lived!

Retrieving her laptop and work bag, Paige returned to set up at the table. Not on one end which she'd normally do, so as not to disrupt Oliver's life too much given he was so generously sharing his home. Nope. Right in the middle to be as much of an inconvenience as possible.

With that in mind, Paige spread out as much as possible. Plonking the violin case on the table, she placed folders with relevant client files on either side of the laptop. Yes, most of her records were electronic but she kept meticulous print copies of everything as well. Just in case she was ever hacked or something else equally calamitous.

She also placed several different notebooks on the table along with a colourful array of Post-it notes – which she could not live without. The last thing on the table was her pencil case containing pens of infinite colour. She'd got into the habit of using a different coloured pen for each client and consequently had quite the collection.

Stupidly it made her happy looking at them. Like she could see the success of her business just by peering into the pencil case.

She'd also snaffled another cupcake which she planned to eat as messily as possible.

Paige worked for a couple of hours, methodically answering emails then running through her daily to-do list before she tackled the proofing of some audio file transcriptions from one of her oldest clients who worked in pharmaceuticals. They'd recently switched to AI for the actual transcription but with a lot of technical medical jargon her client preferred to have an extra set of human eyes to double-check everything was correct.

It was much slower going than usual because the view was exceptionally distracting. There was something soothing and... elemental about the ocean. Even on a grey day with the wind whipping occasional flurries of raindrops against the glass, knowing that the great expanse of water had been around since the very beginning of time was incredibly reassuring.

Life changed but some things didn't.

One day things could be fine, the next they could be tits up. But some things were constant. Like the ocean. The horizon. Paige had been keeping her head down for so long, she'd forgotten to look up. To fix her gaze on a point in the distance and steady herself. Like now, staring at that moody flat line in the distance.

She was still working as the grey leeched from the sky and the view slowly dissolved into the night. The room dimmed around her, the only light coming from her screen and bathing her face. Due to her ear pods, she didn't hear Oliver approaching but a strange prickle at her nape alerted her a second before the fancy light above the table flooded her in a pool of warm yellow.

'You'll go blind in that light,' he said as he strode into the kitchen.

Paige pulled out her ear pods, watching him as he grimaced at the crumbs and the dirty dishes in the sink. 'Thanks.' She smiled at him. 'I lost track of time. The view is very distracting. You're lucky.'

Pausing at the sink, he also stared out over the ocean that was barely visible now. The horizon had long since vanished into sea mist. 'Yes. I am.'

But it sounded kinda bitter and Paige had to stop herself from rolling her eyes. How awful to be forced to live in Daddy's Cornish beach-side cottage while his ex-fiancé is picking up the pieces of her broken heart.

Cry me a river, dude.

Switching his attention to the hamster cage, he stared at the rodent. 'I don't think Pavarotti has used that wheel once.'

Paige was pretty sure he hadn't either. In fact, if he'd moved more than the length of the cage, she'd be surprised. 'I think he's intimated by it at the moment. Give him time.'

Oliver put his elbows on the bench, peering at the hamster, his expression clearly indicating that he didn't think Flower had time to just fanny around getting used to it.

'Maybe he needs a little push?'

For somebody who had clearly not been impressed with having a rodent in his house, Oliver seemed unusually invested in his health.

'Maybe.'

He glanced at her. 'Do you mind if I...?'

'Sure.' Paige waved her hand. 'Have at it.'

Permission granted, Oliver addressed the rodent as he reached into his cage to give the wheel a push. The strip lighting around the outside flashed as the wheel turned. 'See,' Oliver crooned. 'It's fun, my guy. You're going to love it.' And he pushed again for good measure.

Paige's irritation at his poor little rich boy act vanished as Oliver coaxed and cajoled, his voice low and friendly. As he picked up Bunky's pet and placed him onto the wheel, Paige reached for the burner phone in her bag. Suppressing a grin, she shot him another text.

> Here is your latest from HAMSTER FACTS! Did you know European hamsters are critically endangered? Press 1 if you'd like to know what you can do to prevent this unfolding tragedy of extinction. Standard messaging rates may apply.

Without taking his eyes off Flower, Oliver reached into his back pocket and pulled out his phone. Paige had to bite the inside of her cheek when he scowled at the screen and muttered, 'For fuck's sake.'

'Problem?' she asked as she placed the burner in her lap.

Withdrawing both hands from the cage, he shut the door. 'This bloody hamster comes into my life and suddenly I start getting messages from an organisation called Hamster Facts.'

'Hamster Facts?' Paige feigned surprise. 'That's random.'

'Uh huh.'

'But you know what they say about our phones and tech, right? Bots and the like spying on us and all that.'

'Yeah, well...' Oliver's thumbs stabbed at the screen, and, in her lap, the phone buzzed. It killed her not to open it immediately. 'This one just got its ass blocked.'

Throwing his phone down in clear disgust, he returned his attention to Flower/Pavarotti who was now sitting in the wheel where he'd been plonked having not moved one iota. As if he was expecting to be given a ride.

'C'mon dude.' Oliver shook his head. 'It's not the sodding Falkirk Wheel. You gotta do the work.'

Clearly unimpressed by the pep talk, Flower slumped, settling into the bottom of the wheel, his arms and legs akimbo, dangling from either side. Paige had the feeling that her expensive hamster exercise machine was about to become Flower's favourite new couch.

'Okay...' Oliver sighed. 'You win. It's getting dark now but tomorrow is a new day. Rest up.'

He fist-bumped the cage and Paige laughed. Then she castigated herself for laughing and feeling all warm and fuzzy. But seriously, how could this man who was being so cute with a *hamster* so carelessly and callously *jilt his bride* on their wedding day?

Not that it was her job to psychoanalyse him – just explode a few karmic bombs in his life. But still... how?

'Is there a violin in that case or is that where you keep a stash of crumbs for general strewing?'

Paige fought the laughter pressing against her vocal cords. It was going to be hard to be the angel of karma if she kept laughing at his wry sense of humour. She glanced at the instrument. 'Violin. I saw it in the window of an antique shop in town and thought why not?'

'So...' He frowned. 'You play?'

'No,' she lied. Well, maybe 75 per cent lied. She wouldn't be strangled-cat bad but it would take her a while to get the instrument to truly sing.

'Oh. Did you get it for someone else?'

'No. Figured I'd learn how to play it while I was here.'

He opened his mouth to say something then shut it again, clearly bamboozled by the statement. 'Have you played any instrument?'

'I guess. If the triangle counts?'

'Um, no.' He cleared his throat. 'I don't think it does.'

'Yeah, I didn't think so.' Although it was worth saying for the way he hid his alarm so admirably behind a stiff British veneer.

'So, you're just... going to learn the violin? Just like that? Can you read music?'

'Nope.' Now, that was a 100 per cent lie. She wondered if, when a person got to a certain accumulative total, it sent you to hell. Directly to hell. 'Do you?'

He shook his head. 'I was more into drama class than band stuff.'

'It's fine,' she assured as she reached for the case and flipped it open. 'I'm sure there'll be something online. YouTube. Or whatever is the Duolingo for instruments.'

She plucked one of the strings with her fingers and gave an internal wince. It needed tuning *badly*. Which was perfect in every way. Grabbing the bow, she glanced at Oliver. 'How hard can it be? I've seen five-year-olds playing them on TikTok.'

'Mmm,' he said, his brow furrowing as she positioned the violin and raised the bow.

The thing about mastering an instrument was that you also knew how to play it badly. The poor condition and lack of tuning helped but Paige knew exactly where and how to strike the strings to make a truly awful noise. And she did it straight away. It was the worst combination of nails down a chalk board and yes... strangled cat.

The hamster wheel shook as Flower started in alarm. Oliver winced in the same way her father used to, drawing in a breath and blinking rapidly like he'd not only heard something awful but smelled it too. 'Oh. My.'

She smiled at his understated, heavily curated remark. She'd always admired people who could engage their filters before they spoke. That wasn't something her family were known for. Hell, her brother would have just blurted, *Fuck's sake Paige, what did we ever do to you?* And, to be fair, the nerve endings in her ear were still untying themselves from the spasm that note had caused.

'Needs some work,' she admitted.

He was looking at her like she'd just uttered the biggest understatement ever uttered in the history of understatements. 'Practice makes perfect,' he agreed with a fixed smile.

'Right?' Paige lifted the bow again and struck an equally inhuman chord.

Oliver held up his hand hastily. 'I think I'll... leave you to it.'

Pressing her lips together as if in thought, Paige nodded. 'Good idea. No one likes looking like a fool in front of other people.'

Like, say, being *jilted* on your wedding day...

But he clearly wasn't picking up what Paige was putting down. He just looked relieved to be getting out of there. He turned to leave then hesitated, looking back over his shoulder at the cage. 'Umm... I might take Pavarotti with me.'

Paige glanced at the hamster who seemed to be cowering in the far corner of his cage. It was such a sweet consideration Paige almost let out a *nawww*. But then she remembered.

Jilted, Paige. Jilted. *Get a grip*.

She struck a few more screechy chords as Oliver disappeared down the stairs with the cage, stifling a laugh as she heard the door close. Oh, *this* was going to be so much fun.

Picking up the phone on her lap, she read the text he'd stabbed out.

> Listen here, you tosser. There is a particular place in hell for bots. You're blocked!

Paige did laugh then. Because she had plenty more SIM cards and the means to buy more. She could do this for the next two months.

Returning to the violin, she set up her phone on the table in front of her and scrolled to video. Tapping record, she filmed herself playing a particularly slow and torturous (for the benefit of her downstairs audience) rendition of 'Three Blind Mice'.

Given it was one of the foundation pieces when learning the violin, the song was pure muscle memory for Paige although it had been many years since she'd played it so heinously. She remembered how proud she'd been when she'd conquered it. How her parents had winced-clapped heartily and her sister had threatened to decapitate her Ken doll if she ever heard it again.

Stopping the video, she did a quick edit, zooming in and cropping until it was just the instrument, then she attached it to a message and sent it to her co-conspirators.

JUST DESSERTS WHATSAPP GROUP. 17.45 GMT.

PAIGE

> Guess who decided to take up violin?

SIENNA

> Holy crap. That's awful. I love it.

PAIGE

> Sadly, Oliver is not a fan. Bwahahahahahahahaha 😈

SIENNA

> Poor baby 🥺

ASTRID

> Oh the pain! 😜

BELLA

> God, I wish I could have seen his face.

PAIGE

> There was wincing

BELLA

No one does resting wince face like Olly

PAIGE

There wasn't much resting about it.

ASTRID

You're hitting this out of the park, sister.

PAIGE

How are Horrible Harvey plans coming along?

SIENNA

I'm still hatching a plan, but don't worry. He's going down. I promise.

PAIGE

Good. Considering he never went down on me once, I shall enjoy the symbolism of his fall.

ASTRID

Ugh. Why does this not surprise me! 👑

PAIGE

👑 👑 👑

4

Three days later, with the weather still grim, Oliver was hiding out in the media room with Pavarotti trying to put as much distance between them and Paige's violin *practice*. He may not have been a fan of the rodent but there was no way he could expose the creature to the dreadful caterwauling that Paige inflicted on them several times a day.

She was dedicated, he'd give her that. But he was a firm believer in reaching a point in life where some things should never be attempted. That there was a window where taking up certain hobbies was acceptable and then it shut and that was that.

Like windsurfing for instance. And bungee jumping. And the violin.

Seriously, if Paige hadn't been Bella's friend he'd have shown her the door the morning after Pavarotti's night-time escapades.

But, Bella…

He didn't know what the statute of limitations was on his guilt but he had a feeling he'd never quite be able to absolve himself. Why hadn't he spoken up in the weeks prior to the wedding when he'd been feeling more and more uncertain and avoided the total panic of that day that had led him to do such a calamitous, idiotic thing?

It had been the right thing, calling it off. On the morning of, though? And via text? That had been unforgiveable.

He'd been putting his feelings of disquiet down to nerves and the weight of responsibility he suddenly felt to be a good husband. To provide. To be the hunter and gatherer. Although God knew why – he had money and Bella had an amazing job and was independently wealthy. She hadn't needed that from him.

All she'd needed was him to love her.

And that had been the crux of the issue. He'd been panicking about all the other stuff because that had been easier than admitting he didn't love the woman he'd asked to spend the rest of his life with.

Not in the way she needed anyway.

He loved her. Of course he did. He still did. She was one of the best people he knew. But he hadn't been *in* love with her. In fact, he'd known that morning he'd *never* been in love with her.

And that she'd deserved more.

There had been a lot of conjecture in the incessant tabloid coverage about his poor marital role models what with his parents' infamous on-again, off-again relationship and eventual divorce. And maybe they were right because Oliver wasn't entirely sure he knew *how* to love someone.

He'd been with women, had a couple of relationships that had even made it to the three-month mark. But when they'd ended as they inevitably had because he hadn't been able to say the L word, he'd never been heartbroken. And there'd always been plenty of women who'd wanted to date a guy related to Hollywood royalty.

Maybe kids that grew up in a household fraught with marital tension never learned to be open with their hearts. Never trusted feelings to be true.

Bella seemed to understand that from the get-go. Perhaps because they'd been friends first? It certainly hadn't seemed to matter to her that he'd never said the L word and there had been such comfort and ease in that but, as she'd said when they'd first spoken after the jilting – *I just assumed you did and that's why you'd asked me to marry you.*

Which had been a fair enough assumption.

But when it came to standing up on that day in front of 400 people and, well *God,* he supposed – although he'd never been religious – in a ceremony that was all about true, deep, abiding love and solemn commitment, he'd realised he couldn't say them.

Because he hadn't loved Bella like she'd needed him to. And he *liked* her far too much to see her settle for less.

But yeah, in an *Am I The Asshole* reddit post, he would definitely be the asshole. And if a whirling dervish of a woman with questionable taste in clothes and a dubious commitment to veganism who never cleaned up after herself and subjected him to terrible violin practice and bloody *hamsters* was his punishment, then he could suck it up.

The wheel which had been merrily spinning around, its lights glowing a fluorescent rainbow in Oliver's peripheral vision whirred to a halt and he glanced at said hamster.

'Not yet, buddy.' Checking the app attached to the wheel, Oliver used his poshest accent as that seemed to be the one that Pavarotti responded to best. 'Another two minutes.'

The advantage to hiding out with the rodent several times a day was he'd been able to work on his plan to get the animal fit so he wouldn't suddenly drop dead of a heart attack.

His thrice daily texts on hamster facts – they just kept coming at him relentlessly like the fucking Terminator despite him blocking the numbers – had informed him that the animals lived for about two years although the oldest recorded hamster had been four and a half.

Which had become Oliver's goal. Four and half. Because he remembered acutely the death of his beloved turtle when he'd been a kid. Bolt had been given to him by Ernie Cummings, his father's agent, for his fourth birthday. Ernie had told him turtles were a commitment because they lived for twenty to thirty years and if Oliver wasn't up to the job he'd take him back and get him a guppy instead.

Oliver had solemnly declared he was up for the job. And he had been. Even at four he'd taken his responsibility very seriously especially given the adults in his life were too busy bickering to rely on for help. That time with Bolt had been a fabulous distraction from the raised voices of his parents and Oliver had loved and cared for that cool little dude until his mysterious demise a few months later.

To say he'd been devastated at the loss was an understatement. The fact that Bolt's death had coincided with the first time his mother had left had probably amplified those feelings. Or at least that's what a shrink had told him when he'd been thirteen and he'd undergone an assessment as part of his mother's application to the courts for full custody.

Oliver didn't know Paige's nephew but he did know that four-year-olds could feel just as deeply as any adult. Bunky's childhood might not be as anxiety-ridden as Oliver's but there was still no need for him to find out about the grim realities of life at such a tender age.

With a name like Bunky, life would no doubt fuck him over soon enough.

So, aided by the YouTube videos, project Healthy Hamster was launched.

After discovering – unsurprisingly – that food was Pavarotti's main motivator, Oliver had started training the hamster to work for his supper. It hadn't taken as long as he'd thought given Pavarotti was exceptionally motivated but it had taken a while to figure out what food was a balance between healthy and naughty.

It turned out to be grapes. Not the cheapest fruit available in the middle of winter and a world-wide economic crisis in an English county which was not generally known for its grape-growing climate.

Of course the hamster would have champagne tastes...

But, luckily for Oliver and his father's regular posthumous royalty payments, money didn't matter and if getting him to ride the damn wheel meant spending his inheritance on *grapes* then that's what he'd do. He'd gradually wean the animal on to more nutritionally appropriate hamster food, he just had to get him hooked on the routine first.

When the wheel remained stubbornly stationary, Oliver plucked the grape off the coffee table and held it up so Pavarotti could see it from his position on the floor. The little blighter might be being compliant but enthusiasm was a ways off so a little reminder of the end prize never hurt.

The wheel started up again, the rainbow array of lights a blur and Oliver smiled to himself as he placed the grape back on the table and used the remote to pump up the music volume another notch. It was playing the *Rocky* soundtrack both for the motivational benefit of Pavarotti and to drown out whatever nursery rhyme Paige was butchering today.

Turning his attention to the laptop that was balancing on his knees, Oliver stared at the blinking cursor on the screen. He'd been working on an action-adventure script since he'd returned to Cornwall and he knew people in Hollywood – directors, studios, producers – who would look at it seriously because of whose kid he was despite his father not being around any longer.

Ernie, who was in his late seventies now and still going strong, certainly would. In fact, he kept hassling him for it.

But he knew in his bones it waslacklustre. The stakes weren't high enough. Probably because his spook hero – Zac Woodbury – was as wooden as the bespoke blonde floorboards upstairs.

Thanks to his connections he'd done some minor acting roles over the years, a lot of which had ended on the cutting room floor which had oddly not been overly disconcerting. Sure, he'd enjoyed it, he'd certainly bragged about it to date women, but his real passion had been writing and the acting just a side hustle.

His time at USC where he'd studied writing for film and TV had confirmed that. And also confirmed that this script was crap. Which was fine, writers learned their craft through writing crap and getting better. Handing it in, getting feedback and rejections and those dreaded *notes*.

The problem was, the son of Roger Prendergast could not show anyone a crap script. Even when his father was alive he couldn't have but that went double now he was dead because people talked and although he had mixed emotions where his father was concerned, he'd hate to besmirch his name by having a kid who wrote dud scripts.

He didn't want his dad to be a laughing stock. Nor did he want to be pitied or humoured especially in the aftermath of the not-wedding. He certainly didn't want the script to be snapped up and splashed around for publicity purposes then made into some B-grade monstrosity *written by Redondo's runaway groom* playing to empty houses for the ghoulish delight of the tabloids.

So, he was in a weird kind of limbo where he didn't know how to progress or how to fix what was wrong. Not for the first time he thought he should just ditch it all and start afresh with a completely new idea. But new ideas were thin on the ground as well.

Also, he was self-aware enough to realise that this yearning-to-start-again thing probably wasn't about the script at all.

Although God... it was truly a dog of a script.

The door to the stairs opened suddenly and Paige appeared brandishing two steaming mugs. Her hair was its usual tangle of stringy titian curls, her jeans a landscape of mismatched denim patches. Her T-shirt depicted a seagull in sunglasses, a French fry hanging out its beak. The words stamped beneath were – *chip magnet.*

Her perfume followed her like it always did, a zesty spritz of lime. She'd been in his house for less than a week and every time she passed by he got a hankering for tequila shots. Which made him think of things he could lick, sip, suck and Paige was Bella's friend so that was very much *not* helpful.

'I can hear that music all the way upstairs.'

He suppressed the urge to say, *you're welcome* and point out that it was at least real music, not the musical equivalent of the jaws of life tearing through metal. Instead, he said, 'Sorry, motivational music for Pavarotti,' and reached for the remote to flick it off.

Pavarotti took that as a sign to stop his exercise, slowing right down until the wheel came to a standstill. Keeping up his end of the bargain, Oliver pushed three grapes through the bars of the cage. Leaping off the structure in a surprisingly agile manner for such a cumbersome creature, Pavarotti scurried over to his gastronomic treasure and proceeded to gobble his way through the reward.

Oliver tipped his chin at the mugs. 'What do you have there?'

'I had a hankering for hot chocolate. Thought you might like one?'

Trying not to think about the kind of mess that awaited him in the kitchen – spilt milk, chocolate powder, scattered sugar granules – Oliver nodded. 'Thanks.'

She set the mugs down, pushing the remote control out of its usual position with her left hand and accidentally over tipping the drink with her right. His eye twitched at the asymmetry of the remote controls and the milky splash on the sleek glass table. But his irritation didn't last long as she sat beside him, her limey freshness filling his nostrils.

Like a margarita. Christ, the woman was turning him into an alcoholic.

Picking her mug up, she eyed the laptop. 'So, you're not just watching TV down here all day,' she said, blowing on the surface of her drink. 'You write scripts?'

Closing the lid, he placed the computer on the table and picked up his mug. 'I... dabble,' he admitted.

'Pretty inspirational room to do it in.' Her gaze lifted to the top shelf where all his father's awards sat beneath their individual spotlights. 'Or intimidating, I guess.'

Oliver eyed the golden glow of the Oscar. Hell, if *that* wasn't accurate...

'How's it going?'

He grimaced. 'I'm kinda stuck, actually.'

'Being the son of a famous actor doesn't make it come any easier?'

Oliver realised this was the first time she'd mentioned his

father directly in the whole time she'd been under his roof. He was so used to his father being the number one topic of conversation between him and people he didn't really know that it had been refreshing to learn the world actually didn't revolve around his father's career. 'God no. If only. Hell, I studied at USC—'

'USC?'

'University of Southern California. They have a big film campus there and I studied script writing. And even that doesn't make it any easier.'

'Are you blocked?'

Oliver blinked at the question. What would Paige know about that? 'No. More... stymied by expectation.'

'Oh?' She tilted her head a little as she regarded him. 'Yours or someone else's?'

His. Ernie's. His professors at USC. People who knew his parents. The whole fucking entirety of La La Land. He gave a half laugh. 'Both?'

A brief flash of... something crossed her features before she schooled them – impatience? Her lips pressed together as if to stop her from saying what she was thinking.

'Am I allowed to know what type of film you're working on?' she asked instead.

Oliver had always been very private about what he'd written because of the expectation that came with the Prendergast name. He'd even hated having lecturers reading what he wrote. And so it was on the tip of his tongue to tell her to mind her own damn business because it was personal *and* bad.

But perversely because she was, to all intents and purposes, a stranger and hadn't shown any inkling of interest in movie land – or his father – he felt he could talk to Paige. Even maybe *wanted* to.

'It's an action adventure.'

Bending her knees, she slid her feet onto the edge of the table, her toes curling around the smoothed glass edge. They were painted green. Bright lime green. And suddenly he was thinking about day drinking again.

'Ah. That explains why you were watching *Die Hard* in January.'

No. It did not. 'I watch *Die Hard* at least once a month.' And sadly, Zac Woodbury was no John McClane.

'I get that. I watch episode seven, season one of *Outlander* just about every month.'

'Oh?' The popular Netflix show hadn't ever been on his radar but he knew several people who worked on it and that it was a quality show. 'Why that one in particular?'

'It's the wedding episode.'

Well, *of course* it was. 'Ah.'

'Yeah, sorry, I know you're not a fan of the *W* word.'

Okay yeah, he deserved that. Leaving her jibe alone, he asked, 'Why do you watch it so often? What about it makes you keep going back to it?'

Oliver found this endlessly fascinating – what connected people to movies or TV. Why did they return to the same things over and over when there were a million different options vying for their attention? As one of his USC professors used to say, understanding the viewer and what connected them to a script was where the gold lay.

'Is it the sex?'

The question tumbled out before he could stop it. It probably wasn't very appropriate given they'd only cohabitated for five days. It wasn't like they'd talked much in that time so throwing the *S* word into a conversation was probably a little intimate for someone he didn't know that well. But there was no denying after probably the longest dry spell of his adult life and the memory of Paige's naked freckly shoulders replaying a little too often in his head, sex was definitely on his mind.

She wrinkled her nose which drew his gaze to the freckles that popped across the bridge and smattered her cheekbones. Because apparently now he was obsessed with freckles?

'How reductive of you.'

Slightly chastised by her obvious disappointment and then irked at feeling that way, Oliver pushed, 'So, it's not the sex?'

Sighing, she cradled her mug in her lap and turned slightly to face him. 'It's not *just* the sex, although that is *very* good.'

Her expression was so earnest it left Oliver in little doubt.

'Too many sex scenes in my humble opinion seem to make it all about the man. Like they're written for men with gratuitous nudity and the woman being passive or... performative. Like the sex is being *done* to her. The ones in that episode are all about Claire and the build of intimacy and trust between her and Jamie.'

He nodded. The female gaze. It had been taught at USC but he'd not really paid much attention. Not because he was unsympathetic to what Paige was saying but because he wrote action adventure, a genre not known for its exploration of emotion.

Her words from their discussion over *Die Hard* that first day came back to him. *He's doing it for the woman he loves.* Hmm, maybe he needed to rethink the whole emotion thing.

Except that would probably require him to explore the reasons behind his avoidance of that messier part of life and the bloody script would never get done.

'But it's also about Jamie,' she continued, unaware of his festering thoughts. 'We already know he's an honourable man. But it really shines through in this episode because you get to see this big, brave tough He-Man highlander brought to his knees *and gladly so*, by a woman. He's a virgin—'

'He's a virgin?'

She just smiled and nodded. 'But he's not ashamed of it or trying to pretend he's some amazing lover. He's keen and willing to learn, to be tutored. And he doesn't just want to take, or for it to be all about him. He wants to give as well, he wants her to enjoy it.'

'That sounds very *modern* of him.'

'Why?' she demanded. 'Because men 200 years ago were all brutes and assholes? Surely there was a spectrum even then? And nuance? There's so much nuance to Jamie in this episode. He's funny and wry and self-deprecating and charming as well as earnest and serious and controlled. But mostly he's just really… present. It's…' Her fingers fluttered against her throat. 'Very swoony. *He's* very swoony.'

Maybe that was what Zac was missing. He was an honourable man but maybe he needed the swoon factor. Some *emotional* nuance.

'You should really watch it sometime.'

Oliver was thinking he might just do that. In fact, maybe he should watch a bunch of content with Paige. She might not know the technicalities behind things but she could certainly articulate how something made her *feel*.

'Thanks, I will.'

'You know who else is a really good action-adventure hero?'

'Who?'

'Jack Colton.'

Oliver nodded. '*Romancing the Stone*.'

'Uh huh.'

Yeah, Oliver had to admit, he was good. Textbook even. Which had been the whole point of him given he'd been the personification of the romance novelist heroine's romantic fantasies.

'Also, one of the best lines ever written. In my humble opinion.'

Oliver quirked an eyebrow. '"Bastards have brothers"?'

The fact he'd clearly stunned her by his almost encyclopaedic knowledge of film was evident. But it was that little flash of admiration that warmed him on the inside.

'That's the one.'

'It's good,' he admitted.

'Yeah.'

She nodded and they stared at each other in what very much felt like mutual admiration. Oliver wasn't sure if it was over the movie line or over their synchronicity.

'Anyway...' She gave a little shake of her head, downed half of her mug then stood. On the ass of her jeans she had a big yellow *don't worry, be happy* patch and it was definitely *that* she caught him looking at moments later, not the way she filled out those jeans, her round ass cupped to perfection.

Paige Barker was all about the bass.

'I'll leave you to your script,' she murmured, making no comment about where his gaze had been. Crossing to the cage, she picked it up. 'Come on Pavarotti, let's get out of here so Oliver can get back to his action-adventure stuff.'

Quirking an eyebrow, Oliver pointed at her. 'You called him Pavarotti.'

She looked nonplussed for a moment before what she'd said registered. 'Thanks to you the damn thing only answers to that now.'

Oliver laughed. 'Sorry. Not sorry.'

'Bunky is going to be well confused when I get his pet home,' she said as she headed for the stairs.

Like a kid called *Bunky* wasn't going to have name issues anyway...

'Door open or closed?' she asked at the foot of the stairs.

'That depends. Have you finished committing crimes against music for the day?'

Shooting him a sarcastic smile, she said, 'Yes.'

'In that case you can leave it open.'

Oliver couldn't explain how very *nice* it had been hearing someone moving around the house these past days. Even the sound of Paige – a friend of the woman he'd jilted at the aisle – stomping up the stairs now made him feel less... alone. He hadn't really realised how dark and quiet the house was and how isolated he'd been these past months.

It hadn't been uncommon for him not to see or hear another soul for days at a time apart from maybe the occasional muffled voices that came from the beach. Not that there'd been much of those either lately given the shitty January weather. But he didn't need to see a shrink to know that rattling around in a house by oneself and barely getting out wasn't good for his mental health.

No wonder he hadn't been able to see the wood for the trees with the script.

It hadn't been his intention to become a recluse. But the initial tabloid interest had driven him indoors and the winter weather had added extra incentive to stay there. Since having his house guest here, however, he'd started to realise being barricaded inside had been a bit of a safety blanket for him and how even something like cleaning up after hurricane Paige had turned a light on – metaphorically speaking.

Which had to be beneficial, right?

Even if she did remind him of key lime pie and how very much he'd screwed things up with Bella. He felt for sure the universe was probably having a laugh at his expense but if this was his penance then maybe some good could come out of it for him too.

Despite the chaos and the mess and waking every morning to a degree of trepidation over what the day would bring.

Turning back to his laptop, Oliver straightened the remote control before returning his attention to that damn blinking cursor again. Zac was about to blow up a fuel depot but maybe what he needed was a love interest? Somebody to highlight his soft underbelly. Oliver paused and frowned for a bit. Hmmm. He tapped out a note.

Give Zac soft underbelly.

His phone pinged then and he absently plucked it off the arm of the couch where he always placed it when he was sitting in this spot.

> Here's your latest from HAMSTER FACTS! Did you know that in the wild, the female kicks the male out of the burrow at completion of coitus? Little wonder when the event is over and done with in approximately four seconds. Press 1 if you think male hamsters need to be better lovers. Standard messaging rates may apply.

Oliver blinked, temporarily at a loss for words, wondering if today's bot had been AI trained in feminism. Or whether his phone really was listening in to his conversations. Or possibly reading his mind considering how much the *Outlander* discussion had him thinking about sex. And how very long it had been since he'd had any.

Four seconds? He'd be grateful to last that long if he ever got around to *coitus* again.

5

Paige was back in the café again the following Tuesday. She was the only customer, which was just as well given she'd just finished a FaceTime call with the Just Desserts gang, all laughing and joking over their mutual shenanigans.

Bella who was dealing with art gallery owner Chase and Astrid who was working on hockey superstar Aiden were kicking it, but she knew that Sienna had to play a longer game with Horrible Harvey.

She took a restorative bite out of her scone slathered with clotted cream and sipped her full cream milk coffee. Real milk, real cream. This pretending to be vegan thing was a lot harder than she thought it would be. And she hadn't even lost weight from lack of gluten and practically every other joyous food known to man because she was pretty much existing on packets of crisps.

And visiting bakeries a little too often.

Glancing out the window, she spotted the dog from last week again. Two big brown eyes sitting atop a greying muzzle looking at her, his unkempt wind-ruffled hair whipping across his eyes. The dog still looked skinny and freezing.

'Jiya,' she called, keeping an eye on the animal that looked like it was now in a hurry to move on.

'Yes, my bewdy?'

'Does someone own that dog?' A Border Collie around these parts surely had to come off one of the surrounding sheep farms?

'He's a stray. Been hangin' around on and off the last couple o' weeks. People have tried to take him in but he don't seem to mind his own company.'

Paige nodded. But surely, he wouldn't mind a little TLC?

The WI women approached the door then and the dog hurried off as they traipsed in from another blustery walk. It wasn't raining outside but the wind hadn't really let up all week and the sky while still grey wasn't *low* and grey. A couple of times it had even looked like the sun might poke its way through.

It hadn't *yet*. But hey, she lived in hope.

'Hi again,' Dorry greeted as she approached and the others swarmed the counter.

Paige smiled. 'Hey. Another fine Cornish day to be out walking, I see.'

The deep crinkles in the older woman's face split into ravines as she laughed. 'It's what we call bracing around these parts.'

Grinning, Paige cocked an eyebrow. 'So where did you come from, originally?'

'Buckinghamshire born and bred. Married a tin miner, been here ever since.'

Sixty years, Paige recalled from their chat last week. 'Bet you're still not considered local, though, right?'

Another hoot. 'Right.' She glanced out at the sea front. 'You should join us on our walk if you're sticking around for a while.'

Paige also turned her gaze to the view. 'In this? No way. This is red wine and log fire weather. Not walking around the streets weather.'

The dog suddenly appeared on the beach, dashing down to the tide line, running in and out of the shallows chasing the retreat of the waves, getting soaking wet and sandy.

'Jiya says that dog's a stray?' Paige said. 'Surely someone must be missing him?'

'The vet scanned him when he first appeared a fortnight ago. She says there's no chip and he's not wearing a collar. Nor has anyone come looking for him either. She was going to take him to the shelter but he escaped when she had her back turned and he's been a bit of a ghost ever since. Here one moment, gone the next. There's been notices put in all the local surrounding villages' Facebook groups but no one's claimed him so far.'

'*Dorry.*' Elizabeth's imperious voice travelled easily across the café. 'You're up. Jiya doesn't have all day.'

Paige swallowed down the urge to laugh out loud at the way Doris looked pointedly around at the empty café. 'Coming, Elizabeth,' she replied placidly before turning back to Paige to mouth, 'Bossy boots.'

Pressing her lips together, Paige said, 'See you later.'

'Maybe for the walk next week?'

Dorry did not give up. 'Maybe. If the weather's better.'

Paige returned her attention to the beach front as Dorry joined her girl gang. The poor mutt looked like such a forlorn figure on the freezing deserted beach, amusing himself in the hideous weather. Sighing, Paige wrapped the second scone she hadn't got around to plying in jam and cream in a paper napkin and shoved it in her jacket pocket.

Quickly downing the last of her tea, she stood. 'Bye ladies, bye Jiya.'

Everyone bade her goodbye and despite every sensibility she owned warning her not to go down to the beach and possibly catch her death like some nineteenth-century romance heroine, Paige's feet took her there anyway.

She probably shouldn't be engaging with a stray dog but considering how sedentary her job was, she could *definitely* do with a spot of *bracing* air.

Flipping up her hood on her Red-Riding-Hood-esque cape she'd found at a charity shop, Paige hunched into her coat beneath, her fingers wrapping around the scone in the left pocket.

Stepping onto the sand, she immediately noticed, despite the harbour being relatively calm, the flotsam and jetsam of the churning sea deposited on the shore. Twisted piles of dense, wet seaweed, the odd plastic bottle, gnarly driftwood, bits of old tangled fishing net and an array of shells were scattered in haphazard abandon.

It was as if the ocean had been tipped upside down and shaken onto the beach.

Paige made her way slowly toward where the dog was running back and forth, chasing the tide, barking at the water when it caught up with him. She stood and watched him for long minutes clearly enjoying himself. He might be a stray, he might need some meat on his bones, but up close, he didn't look like he was feeling sorry for himself either.

On the contrary, he looked like he was enjoying life.

Finally, the dog noticed her standing off to one side and plonked his ass on the sand, his head turning from side to side as he regarded her solemnly, a pink tongue lolling from his mouth. He whined a little, his legs trembling as if he'd suddenly remembered it was January and he was freezing his bollocks off.

'Hey there,' Paige murmured as she slowly approached, keeping her voice neutral and a smile on her dial. 'You got a home, boy? Or are you really a ghost?'

The dog didn't say or do anything for several beats then took off along the beach, nose down, sniffing at various objects scattered across the sand. *Ooo*-kay then. That was successful. But, before she knew it, he was back, a crusty, faded tennis ball that had clearly seen far better days clamped between his jaws.

He brought it to her, depositing it gently at Paige's feet.

'Oh, you like to play fetch, huh?'

Bending over, Paige picked up the ball. It was rough, cold and wet against her fingers but she didn't mind as she pulled her arm back to toss it, the dog never taking its eyes off the ball. Paige let it fly in the direction of the pier, hurling it as far as she could and the dog took off, a blur of limbs, tail and fur. Which only went to prove that he must have been someone's because he'd obviously been taught to fetch.

He caught it on the third bounce and had it back at her feet within seconds and Paige dutifully picked it up and threw it again. And again. And again. After ten minutes, though, her face was burning from the slap of cold wind and her fingers were red and practically numb. Pulling the scone from her pocket, she offered that to the dog instead.

He dropped the ball like it was dead to him.

Paige crouched beside the mutt as he scoffed down the offering. 'You like that huh, boy?' She petted his head, scratching behind his ears which was about the only place on his body that wasn't wet and sandy. 'Better with jam and clotted cream, trust me.'

The dog angled his head a little as if to direct Paige to the sweet spot and she smiled as she obliged. 'What's your name then, boy? Are you a Max? Or a Beau? Or is it slightly grander? Are you a Zeus? Or an Apollo?'

None of the names seemed to have an effect on him as Paige petted.

'Are you a ghost? Should I call you Casper? Yeah.' Paige nodded. 'You look like a Casper. Is someone missing you, Casper, or did you run away for a good reason, huh?'

He looked in good condition and hadn't cowered or been mistrustful with Paige. In fact, quite the opposite – he'd trusted her immediately.

Clearly done with the twenty questions, the dog picked up the ball again and dropped it near Paige's knee. 'Sorry, Casper,' she said on a laugh as she stood. 'If I stick around outside any longer I'm going to turn into a Popsicle.'

The dog stared at her with his big brown eyes and whined a little. And if he'd done it deliberately to make Paige feel guilty, it worked. But her toes were officially frozen and her lungs were now aching from the constant shock of cold air.

A thought crossed her mind. A deliciously delightfully wicked thought. 'You wanna come home with me?'

Both Jiya and Dorry had said the dog had resisted attempts at offering refuge so Paige wasn't sure if he'd go for it and she sure as hell wasn't going to drag the creature into the car against its will. But if he did go for it? She could only imagine Oliver's face if she turned up with the sodden, bedraggled animal threatening to besmirch all that blinding white.

Yeah. He'd probably really hate that. He'd only grudgingly accepted Pavarotti.

The dog however had different ideas, picking up the ball and trotting away in the opposite direction. And that, Paige supposed, was that. Still, she was disappointed. And not just because she'd miss out on some fun and games with Oliver but also, it was cold and wet and the thought of this dog out in the January weather just didn't sit right.

But, she couldn't force the animal into a warm, dry, freaking luxurious beach-side house of a famous dead British actor, could she?

As it turned out, she needn't have worried. Casper was lying on the pavement, manky ball from the beach sitting beside him, waiting for her when she got back to the Mini half an hour later, two grocery bags in tow. Paige didn't know how the dog knew it was her car – or Oliver's car to be precise. Maybe he *was* a ghost dog. She was just inordinately glad to see him as he lifted his head from the cold concrete of the footpath and wagged his tail.

'Casper,' she greeted with a grin and the dog stood, picking up the ball and wagging his tail some more.

If anything, he was even filthier than when she'd left him on the beach. He looked as if he'd detoured across a field on his jaunt to the car, finding every muddy wallow and possibly cow pat along the way. He was a total disaster zone and not even Paige could countenance putting him in the front seat.

Oliver probably deserved it and more, but she'd become quite partial to the pristine internal condition of the car and just couldn't quite bring herself to do it.

'Okay, but you're going in the back, mister and into a bath as soon as we get home.' Paige faltered at the ease with which that word had rolled off her tongue. It was not her home. It was *Oliver's* home. Thanks to Harvey she'd probably never have her own home, never feel able to put down roots.

Pushing *that* aside, she peered sternly at the dog. 'That is non-negotiable.'

The dog seemed agreeable and when she opened the boot,

he obligingly jumped in, dropping the ball. But, as she was stashing her bags beside him, he decided to renege on the deal. In a blur of fur, he took another leap from the boot to the back seat and then, like he was used to manoeuvring around things, squeezed between the two front seats to claim the passenger one as his own, leaving a trail of sand and dirt in his wake.

Yeah, that was not the first time the dog had done that.

'Casper!' she gasped but all Paige could see from the boot were two ears fully pricked to attention and the swish of his tail.

Shutting the boot, Paige went around to the driver's side and opened the door, prepared to chastise the animal. Crossing her arms, she injected a note of warning into her voice. 'Casper.'

But Casper refused to even glance in her direction, his muzzle straight ahead as if she'd assigned him a role as navigator and he was ready and raring to go. Paige stared in dismay at the mud and sand smudges that decorated both the back and front seats.

Oliver would be pissed. She smiled to herself – *perfect*.

'Hey Casper,' she crooned as she reached for her phone.

The dog, obviously an expert in tone – even more evidence that he not only belonged to somebody but had been highly trained – turned his head with a tail thump, his tongue lolling out of his mouth. He looked right at her, the fur on his face and ruff utterly filthy, like he'd been dipped in a diluted mud-and-sand-pie mix.

She shook her head at him and snapped a pic. Climbing in the car, she shut the door and quickly sent it to the girls.

JUST DESSERTS WHATSAPP GROUP. 09.45 GMT.

PAIGE

Guess who's coming home with me?

ASTRID

Is that a dog?

PAIGE

It sure is! I've called him Casper. The menagerie grows.

SIENNA

Jaysus. Where did you find that? It looks like the creature from the black swamp.

BELLA

Olly will have apoplexy! I approve this message 100%

* * *

Oliver didn't think he was rare among men to admit that he enjoyed taking his morning constitutional. Maybe women did too – it wasn't a conversation he'd ever had with one – but plenty of dudes he knew freely admitted the same. There was nothing quite as satisfying as those few peaceful minutes sitting on the *throne* – so to speak – flicking through a magazine as bodily functions did their thing.

Made a man feel like a king for a few moments. Like he could conquer the world. Yeah, it sounded really dumb but he didn't make the rules.

This morning he was taking his in the toilet that adjoined a bathroom servicing the living area, when he thought he heard the garage door open. Paige must be back from town. Turning to the loo roll, he frowned. Someone – Paige, *of course* – had put the bloody thing on the wrong way.

What the hell?

Everyone knew there was a right way and a wrong way. The paper had to come over the top of the roll, not from underneath.

It was like... *science*. For fuck's sake, it was like finding the damn remote controls scattered all around the media room instead of lined up in a row on the coffee table where they belonged. Or his CDs replaced (when she bothered) willy-nilly on the shelf instead of following his carefully alphabetised system.

Seriously, since Paige had come to stay, nothing was the right way. She was like a *reverse* Mary Poppins, taking all things ordered and creating chaos.

And now this. Apparently, he couldn't even take a morning dump without being inconvenienced, yet again, by the woman who had blown into his life only a week ago. He wasn't sure how much more he could take of it – she really was getting on his last nerve.

And she wasn't leaving until the *end of next month*!

Irritated, he turned the toilet roll around. What kind of heathens didn't know the unwritten rule of toilet paper? Had she been raised by wolves? He blinked. Actually... where *did* she come from? He realised they'd never really spoken a whole lot about her.

He knew she had a brother and a sister and a nephew called Bunky and a niece called Lulu. *That was it.* He supposed they didn't talk a whole helluva lot. Which probably had a lot to do with him trying to avoid her because of a) the general chaos that surrounded her and b) those damn freckles which drove him just a little bit crazy and made him think – in the moments when she wasn't being Mary Poppins' evil twin – that maybe he could take a whole lot more of her.

But she knew about way more intimate things where he was concerned. His struggles with his script for example. *And* what he'd done to Bella.

He was just exiting the bathroom after washing his hands when he heard a strange kind of clicking noise. Frowning, he turned his head to locate it only to find some kind of feral animal trotting into the hallway from the door that linked the garage with the rest of the house. Paige, in some kind of cape contraption, her hair a veritable mass of knotty, windswept curls, followed closely behind.

What the...? She *had* to be joking. A strange animal and toilet roll the wrong way around?

'Stop.' He held up his hand and, to give them their due, both Paige and the animal – a dog – did halt. In fact, the animal, which looked like it had been rolled in sand, grass and mud, sat his ass on the pristine cleanliness of his polished blonde wooden floorboards. 'That... *thing*, is not coming into my house.'

'Shhh.' Paige looked at him like he was about to produce a gun and shoot the animal. 'It's okay lovely,' she crooned as she glanced at the dog. 'Daddy didn't mean it.'

Oliver almost choked. Lovely? Daddy? *Nope*. 'Oh, hell no.'

'Oliver. Casper's a stray. I know you don't have any idea how cold it is out there because I haven't seen you leave the house but trust me, it is.'

Oliver had been in Cornwall in January enough to know *exactly* how cold it was which was *exactly* why he wasn't venturing out. Mostly. And if he hadn't, the pink in her cheeks would have told him anyway.

'He has nowhere to go.'

The dog looked at him with big brown eyes, a string of drool forming around the area where a scruffy-looking ball was lodged in his mouth. A twinge of guilt hit Oliver square in the solar plexus. 'How do you know he'd called Casper if he's a stray?'

He rolled her eyes at him. 'I don't. But we have to call him something.'

'Um... no we don't!' For God's sake, he had a fucking

hamster in his life he didn't want. He certainly didn't need a mangy-looking dog. Oliver shoved a hand through his hair. 'Where did you even find him?'

'He hopped in the car.'

Oh, bollocks. The creature had been *in his car*? Oliver shuddered to think what state it was in. 'Just... jumped in?'

'I've seen him around town the last few times. He doesn't have a collar and he doesn't have a chip and no one knows where he's come from and people have apparently tried to take him in but he keeps evading them.'

'He didn't evade you.'

A small smile played on her mouth as she shrugged. 'I guess I'm irresistible.'

Oliver glanced at the dog who looked back at him with a *dude, it's true* expression and he wondered if anyone ever said no to her. Or was it that they just struggled to escape the centrifugal force of her as she spun around spreading the chaos of metabolically challenged hamsters and filthy strays.

And fucking loo rolls.

As if sensing he was about to capitulate, she walked toward him, peeling off her cape to reveal a raggedy ass jacket that looked like it had inspired Dolly Parton's Coat of Many Colours. 'I called the vet, she knows I've taken Casper home.' She unzipped the coat then and shrugged out of it to reveal another classic T-shirt.

Surely not everyone was Kung Fu fighting.

He would have laughed out loud normally but the shirt was V-necked and he was distracted by the dusting of freckles across her décolletage.

'It'll just be until someone claims him. There have been notices put up on all the local Facebook groups and church halls in the district.'

She stopped as she drew level with him, her zesty lime fragrance surrounding her like a reverse forcefield – attracting not repelling.

'I couldn't leave him out in the cold. Not when he looked at me with those eyes.'

Oliver glanced at the dog who gave him *the eyes* and sighed. 'Fine.' Lifting his gaze to Paige, he said, 'But this is *only* temporary.'

She nodded quickly. 'One hundred per cent. Just until his owner comes forward.'

'And that ball.' He pointed to it. 'Is not coming in the house.'

As if he absolutely knew which side his bread was buttered on, Casper dropped the ball in an instant and it fell to the floor with a flat, wet thunk. *Gross.* Oliver shook his head as he turned his attention back to Paige.

'He's not allowed on any of the furniture.'

'Of course.'

'He's only allowed on this level and in the media room. Not upstairs on the beds.'

'No beds. Check.'

Oliver chugged out a breath as he looked from the woman to the dog and back to the woman again. They were both patiently awaiting his next edict. Like he was some damn dictator, but he needed to claw back some control here or there'd be worse things than loo rolls the wrong way around.

Although what *that* could possibly be he couldn't imagine. The zombie apocalypse?

'He needs a wash before he goes any further.' He pointed at the bathroom door beside him. 'Use the shower.'

God knew the kind of ring Casper's degree of filthiness would leave in a bathtub. Ninth circle of hell ring, for sure.

She smiled and gave him a little salute. 'Aye, aye, sir.'

Oliver ignored how her eyes glowed and the way her mouth curved upwards. And just how much that little salute echoed through the sudden heat in his blood.

'Come on then Casper, you heard Daddy, it's shower time.'

Moving aside, his back to the wall to allow them passage, Oliver gritted his teeth. Do not put Paige – *Bella's friend* – and Daddy in the same sentence.

The dog moved unhurriedly, his toenails clicking on the floorboards as she opened the bathroom door and he ambled in. She followed but drew to a halt when he said, 'Paige?'

Her fingers wrapped around the door frame as she looked over her shoulder at him, all big hazel eyes and freckles and his blood heated a little more.

'Uh huh?'

'Stay away from the damn pear tree down the end of the road.'

Her brows scrunched together, confusion clouding her eyes. 'Um... okay?'

'Just in case there happens to be a bloody orphaned partridge in need of a home.'

It took a beat but then her frown smoothed out and her mouth kicked up at the sides and she laughed. And then he was laughing because this woman was turning his house into a bloody zoo and he should be mad as hell. He *was* mad as hell, damn it. But there was something so delightfully *unhinged* about it, he couldn't help but laugh.

'No partridges, I promise,' she murmured and then disappeared into the bathroom.

Right. Like he was going to take that to the bank.

6

'Paige!'

The irritation in Oliver's voice carried all the way up the stairs to Paige who was sitting at the table, ostensibly working but actually messaging with Bella. 'Oops,' she murmured to Pavarotti who had instantly stopped running on his wheel at the sound of Oliver's voice.

Pavarotti had a total dude crush on Oliver.

'Someone's wearing his cranky pants today.'

PAIGE

> Gotta go, methinks Oliver is having trouble finding the remote control again.

BELLA

> Where'd you hide it this time?

PAIGE

> I can neither confirm nor deny that it may have *slipped* down between the side and the cushion.

> **BELLA**
> You are so evil for messing up his system like that.

> **PAIGE**
> Who? Moi? 😇

She signed off then before another, '*Paige!*' thundered up to greet her.

Smiling, she headed down the stairs. 'You bellowed?' she said as she stepped into the media room. Casper, thoroughly at home after only two days, lay stretched out on the couch, his tail thumping in greeting.

'Where's the damn remote control?' he demanded, his cheek kissing the floor as he peered beneath the couch.

Paige clamped her lips together to stop from laughing. 'Have you checked under the dog?'

Oliver climbed to his feet. 'Yes.'

She pressed her lips even harder as she took in the lolling dog all freshly spruced, brown and white again, his fur snowy soft, looking like the sofa was not only his but that it had been made especially for him.

Paige folded her arms. 'I thought he was only allowed on the floor in front of the fire?'

Shoving his hands on his hips, Oliver was distracted as he looked around for any obvious signs of the remote Paige had hidden last night after he went to bed. 'Yeah, he's not great at following commands.'

She narrowed her eyes at the dog. Paige was pretty sure Casper understood far more than he was letting on. In fact, she'd even hazard a guess after he'd dropped that damn ball in the hallway like it had been made of lava, that he was not only highly trained but highly intelligent.

He certainly had Oliver figured out anyway.

Sure, Oliver might outwardly protest their presence but Paige knew Pavarotti perked up whenever he heard Oliver's voice and she'd bet her last penny Casper would be sleeping on the end of Oliver's bed before too long.

'The remote?'

Dragging her attention back to the problem at hand, Paige put on a good display searching for an item whose location she already knew. 'I swear it was on the arm of the chair when I finished watching last night,' she murmured, tapping her index finger against her mouth feigning concentration. 'Maybe it... fell down the side of the cushion? Did you look there?'

He glared at her impatiently. 'Yes.'

Well... she *knew* it was there so he couldn't have looked too damn hard. Although she had *crammed* it down.

Quirking an eyebrow at him, Paige made a huge show of crossing to the couch and feeling down between the cushion and the arm. She rummaged around for a bit, digging her fingers in hard towards the back, her fingertips just scraping it on a second sweep.

Man, she really *had* crammed it in there.

Giving a triumphant little squeak, she yanked it out. 'Well, whaddya know,' she said, brandishing it.

He huffed out an annoyed breath, his eyebrows forming a deep V. 'I did search there,' he muttered, holding out his hand. 'I must have unknowingly knocked it further back.'

Paige slapped it into his palm like he was a surgeon and she was passing him an instrument. 'Or you just had a *boy* look.'

'Or, you could leave the remote on the coffee table next to the other ones where it actually belongs and I wouldn't have to spend the first hour of my day, looking for it.'

'Considering that's about the most energetic thing you do all day, you should be thanking me. Think of it as your cardio.'

She was aware of the dog's head ping-ponging from one to the other. Christ, she'd been here for ten days and they were already sounding like an old bickering couple. If only there wasn't that zip in her blood right now. Or that funny breathless feeling causing her chest to rise and fall a little faster. Something Oliver had clearly noted as his gaze dropped briefly before returning to meet hers.

From the outset, Paige had thought undertaking this exercise in karma would be fun. She'd definitely felt it was justified. Why should he be able to jilt Bella at the aisle and just carry on with zero consequences or disruption in his life? But she'd not realised it would be... stimulating on levels she didn't even want to think about.

The last four years she'd been going through the motions. Getting by. Until this little challenge had come along and... excited her. And not just because Oliver Prendergast was a bastard getting his comeuppance.

Not if that hitch in her breath was anything to go by.

Casper gave a little whine then, like he couldn't bear it when Mummy and Daddy fought, which was enough to break through the sudden weird tension. 'It's okay, lovely,' Paige crooned, crouching beside the couch to run her hand up and down the dog's side which he lapped up like it was his due.

Oliver sat his ass down in his usual spot beside Casper, flicking on the television before making a production of placing the remote back in its place. If it was meant to irritate her, it did but then he slipped his hand onto Casper's head and absently toyed with his ear and it was hard to stay irritated with a guy who petted a dog he hadn't even wanted two days ago.

Raising his foot, Oliver placed it against the edge of the

coffee table. It wasn't the first time she'd seen him barefoot; in fact, that was pretty much his state of being, but it was, owing to her crouched position, the first time she'd been this close to one of his bare feet and lordy they were *big*. She supposed it stood to reason given the general symmetry of the human body. He was a tall guy after all but, yeah... *wow*.

Preferring not to think about the size of his feet, Paige also sat her ass on the couch, the other side of the dog. 'What are we watching?'

He frowned. 'Aren't you working?'

'I can take a break for a while.' Especially if her mere presence was going to annoy the crap out of him. Bonus points for that!

'It's a TV show based in the US. *Inside the Actors Studio*. They interview a lot of actors but also directors and writers.'

Paige shrugged. 'Okay.' She settled back into the couch. 'Cool.'

But before the opening music had even finished she noticed a little pile of ripped-up paper on the coffee table that looked like the remnants of an envelope that had clearly been torn up with the letter still inside it. She assumed it was the letter she'd put there earlier after she'd picked up the post off the doormat this morning.

Most of the delivered mail since she'd been living here had been the usual array of junk mail – shopping catalogues, sales promotions and flyers with discount coupons. An actual letter with a stamp had been a real curiosity.

Who even wrote letters these days? Didn't everyone just email?

'Is that the letter from earlier?' she asked.

He didn't take his eyes off the screen. 'Yep.'

'You didn't open it?'

'Nope.'

'But you ripped it up anyway?'

'Yep.'

'So, you know what was in it?' she pressed, casting him a sideways glance. 'Or, you didn't care what was in it?'

He grimaced but still didn't look away from the screen. 'Both.'

'Okay...' Applause was happening on the TV as Paige sat forward a little, casting her eyes over the torn paper, wishing she'd scrutinised it closer when she'd picked it up. But, other than the first-class stamp, there'd been no indication of who it was from. No return name or address on the back – that had been the first thing she'd checked.

'Is it some kind of final notice? Not paying your bills, Oliver?'

'Nope.'

'Some kind of survey maybe?'

'Nope.'

'Ooh.' She clicked her fingers as a thought suddenly occurred to her. 'Is it a secret admirer?' He was a rich good-looking guy with huge *feet* after all.

Oliver hit pause on the remote and looked at her like he was gathering patience from God himself. 'If you *must* know, it's from a publisher. They want to give me a bunch of money to write my father's biography.'

'Oh.' Now that she hadn't expected. 'How much is a bunch?'

'A hundred grand.'

She blinked as she sat back in her seat. Holy fuck-a-doodle-do. 'That's... a lot of money.'

'I don't need the money.'

Of course, a hundred thousand pounds to him was just a drop in the ocean she supposed but hell, if someone offered her the kind of money that would pay off her student debt in one hit, to do something – not of a sexual nature – she sure as shit wouldn't be tearing up their letters.

She'd be framing them.

'So,' she dismissed, 'give it to charity.'

He nodded after a beat as if it was a possibility and Paige half turned to face him, assessing his closed profile. 'If it's not about the money, it's about what? You just... don't want to?'

'I do not.'

'Because it's too close? Too soon? Too personal?'

He shook his head. 'I'm not a biographer. I'm a script writer.'

Paige glanced at the laptop, the lid down, no little white glowing light on the side to indicate it was even on. Same as it had been earlier. She was pretty sure it hadn't moved from that exact spot these past couple of days. All she'd seen him do with that thing was alternate between staring aimlessly at the screen and avoiding it altogether by watching other people's scripts in action on the television.

The rest of the time had been taken up by becoming a hamster's personal trainer.

She'd understand if it was just too damn raw still to be trawling through the emotional ashes of one of the most foundational relationships in a person's life. But quibbling about the kind of writer he was, was something else entirely.

'But are you?' She cocked an eyebrow. 'Really? I don't see a whole lot of writing going on at the moment.'

Paige hadn't thought she'd be using something like this to push Oliver Prendergast out of his comfort zone but she was nothing if not adaptable and she would use whatever was at her disposal, including some home truths.

'I told you, I'm just... stuck at the moment.'

'Have you ever thought you're stuck because script writing isn't your calling?'

He snorted. 'No.'

'Really? What if you're actually meant to write books? Or this one book, anyway.'

'They have people they can pay, a *lot less*, to do a biography on my father.'

'Yeah. But not one who could write it like you could, right? The way only a son could. The true, inside story. That kind of thing.'

He hesitated for a moment and Paige wondered if she'd struck a chord before his jaw tightened. 'Yeah, well too bad. It's not happening and I wished they'd just bloody lay off with the whole, the world needs to hear your homage thing like it's the expected thing to do for the kid of a famous dead actor, because it's making it really fucking hard to concentrate on the thing I'm actually supposed to be writing.'

Paige blinked. She couldn't believe what she was hearing. This guy of enormous privilege whining about doing something pretty damn amazing. Something he was uniquely qualified to do. She knew a lot of writers who'd trade their souls – and their fancy Macs – for a £100k commission.

'Poor you, huh?' she said, their eyes meeting. 'Publishers throwing money at you like that when you're all *stuck*.' She clutched her chest dramatically. 'People expecting too much of you.' Dropping her hand, she shook her head. 'Welcome to the real world, Oliver. Where people expect too much of you all the damn time.'

Did he realise what it was like in the real world? Locked away in his posh house by the beach with little golden statues to keep him company, where he didn't have to worry about a job and mundane things like how he was going to eat or pay the bills.

She hadn't had that privilege when pictures and videos of

her had landed in every student and faculty inbox at Oxford. As well as several porn sites. She hadn't been able to just sit and wallow in her misfortune which was, unlike Oliver, *not* self-inflicted.

Sure, holing up in her old bedroom in her parents' house and not ever coming out had been attractive and she *had* indulged for a couple of weeks. But, as a poor ex-law student, it hadn't been a plan for the rest of her life. And although she might not be living large or earning a fortune, she had carved out a niche for herself.

Even if she was hiding behind a peach emoji.

And having Richie Rich here sitting around on this couch all day bemoaning his lot was officially getting on her last nerve.

Oliver looked discomforted as he said, 'I'm prioritising the script.'

Once again, she glanced at the disused laptop. Yeah, she could see that…

Paige changed tack. 'You know sometimes when you're having issues with something you're writing, actually working on something else, something different, can help clarify things for the first project.'

He quirked an eyebrow. 'And you know this how?'

'I do VA stuff for quite a few authors.' And before she put her brain full into gear she was offering her services. 'If you like, I can help you.'

Oliver contemplated her offer for a beat. 'How?'

'Lots of ways. I can be a beta reader for a start.'

'Have you done that before?'

'No, but I am a voracious reader. One who knows nothing about your father or your relationship with him so I'm coming at it with no preconceived ideas or expectations. And as a neutral third party, you could bounce ideas off me. I can also proofread it as you go or do line editing. I can work on an outline with you. I can do up a schedule for you to keep you on track and then nag you about it every day I'm here.'

He gave a half laugh. 'Yeah, I reckon you'd excel at that.'

Paige looked at him, deadpan. 'I excel at *everything*.' It was true, from her law degree to her business, Paige had always kicked ass.

'Yeah.' He nodded slowly, his eyes locking on hers. 'I bet you do.'

It was possibly the nicest thing a man had ever said to her. For a bastard, he was a pretty nice guy. Which was not what she should be thinking or feeling about Redondo's runaway groom. Clearing her throat, she got back on track. 'So? What d'you think?'

Oliver blew out a noisy breath. 'I... wouldn't know where to start.'

'From the beginning?'

'I don't know how much I remember of that.'

'Okay, so...' Paige shrugged. 'Don't tell it chronologically.' She moved around more so she was sitting sideways on the couch completely facing him now, one leg tucked under her, the other foot on the floor. 'Go back and forth. Jump around. I can help you collate it into something more cohesive at the end. What's the first memory that pops to mind when you think of your father?'

He glanced up at the trophy stash. 'Him winning those I suppose.'

Paige shook her head. 'No. I don't mean things. Or clips of his acceptance speeches I can go and look up on YouTube. I mean something private. Something about him being your *dad*. Not a famous actor.'

'Our relationship was...' He hesitated. 'Complicated.'

'You're not on your lonesome there, Oliver. Lots of people have complicated relationships with their parents. It's probably what will appeal to readers the most and exactly what the publisher wants.'

'If they're after some scandalous tell-all, they'll be disappointed.'

Paige suppressed a smile at how painfully English he sounded when affronted. But she hadn't missed the fact that he was already talking about it like it was going to happen. 'It doesn't have to be that but no one wants to read about a perfectly happy family blessed with unicorns and rainbows. They want to know that famous people grapple with the same issues as they do. And who knows, maybe it'll be cathartic for you if it's not something you've properly processed yet.'

She didn't have to be a shrink to know he clearly *hadn't* processed things yet. Maybe him doing something so heinous as jilting Bella at the aisle had something to do with his unresolved issues. He had after all, according to Bella, proposed to her not long after his father had died.

'Maybe look at it as an opportunity to work through some things. Don't take their money right now. Don't write the book for them. Write it for *you*. And then decide what you want to do with it.'

He regarded her for long moments. 'You're good at this.'

She smiled. 'You're catching on.'

A grudging answering smile touched his lips as he flopped his head back against the couch and stared at the ceiling as if he might find the answer there.

'He had this scarf.' Oliver murmured eventually. 'A red scarf. It was cashmere. And really soft with fringes on either end that I remember used to tickle my face. My earliest memory of him is standing at an airport gate watching him walk down the gangway to the plane he was taking to America for some role or other and everyone else was wearing black and brown and grey and there was my father, this pop of colour bobbing up ahead, getting further and further away from me.'

His clear affection for his father warmed his voice and pulled at her heart strings. 'Okay then,' she said quietly. 'Start there.'

* * *

A few days later, Oliver was once again staring at a blinking cursor but this time it was a Word document and this time it was blank. He'd been writing and deleting the same thousand or so words since Paige had come up with this harebrained scheme.

So, maybe it wasn't just that he was stuck on the *script*. Maybe his writing was *generally* stuck. Maybe he *was* experiencing writer's block.

Considering he'd written comparatively little in his life, that was slightly worrying.

Or maybe every time he thought back to that moment in the airport he remembered the gut clash of emotion. Pride and love butting up against a staggering sense of abandonment.

After all, he didn't need £100k. He didn't need to pull in any income for the rest of his life. His father's estate was significant and the royalties off his work alone would keep Oliver more than comfortable for the rest of his life.

Did he really want to pick that scab?

Or maybe it was just the godawful screech of 'Frère Jacques' upstairs that was putting him off his game. Maybe he needed to invest in a proper soundproof door? He was pretty sure even the seagulls that sat incessantly on the balcony railing upstairs buggered off the second Paige picked up her bow.

Triple glazing or not.

'What do you reckon, Pavarotti?' He glanced over at the rodent running on his wheel like he was training for a marathon. 'Is Mumsy getting *any* better do you think?'

Taking the animal's silence as a judgement on her lack of ability, Oliver nodded. He cast his eye over Casper who had decided his rightful place in this world was on the couch next to Oliver. And now he no longer looked like the creature from the swamp, Oliver had to admit, the company was nice.

And, unlike Paige, the dog didn't judge him when he turned the TV on instead of reaching for the laptop.

Oliver couldn't quite believe how quickly his life had turned around. Two weeks ago he was living a perfectly happy existence with just himself for company. Today he was living with a distractingly curvy woman with red hair, freckles and a great rack, a very large (actually less large now) hamster with a wild Trump-esque quiff and a stray dog who filled up his life in ways that were exceptionally inconvenient.

Had he wanted any of them? No. Would he be sad if they all left tomorrow? No – *probably*. But, here he was and it... wasn't awful.

The screeching suddenly stopped from upstairs and he, the rodent and the dog, all held their breath and listened. Was there to be any more massacring of music or would today's session be mercifully over?

When it didn't resume, Oliver's head fell back against the cushion. 'Halle-fucking-lujah,' he muttered.

Casper's tail thumped against the couch as if in agreement and Pavarotti slowed his roll until the flashing lights stopped and the wheel came to a standstill. Had he been using the sound of the wheel in motion to block out the sound of Paige on the violin?

Huh... Maybe the rodent wasn't as dumb as he looked.

A minute later, footsteps alerted Oliver to Paige descending and he knew she'd be coming down for an update and then looking at him all *disappointed* if he'd yet again failed to produce some kind of output for the morning.

She would have made a great teacher, he thought. Or maybe a sperm bank nurse, urging masturbators into greater deposits and subtly sperm shaming them for poor yields.

He rewrote the same paragraph he'd deleted an hour ago. He knew it word for word because he'd written and deleted it multiple times over the last few days.

'I think I'm improving,' she announced as she entered the room. 'The bow feels like it's gliding more naturally.'

'Uh huh,' Oliver murmured noncommittally as both animals side-eyed him in a way that left him in little doubt they felt *he* should be the one to tell her she was *not* – in any way, shape or form – improving.

Yeah... that wasn't happening.

'What about you?' she asked, sitting on the single chair. 'Is it coming any easier?'

Oliver shook his head. 'Not really.'

'Okay.' She nodded like she understood but clearly, she didn't. 'Do you know why that might be? Maybe it's not the right scene to be working on right now? What if you worked on a different scene? You know you can bounce ideas off me if you want?'

Oliver would rather eat Pavarotti's hamster pellets than do that with someone who had no experience with this kind of work. 'Thank you for the offer but creatives' brains work differently to other people's.'

Oh bloody hell, he sounded like a self-important wanker. He winced internally.

She quirked an eyebrow. 'How many words have you written so far?'

'In total?'

'Uh huh.'

Oliver's gaze dropped to the word count in the lower left corner. Oh Jesus. He cleared his throat. 'Fifty-nine.'

She smiled but he could see it was strained. 'And how many words have you deleted these past three days?'

'Probably about fifty-nine hundred.'

She nodded. 'Right.'

'It's a process...'

'It's a shockingly inefficient process.' Looking at him like he was a mildly annoying student and she was the teacher – a curvy, freckly fiend of a teacher – she pursed her lips. 'Have you ever thought of ditching the laptop and using pen and paper? One of the authors I VA for, she always hand writes her first draft. Says it helps her tap into her creativity better than using a screen.'

Oliver blinked. How very primitive... *And she called him inefficient.* She'd be suggesting he use a typewriter next! 'Yeah, I don't think that would work for me.'

She quirked an imperious eyebrow like he'd got the answer wrong and was moments away from a rap over the knuckles. 'Why not?'

'If the universe had wanted us to hand write, it wouldn't have given us Steve Jobs.'

Rolling her eyes at him, she regarded him again for long moments as she absently chewed her bottom lip, looking at him like he was a problem to be solved. Like he was Maria von Trapp and she was the Mother Superior.

'Okay.' She nodded then as if she knew the answer. Standing, she announced, 'What you need is a change of scenery.'

Oliver frowned. 'A change of scenery?'

'Yes.' Striding over to the door that opened out directly onto the beach, she threw back the curtain. It had been shut since winter had thrown its stormy tantrum at the beginning of the month. 'You need to get out there, walk a little. Blow some cobwebs out. Use your phone to record if anything comes to mind.'

Casper, who had been about as inert as neon since he'd entered the house last week, suddenly sat up, leaped to the floor and rushed to the doors, his nose pressing to the glass as he gave an excited bark, his tail wagging like a freaking fan.

Oliver cast an eye at the grey weather. 'I don't think that would help.'

'Well, you won't know until you try, right?' She slid a hand to her hip and stared him down like he was being truly recalcitrant now and she was on her last nerve. 'Don't look at it as trying to write your book. Just, take the dog for a walk.' Casper barked again. 'Throw a ball for a while. You never know what might shake loose.'

And therein lay the problem. Oliver wasn't sure he was ready for what might *shake loose*. He had no doubt that writing his father's biography was something he was capable of doing. He just wasn't convinced he *should* do it.

It had been eighteen months and he didn't think that was enough distance to go poking at all the old bruises.

'I might be recognised.'

She eyed him like he was being a total twat which, of course, he was, but him going out there to confront stuff felt a little too emotionally perilous.

Swivelling her head, Paige peered out of the smoky glass of the sliding door. 'There's three people out there. Wear a beanie. You'll be fine.'

Oliver glanced at Casper, who wagged his tail furiously. He was clearly going to be no back-up. Flicking his gaze to Pavarotti for some solidarity, Oliver was confronted with a shit ton of hamster judgement. He quirked an eyebrow at the rodent. *Really, dude?* Criticism from someone addicted to Dib Dabs?

'You should get out anyway,' Paige mused, breaking into the mental telepathy between him and the hamster. 'Stay indoors much longer you'll be paler than Casper.'

Looking at the frigid jade of the ocean, Oliver figured the only thing he was at real risk of was freezing his bollocks off but at least outside he'd be free from the judgement of an obese hamster and a woman who was looking at him like he was a complete wastrel.

'Fine,' he huffed. 'But only for some damn peace and quiet.'

She smiled triumphantly, completely unconcerned by his annoyance. 'Whatever works.'

7

Ten minutes later, hunched into his jacket with a beanie pulled low, Oliver found himself on the beach, an excited Casper racing ahead like it was the first time he'd ever seen sand. He'd only got ten paces when his phone buzzed in his pocket.

Paige.

Nope. More fucking hamster bullshit.

> Here is your latest from HAMSTER FACTS! Did you know hamsters are highly trainable? They especially love the challenge of a maze. It has even been reported that a Siberian hamster in Sitka, Alaska, called Bear, knows how to recognise letters! Comment YES! if you think hamsters are truly a-maze-ing! Standard charges apply.

What the... *recognise letters*? Go home, hamster weirdo, you're drunk. The Hamster Facts person had clearly lost the plot.

Although, if it was true, maybe he could train Pavarotti to write the bloody book!

Shoving the phone and his hand back into his pocket, Oliver trudged along the beach. It wasn't windy but it was still bitingly cold, the chilly air burning his lungs. The ocean was still a frosty jade, making his testicles retract just looking at it, but it was calm, lapping at the beach with a tiny little frill of foam as it curled in to kiss the sand.

A frill that Casper was currently barking at, chasing the water as it ebbed, running away from it as it pushed forward again to terminate in another little curl of foam. A flock of seagulls landed nearby, their yellow beaks a bright splash against the dull background and Casper forgot all about chasing waves, taking off after them, announcing his imminent arrival with an excited bark, causing them to scatter.

It unleashed a memory from when he was a kid and he used to come to the beach house for his summer holidays. He must have been four or five, eating fish and chips on the beach with his dad. He remembered his father wore a pair of Speedos, his athletic frame a deep nut brown from his tanning salon addiction. Oliver had felt very special with practically everyone on the beach whispering and pointing at them because of his dad. Because they loved his dad. Which he totally understood because he loved his dad too.

A gull had swooped down and stolen a chip right out of his hand and Oliver had cried. More from the shock of it than the loss of the chip. His father had laughed initially but when Oliver had continued crying, he'd clearly been embarrassed by his son's emotional display, quipping to people nearby, 'Anybody'd think the kid had lost the part of Hamlet to an *American*.'

There'd been general laughter and he'd even signed an autograph and he may have only been young but Oliver could still remember realising that he wasn't the centre of his father's world.

Pulling his phone out of his pocket, Oliver navigated to his notes app and tapped the microphone and started to talk. 'I loved my father but nowhere near as much as he loved himself.'

And then he couldn't stop talking.

* * *

After almost an hour had passed and Oliver hadn't returned, Paige, who'd been sitting at the table attending to some urgent work that had landed, stopped what she was doing and opened the door to the deck. Frigid air slapped her in the face as she crossed to the railing, her eyes squinting as she identified the man and dog at the far end of the beach trudging back in her direction. Casper was giddily running about, alternating between chasing waves and chasing gulls.

Oliver was holding his phone close to his mouth which *was* moving and she smiled.

Was he making headway on the book? Or possibly leaving her a disgruntled voice mail about catching his death out on the beach. If it was the former she was going to be smug AF and planned to mention her brilliance as much as possible. If it was the latter, she'd delight in sending it to the Just Desserts WhatsApp chat.

Slipping back into the house, she resumed her work until she heard him enter via the downstairs door twenty minutes later. She could hear him talking to Casper and Paige smiled to herself again. She'd been doing that a lot where Oliver was concerned but seriously, for a man who'd professed to neither liking nor wanting a dog and a hamster, he seemed quite smitten with both of them.

'Hey,' Oliver greeted as he approached from behind.

As if she hadn't been spying on him from the deck, Paige turned, placing her arm along the back of the chair. 'Hey.'

He was pulling his beanie off, his dirty blond hair totally dishevelled and yet somehow disarmingly attractive in his faded jeans and chunky cable knit jumper. Had it been her letting her curls free from prolonged enclosure in a beanie, she'd have looked like she'd stuck her fingers in an electrical socket but no, Oliver bloody Prendergast looked like he'd just stepped out of the pages of an Old Spice commercial.

His cheeks were pink and his eyes bright and he didn't seem remotely cranky about the soggy dog beside him tracking sandy footprints across the pristine floorboards.

'You look pleased with yourself.'

He just nodded and smiled and somehow that had more of an effect on her than if he'd raved effusively. 'It was productive?'

'It was very productive.'

And he looked as if a load had been taken off his shoulders and that hit her straight in the solar plexus. She was here in this house to mess with his life a little. To throw a spanner in whatever works she could and this was the very opposite of that. She wasn't supposed to be helping him. But to see him like this – so... lit up, so engaged. It filled her in a way that nothing else had since she'd had to walk away from her law degree.

The success of her business had been fulfilling and a way to show the world that she'd moved on. But this? It filled an entirely different cavity inside her, one that yearned for an emotional connection she'd denied herself for so very long.

And that was as alarming as it was tantalising.

'So...' She wiggled her eyebrows to lighten the moment. 'I was right?'

He gave a half laugh. 'Yes.'

Pressing her lips together, Paige cupped a hand around her ear. 'I'm sorry, I don't think I heard you properly?'

He rolled his eyes. 'Yes, Paige Barker. You were right.'

'You do know I'm going to be unbearably conceited now, right?'

'I would expect nothing less.'

They smiled at each other then, for a stupidly long amount of time. Clearly weirded out by the prolonged interval of silence, Casper gave a little yippy bark which thankfully shattered the strange moment.

'Were you serious about helping me? With the transcribing.'

Paige blinked, getting her head back in the game. 'Sure. Absolutely.' She could still do that and screw with him in other ways, right?

'It's a bit all over the place, just stories I remember from when I was a kid.'

'That's fine. Why don't you download what you have into a Word doc or message it to me, whatever works and I can go from there. I can do a clean version and also start to sort things into some kind of chronological order so it'll help structure wise later.'

He nodded. 'I'm not sure of the quality, the wind blew up towards the end and probably interfered with the audio.'

'It's fine. If there's anything I can't figure out, I'll flag it. Have you thought about using an app like Dragon or something similar that actually learns your voice and the transcribing is much cleaner?'

'No.' He shook his head. 'But I'll look into it. Right after I get this one' – he glanced down at the wet dog – 'cleaned up.'

The one in question wagged his tail and stared adoringly at Oliver, clearly knowing he was in no danger of being disciplined over his bedraggled state.

Oliver ruffled the dog's head. 'You are an utter disgrace.'

But it was said with complete affection and Paige found herself, once again, all warm and fuzzy on the inside. *Gah!* It was starting to become a pattern. If she wasn't careful, it could become a habit. Helping Oliver with his father's biography was one thing. Getting the warm and fuzzies every time he looked at the dog was another.

She had to remember why she was here – he'd jilted Bella on the morning of their wedding. The affection of a stray dog didn't expunge that.

As if to remind her of her mission, her phone chimed a notification from the Just Desserts WhatsApp group. She knew it was them because she'd chosen a popping champagne cork as the sound.

Perfect timing.

Grateful for the interruption, she turned to pick up the device, her fingers stalling as Oliver said, 'You have two phones?'

A spike of adrenaline flushed into her system. *Fuuck.* The hamster phone – not quite as sexy as the bat phone but appropriate – was sitting out next to her actual phone, plain as day. *Careless.*

'You some kind of Jason Bourne?'

He laughed, clearly thinking the preposterous idea amusing. Except she *was* carrying out secret nefarious stuff so his joke was a little too close for comfort. She'd been having great fun making up shit about hamsters but she really needed to be more careful with this double life she was living. She might not be selling state secrets but what she was doing here was a secret from him.

'Oh yeah...' Paige forced both her voice and her actions to be casual as she picked up her phone. 'One personal, one for work. I like to keep my worlds separate.'

'Kinda like a... spy?'

She glanced at him and he was smiling again and the warmth was back despite the situation. 'Well, I could tell you the truth but then I'd have to kill you.'

His smile slowly faded, as their gazes locked. The breath practically stopped in Paige's lungs and she mentally kicked herself. For God's sake, she probably sounded like she was flirting with him. And she definitely *was not* flirting. She'd been... deflecting.

Quickly she added, 'And you have a dog to wash and a book to write.'

But for once, he didn't seem pained by either task, he just nodded before looking at Casper and saying, 'You heard her, dude, you're filthy.'

It probably shouldn't be a turn on that he'd said filthy, especially after Harvey had defiled their sex life by sharing it with the world. But the way Oliver said it with zero connotation and 1000 per cent posh Brit, reminded her that once upon a time, she'd loved getting a bit freaky between the sheets.

'Let's get you respectable,' Oliver continued cluelessly as he left with the dog close on his heels to what must surely be smoke billowing out from between her thighs and the clash of a hundred *not* very respectable thoughts running through her head.

* * *

By the time the following Tuesday rocked around, Paige had rationalised her uncharacteristic reaction to Oliver as purely hormonal. She was clearly ovulating and she never knew how the fuck that was going to pan out so, off-limit thoughts about Bella's ex were just this month's little gift from her ovaries.

It was so much *fun* being a woman.

To compensate she'd gone full VA-from-hell mode, ruthlessly organising and cataloguing his daily oral epistles while leaving coffee rings on every available surface, deliberately letting Pavarotti out which involved a two-hour hamster hunt and losing an earring down the sink which she pretended was a family heirloom and simply must be retrieved.

Oliver had suggested calling a plumber but she'd raised an eyebrow, clearly questioning his masculinity and he'd sighed and asked the great god Google for help because it hadn't taken a mind reader to figure out Oliver Prendergast had never got his hands dirty in his life.

When he'd finally fished it out despite the general dishevelment from a soaking of gross S-bend water, he'd looked exceptionally pleased with himself and damn if that wasn't just plain fucking adorable.

She knew a dozen men in her family alone who could unclog an S-bend without having to do a YouTube tutorial prior but somehow Oliver looking all blue collar as he triumphantly raised her two-pound charity shop earring – the little plastic rhinestone winking as it swung from his fingers – made her want to do him under the sink.

Gah!

But, she'd steadfastly ignored all of it. Unlike his writing which she found impossible to dismiss. Paige had made a career out of transcribing various clients' words into letters, booklets, manuals or whatever document they wanted with zero emotional investment. True they were generally dry business tomes dealing with policy and procedural matters or boring, impersonal company memos and correspondence so they were easy to deal with usually while music blasted into her eardrums.

Oliver's writings were about as personal as was possible to

be and utterly absorbing. The stories as they came in each day tugged at her heart strings. A boy with a father who he adored even through interactions that seemed brief and perfunctory to Paige and, she suspected Oliver, but obviously meant everything to the younger version of himself.

A boy with a mother who understood that her husband was too absorbed by a cutthroat industry and riding the wave of his fame to cultivate a rich family life but had assured young Oliver he was doing the best he could even though adult Oliver had mused in his recordings that she, too, had felt passed over. He recounted a tale when he'd been seven and he'd overheard her telling a friend that becoming emotionally dependent on Roger was pointless because he just didn't love her enough to make losing herself worthwhile.

It wasn't – thus far – a typical tale of fame and drugs and adultery like so many Hollywood biographies but she could *feel* Oliver's struggle for true connection with his father. The way his pride and admiration warred with his yearning for more. In the stories so far, Roger hadn't ignored his young son but Oliver had clearly felt the moments of greatest affection from his father were the moments when a camera was around.

The more she read, the more she disliked the famed Hollywood actor. Roger Prendergast may have been able to buy and sell her father dozens of times over but Paige had always been secure in her father's love and his affection had never felt budgeted or performative.

It made her feel wretched for Oliver and it wasn't what she wanted to feel. He'd wronged her friend, she was supposed to be feeling vengeful. Which was exactly what she was grappling with at Jiya's café when Doris and her WI crew crowded inside. The weather was overcast and chilly – just for something different...

The women waved to her as Doris walked over for her usual chat. Instead of her trademark smile however, a frown turned the lines on her forehead into deep furrows.

'You looked like you lost a pound and found a penny,' Paige said.

Doris *hmphed*. 'Pippa broke her ankle on the weekend,' she muttered with no preamble.

Paige blinked. Was she supposed to know who Pippa was? Although the name did sound familiar. 'Pippa?'

'Geraldine's great-niece? From ITV? And our guest speaker on Thursday?'

'Oh yes.' Paige nodded. She remembered now.

'She's apparently fine,' Doris continued. 'Had it pinned and plated yesterday and is being discharged today. I honestly don't see why she couldn't make it tomorrow; we offered to send a car but she declined which is very inconvenient. I mean, really, millennials never had it so easy. Whatever happened to carry on?'

Paige pressed her lips together at Dorry's obvious dismay. It was clearly very *un-British* of Pippa to let down the WI in their hour of need. But having broken her wrist several years ago and been shitfaced on pain killers for an entire week during which time she'd hadn't been able to string a sentence together let alone perform coherently as a guest speaker, Paige wasn't so quick to judge.

'Everyone is so terribly disappointed and now I have to scramble around for someone else to fill the spot at such short notice. Rebecca volunteered to talk about that time she was an extra on the second *James Bond* film but there's only so many times you can hear about what a gentleman David Niven was and how many times she shagged the head stuntman who apparently was hung like a donkey.'

Paige blinked. That did seem like a lot of TMI for a WI meeting.

Dorry sighed. 'Everyone was so looking forward to hearing some real insight into the film and TV industry.'

Before there was a chance to fully think it through, Paige was already opening her mouth. 'What would you say if I not only knew the son of a famous British Shakespearian actor who made it big in Hollywood but that he is currently living in St Ives. *And* is also a script writer?'

Well, that was a bit of a stretch but he had written scripts. Or partially written anyway. And he'd hate it which made it about as perfect as it could be.

Win/win.

It was Doris's turn to blink. 'You know Roger Prendergast's son?'

Paige supposed given the tabloid coverage of him being in St Ives all those months ago, it wouldn't take someone as switched on as Doris to put two and two together.

'I do.' She wasn't about to admit to living with him lest she have the entire WI turn up on her doorstep.

Although…

'That would be amazing!' Doris's eyes sparkled. 'Would he say yes, do you think?'

'Of course. We're like this,' she said, lying her ass off as she crossed one finger over the top of the other to demonstrate said closeness. 'I reckon he'd love to help out the WI.'

Given it had taken her weeks to pry him off his couch to just step outside the door to the beach, she knew for sure he was going to hate it. Paige couldn't wait to see his face when she sprung it on him. 'I'm sure he wouldn't even mind bringing along one of his dad's BAFTAs, probably the Oscar statue too.'

Doris's eyes practically bugged right out of her head she was so incandescent with excitement. Paige felt a momentary twinge about using an unsuspecting WI in her payback plan for Oliver. But it *was* doing them a favour. And if it just so happened to completely inconvenience Oliver at the same time then even better.

'Oh my.' Doris pressed her hand to her chest like she was about to take a fit of the vapours. 'That's better than anything Pippa could offer.'

Paige figured poor Pippa had enough on her hands to be miffed over being one-upped by an Oscar statue.

'Ladies!' Doris turned to the group giving their coffee orders, beaming like a freaking lighthouse. 'We have a replacement for Pippa that's going to blow your minds.'

And that was it, there was no going back now.

* * *

'No. *Absolutely not*. One hundred per cent no.'

'Oliver.' Paige, expecting resistance, folded her arms and adopted her sternest expression. She'd waited until later that night when he was watching one of his favourite movies in the media room before she dropped her bombshell. 'It's the WI. They're a national institution. You can't say no to them.'

The overhead lights were out, the flickering of the screen casting shadows on the walls and across their faces. Oliver paused the movie, the shadows freezing in place as Oliver also folded his arms and returned her gaze unflinchingly. 'Watch me.'

Casper, who was lying on the couch between them, whined slightly, obviously unhappy about the tension between his humans. 'You want to say no to a bunch of women whose mothers and grandmothers practically ran the country through two world wars? You're a braver person than I am. They *know* things, Oliver.'

There was no response. Just unblinking resolve.

'Besides, I've already told them you would.'

'Well *un*-tell them.'

She shook her head, her curls bouncing. 'It's impossible. It's a done deal. I promised Doris. They're expecting you and they're so excited. Myrtle is making a batch of her scones which are reputedly the best in the county.'

Oliver gaped. 'How can you be in town for just over three weeks and already know Doris and Myrtle from the bloody WI?'

'Because I'm not an anti-social hermit. I met them at Jiya's café in town and we got talking.' She bugged her eyes. 'This may come as a surprise but people actually like me.'

Before she got plastered all over the internet, Paige had been very social. She made friends easily and liked to chat to random people at a coffee shop or on the Underground. The revenge porn had made her more guarded, pushed her into a shell and she was only just starting to realise this exercise she was undertaking with Oliver was dragging her out of her comfort zone as well.

He opened his mouth as if about to rebut what she'd said then shut it again before saying, 'No. It doesn't surprise me.'

Paige wasn't sure if it was a compliment and refused to dig for more info but her body was taking it as one anyway, flushing with pleasure. Not sexy times pleasure but pleasure at being appreciated. God knew if anyone had a reason to not like her, especially after her campaign of discomfort by a thousand paper cuts, it was Oliver but he was regarding her earnestly and the only conclusion she could draw was that he liked her, too?

Despite the constant irritant she'd been to him these past weeks.

She wished she knew how to answer that but she didn't so she pushed on while he was seemingly amenable to her presence.

'So that's a yes then?'

There was another beat or two of intense regard before he threw back his head and laughed. 'Only you,' he said, rolling his head to the side as his laughter settled, 'would turn a compliment into something completely different.'

His eyes settled on hers and even hooded in shadows, the intensity of their Roger Prendergast blueness pierced right through to her brain.

'It would mean so much to them,' she pressed. 'Wouldn't you like to know that you made a bunch of little old ladies happy?'

If Paige thought she had him, she was wrong. Oliver Prendergast decided to play hard ball instead. 'I'll trade you.'

She frowned. She didn't like the sound of that but if it got her what she wanted then... 'Okay. I'm listening.'

'If I do this, you only practice that damn violin when I'm on the beach.'

Paige stifled a smile. Every time he winced during her practice sessions it felt like another little paper cut for Bella. 'But I'm getting better. Pavarotti likes it so much, he jumps straight on his wheel when he hears it. It's like he has his own personal workout orchestra.'

Oliver snorted. 'I hate to be the one to break this to you but he gets on the wheel as soon as you start up that bloody racket so he can drown you out.'

She suspected Oliver was right which should have been annoying but instead the fact that he knew the hamster so well was just charming as all giddy up. 'Okay fine. Deal.'

Paige stuck out her hand and he took it but she was not prepared for the surge of heat that trekked up her arm as they shook. Nor was he if the way he looked at their joined hands was any indication.

What was even happening now?

Withdrawing her hand, she said briskly, 'On one condition.'

'Nope. It is unconditional. Do not pass go. No correspondence will be entered into.'

'Hey, you started the haggling, not me.'

'I think the term you're after is negotiations.'

He sounded so stuffy when he said it but his very British accuracy appealed to the baby lawyer in her which once again strengthened her resolve to keep making life uncomfortable for Oliver because, damn it, she'd have made an excellent lawyer.

'They would love for you to bring along the BAFTA.' She glanced up at the row of awards that, even in the darkened environment, dominated the room in all their cold, gleaming glory. 'And the Oscar. Kinda like show and tell.'

Oliver gaped at her like she'd asked him to do the talk naked. 'That Oscar is insured for a million quid!'

It was Paige's turn to gape as she turned her eyes on the golden statue standing erect as an army colonel and possibly as arrogant as one too. *Wow.* 'Okay, that's a lot.'

'It's an *Oscar*. A best actor Oscar. One of the most coveted awards in the world. And rare. There's only been 103 recipients to date.'

Paige had assumed the gleaming hardware above was reasonably valuable but that figure set her back on her feet.

'Other than a monthly feather dusting from the cleaner, it hasn't been touched since it was set up there next to the others over a decade ago.'

Frowning, Paige dragged her gaze off it to Oliver. 'What? Your father didn't get it down and look at it every now and then? Show his buddies? Surely you've done the same?'

'Of course not, I've never touched it. I've never touched any of them.'

He'd *never* touched any of them?

'They're there to be looked at. To be admired.'

Look but don't touch. It sounded very much like Oliver's relationship with his father from what she'd gleaned from the recordings. Oliver could look but he couldn't touch. Roger Prendergast could be loved and admired – in fact he both craved and demanded it – but only at a distance.

'Haven't you ever wanted to?' Paige knew if her father had a gold Oscar to his name, everyone in the family would have pictures holding it. Hell, she and her siblings would have each taken it to school for show and tell, at his insistence. It would no doubt have come home with hundreds of sticky finger prints dulling its shine and he'd have just given it a quick polish – probably with the tail of whatever shirt he was wearing – and popped it back on the shelf in his shed or maybe in the loo.

Wasn't that where Emma Thompson kept hers?

He shrugged. 'Sure. I guess.'

'Then why haven't you?' She didn't need to say, *Your dad's not around any more to police or object*, it was implied.

'I guess it's never felt like... the right moment?'

Paige wondered what that moment might be and if it would ever occur but instead of pressing him on it, she just nodded. 'I had a great-aunt once, Bessie, who as a young woman, fell in love with an antique china tea set with a delicate bluebell pattern that she'd seen in a local dealer's window. She couldn't afford it, so she negotiated with the owner to pay it off at a sixpence a week. It took her a year but she did it.'

He quirked an eyebrow. 'Am I Great-aunt Bessie in this equation?'

Ignoring him, Paige continued her story. 'It was her pride

and joy and even as a kid I could see why. It was so pretty, the flowers all hand painted, the porcelain so delicate that when the sun shined on it you could almost see through it. Every time we visited I asked if we could use it for morning tea but she'd just ruffle my hair and laugh and say she was saving it for a very special occasion, like the Queen visiting.'

'Let me guess,' he said derisively, 'the Queen never visited?'

Paige's lips twitched. 'Nope, she never did. She died when I was fourteen having never actually drunk tea or served cakes from it. She'd *loved* it and waited to use it for over fifty years and she never did.'

The set had gone to her daughter who had sold it to a dealer a few months later which made Paige sad all over again remembering it now.

'Your point being, life's short, don't wait for the right moment?'

'My point being, get the damn Oscar down and spread some of that Hollywood stardust around to some little old ladies from the local WI.'

And for yourself. Get it down and see that it's a one-foot-tall *bauble* awarded at a moment in time and not a statement of a person's worth or character. Nor was it a divining rod for a person's success. Maybe at eye level it would be less intimidating. Maybe Oliver could see that it was just an object that had only as much power as he gave it.

Although Paige wisely said none of that.

'Have you never just done something for someone for no other reason than because you knew it would please them?'

Surely, if more people in this world did that there'd be less Horrible Harveys.

He regarded her for long moments as if he was seriously considering the question which was clearly vexing him if the scowl spreading across his ridiculously attractive features was any indication.

Even scowling he managed to look effortlessly sexy.

'Okay fine,' he huffed. 'You have a deal. I take the awards and you never play that damn instrument in my presence again.'

Paige nodded with zero smugness and left the room before he changed his mind.

8
―――

Oliver hadn't known what to expect in the WI hall but it hadn't been a giant rainbow flag hanging on the wall behind the raised stage and what felt like every poster from every movie and stage play his father had ever starred in, decorating the walls.

It was a sweet gesture but it was also *a lot* and he almost backed out in the first minute. But then Paige's words came back to him.

Have you never just done something for someone for no other reason than because you knew it would please them?

The answer to that had been easy – yes. For Bella. And where had that got him? A red-headed whirling dervish with a hamster in a cage on his doorstep. But her prompt had reminded him why he'd said yes to Bella in the first place.

Guilt. Repentance. And talking to the WI somehow felt all part and parcel of that. Plus, he didn't really want to turn out like Great-aunt Bessie.

For fuck's sake, he'd known Paige for three weeks and already knew about her aunt with a china fetish.

What was even happening now?

Still, standing in front of them all, their eager faces smiling at him, Oliver wished he'd inherited his father's ease with strangers. Just being around him had given Oliver confidence and he missed him fiercely in this moment. But then he found Paige in the audience smiling and nodding at him and he relaxed.

If she could turn up here today, her hair scrunched into tiny balls all over her head, secured with multi-coloured bands *and* in a jumpsuit that looked like it had been inspired by a Tellytubby orgy without a single qualm, he could certainly give his standard spiel about his father – the one everyone wanted to hear – and be back home on the couch next to Casper in an hour.

So, mentally wrapping his father's red cashmere scarf around his neck, he launched into the version everyone knew, and the appreciative audience lapped it up without interruption. Laughing at the funny anecdotes, clutching their hearts when he told the story of the night his father had proposed to his mother and hanging on his every word about when Roger finally won his Oscar.

There were questions – none he hadn't answered before about a zillion times – and then it was all over and he was being ushered to a table where the BAFTA and Oscar had been placed and was given a plate of Meryl's scones with Edna's strawberry jam and locally sourced clotted cream.

Of course, there were also pictures, phones coming out everywhere to snap a memento of the day and then Doris haranguing everyone to pose both individually and as a group with him for the quarterly newsletter which apparently came out next week. Oliver had a moment of worry that they might find their way on to social media but it wasn't like the paps didn't know he was in Cornwall.

He'd just become a boring recluse. Attending a WI meeting would only confirm it.

People asked politely if they could touch and hold the Oscar for their photos and he nodded amiably. Paige was right, the awards were far less intimidating taken down from on high. And if he was going to break his father's strict no-touching rule, he might as well do it with a bang.

'C'mon, Paige – your turn,' Doris bossed as she interrupted a conversation Paige was having nearby with someone he thought was called Caroline.

She turned, a ham and cheese sandwich triangle in her hand and he almost laughed out loud. 'You are seriously the worst vegan ever.'

Shrugging, she said, 'Let's just call me... vegan curious.'

'Or maybe, a carnivore with occasional vegan tendencies?'

Her mouth twitched a little but she didn't get a chance for a comeback as Doris got them back on track. 'Over here Paige. A photo with Oliver and Oscar.'

'Oh no.' Paige shook her head, her alien-like bobbles unmoving on her head. Anybody else would have looked ridiculous but Paige just looked like... well, Paige. The one that had landed on his doorstep in a windswept frizz of red curls and ridiculous T-shirt slogans like the one she was wearing today beneath her heavy ex-army surplus duffle.

In my defence, I was left unsupervised.

'I don't do pictures.'

Doris scoffed. 'Nonsense. If it wasn't for you, we wouldn't have had this marvellous morning that is going to be talked about for the next decade. Far more exciting than anything Pippa could have offered. You *must*.'

Oliver watched as Paige plastered on a smile but there was a slight wariness to her expression. Clearly, she wasn't comfortable with the idea. Which made him wonder if it was a camera-shy thing or a *him* thing.

'Seriously, I take a hideous picture. Even my baby photos are awful. I'm the most unphotogenic person you'll ever meet. Just mention my name if you want to put something in the magazine.'

Doris looked like she was about to push some more and Oliver watched as a flash of what looked like... *anxiety?* flared in Paige's hazel eyes before the shutters came down.

'Dorry,' he said, diverting the older woman who preened a little at his use of her pet name. 'I was surprised to see the rainbow flag. I hope you don't mind me saying but I wouldn't have thought the WI was a bastion of progressive ideology.'

Diverted, Doris gave a chuckle. 'We do have a conservative reputation that's for sure, but a few years ago Caroline and Nell – she couldn't make it today – were both widowed within a few weeks of each other. They'd been good friends for years and then, a year later they were lezzers.'

Oliver choked on his sip of tea at the word choice. He couldn't decide if he was weirded out more by a word he was pretty sure was very unPC coming from a non-lesbian person or the fact that it had come out of the mouth of an octogenarian who was wearing a string of pearls around her neck.

The pearls, she'd told him, were in honour of Oscar.

Doris ploughed on through Oliver's coughing fit while Paige patted him on the back. 'And they were moving in together.'

Caroline, obviously hearing her name, joined them, nodding and beaming. 'Yep, lesbians,' she said as if she was still couldn't quite believe it herself. 'Took us both by surprise. But it did explain why I was always fascinated with boobs.'

More than a little fascinated with boobs himself, Oliver could understand.

'They were nervous coming out to us,' Doris recounted. 'Thought we might kick them out of the group. Utter nonsense.' She tutted, clearly still affronted by the notion. 'Caro and Nell are as much a part of our group as anyone else. So, unbeknownst to them we held several secret craft night sessions and patchworked the rainbow flag from scraps of fabric from our own clothes so they knew they would always be welcome.'

'It was such a relief,' Caroline chimed in, smiling at Doris, her eyes all misty.

'Love is love.' Doris grinned.

Oliver, now recovered, raised his tea cup. 'Amen.'

The other three did the same and he caught Paige's eye as they all tapped them together with a muted *clink*. She was eyeing him with an expression he couldn't quite decipher. Like she was trying to puzzle him out? Maybe passing judgement?

Whatever it was, it was intense for a beat or two then she seemed to snap out of it and smiled at him, a genuine smile and he felt like he'd passed some kind of test he hadn't known he'd been sitting.

Maybe for the first time she was seeing him as a good guy instead of the asshole who jilted her friend at the altar. More importantly, maybe he was, too?

* * *

Oliver was contemplating that fact later that night sitting in the darkened media room as he stared down the Oscar – the BAFTA had been returned to its shelf on high – and a bottle of his father's expensive vintage cognac which had also been under a *don't touch* order.

In for a penny, in for a pound, right?

It had been a cathartic day in lots of ways. And a much

longer one than he'd initially hoped. Far from being home within the hour, it took almost four hours to depart the hall. Every time he'd tried to edge away, someone else would pounce, regaling him with some Roger Prendergast anecdote or other from St Ives or talk about how something had resonated for them in one of his plays or films.

He'd even been shown pictures of single daughters and granddaughters.

Not to mention that somehow, he'd been finagled into letting the six-year-old grandson of one of the women take the Oscar to school when it was his turn for show and tell.

Maybe they'd been spiking his endless cups of tea with gin.

He laughed at the thought mostly because it was preposterous but also because he'd had three generous slugs of the cognac and was on his way to hammered. Casper was upstairs somewhere with Paige who'd been head down in some work ever since they'd arrived home. Pavarotti was asleep in his cage, the lights of the flickering television shining in the reddy-gold streaks of his seemingly untamable quiff.

It was quiet, apart from *Groundhog Day* playing on the screen but the volume was low and Oliver was barely paying it any attention as he stared at the Oscar. Seeing him being treated today like a curiosity – a fancy one for sure but still a curiosity – and not some revered precious jewel had been normalising.

And the pleasure the WI women had derived from holding it, the pleasure *he'd* derived from watching them had helped break down the mystique of it. Oscar could be touched and held and enjoyed and that was okay.

Their stories today had also given him a deeper insight to his father. He was well used to hearing important people talk about his father's acting greatness. Critics and peers and industry boffins. About his abundant talent, his formal training, his unrivalled technique – *blah blah blah*. But that wasn't what the WI women had talked about. They'd talked about how something in a film had touched them or meant something to them in some way and it felt authentic rather than pandering or ego stroking.

And it had made him see his father in a different light. Not as a performer but as a conduit for people's memories and emotions. It had certainly given him something to think about as he went forward with the book. More nuance and context.

He'd been grumpy all over again this morning as a painfully chipper Paige had dragged him to the hall but he was inordinately pleased he'd gone. For the first time in a long time he'd seen his father as a human being, something he'd felt less and less as he'd grown from a boy into a young adult.

Moving to the States to live with his father when he'd been fifteen had been his attempt to bridge that gap and they'd gone on to have what many of his friends would describe as an enviable relationship. Roger had been happy to have Oliver with him and very keen that they have a grown-up relationship.

That they be buds. Pals. But, deep down, Oliver had craved a deeper connection with his father. He'd wanted a dad. Not another friend. And he'd re-discovered a little of his dad with these women today.

His phone pinged and he reached for it absently.

> Here's your latest from HAMSTER FACTS! Did you know hamsters love toys? No – not that kind.

Oliver blinked. Either he was drunker than he thought or the work experience kid had been let loose with the texts today. For pure amusement value, he'd given up blocking them ages ago.

> As well as wheels they love balls, tunnels and are especially fond of chew toys. Stimulate them daily by switching up their environment on the regular. Press 1 for links to recommended hamster safe products. Standard messaging rates may apply.

Oliver glanced over at the sleeping rodent. Chew toys, huh? His gaze swivelled to the Oscar, his golden hue a little dull in the dark without his spotlight glowing glory upon him. A smile spread across his face as a delightfully tipsy idea floated to the surface.

Pushing to his feet he grabbed Oscar around the middle and took three strides to Pavarotti's cage. The rodent stirred when Oliver lifted the latch, one eyelid fluttering open, blearily assessing his visitor then shutting again. He was clearly too exhausted from his new fitness regime to be bothered by the interruption especially from his bro dude.

'Sorry, old mate,' Oliver said to Oscar, 'I'll break you out after a couple of days.'

Manoeuvring the one foot, eight-pound statue into the corner of the cage just behind the amazing wheel of lights and colour, he smiled to himself as he settled it into the nesting fluff. He wasn't sure how Pavarotti would take the intimidating proportions in the morning or the fact his cage was rapidly resembling some kind of bizarre Las Vegas-style theme park but, with his cognac goggles firmly in place, Oliver thought it was hilarious.

Heading back to the couch, he admired his handiwork. Oscar look dour as ever and maybe the shock of waking to a one foot golden, graven statue in the morning may not be good for Pavarotti's heart but it sure as fuck felt damn good right now.

His father would be *pissed*. And somehow that felt extra good.

Oliver raised his glass in salute. 'Cheers.' And took another slug.

Muted footsteps from behind alerted him to the imminent arrival of Paige but it was Casper who arrived first, leaping onto the couch and assuming his regular position stretched out on his side, his head propped on top of Oliver's thigh.

'Hey bud,' Oliver crooned and absently fondled a soft, floppy ear, earning himself a couple of tails thumps.

'You *are* still down here,' Paige said as she rounded the couch in the semi dark and took a seat on the end cushion that Casper had so graciously left for her. 'It was so quiet I thought you must have gone to bed. You normally have the TV up so loud I can follow along upstairs.'

Oliver shrugged. 'No point having the best surround sound system money can buy if you're not going to use it.'

She was wearing a polar fleece tiger onesie – because of course she was. But her hair was out of those ridiculous balls and was fluffed around her head in its usual disorder and the central zipper of the onesie ended at a point between her breasts that left a generous amount of cleavage exposed.

He was reminded of Caroline's quip today about breasts and his gaze lingered on the pillowy flesh. If he pulled on that zipper would she just peel out of that thing like a banana? Blinking at the crazy thought, he took another drink. Do not go *there,* knob head.

After the way he'd treated Bella, it was a miracle this woman hadn't murdered him in his sleep as some kind of sisterhood revenge. The last thing he needed was to develop some kind of sexual fixation on his jilted bride's friend. Paige might be tolerating him because he'd been able to help her out of an accommodation bind but women stuck together.

Everyone knew that.

Still, maybe he could just lay his head there where it looked all warm and soft and drift off to sleep. Or maybe he was drunker than he thought...

She glanced at the top shelf above before turning her gaze on him, a tiny frown knitting her brows together in a little V, reminding him of the V of her cleavage, all soft and squishy.

Jesus, *dude*... get your shit together.

'Where's Oscar?'

He pointed. 'In there.'

She turned her attention to the cage, squinting into the dark, her eyes widening a little as they zeroed in on the statue dominating the cage like some ridiculous golden phallus.

'*Ohhh*-kay,' she murmured as her gaze pulled back to him before moving quickly to the bottle on the table. 'Are you drunk?'

'Nope. Not yet. Well...' Oliver grinned. 'Perhaps a tiny bit tipsy.'

'I see. And what are we drinking?'

'My father's very best vintage cognac he'd been saving up for who knew what.'

'Ah...' She nodded. 'We're having a little day of rebellion then?'

Oliver laughed, short and sharp. He liked that Paige was insightful and not reticent to speak her mind round him. Too many people in his life had pulled their punches because of who his father was. Even Bella had rarely called him on his bullshit.

'Something like that.' He lifted the bottle. 'You want one?'

'No.' She shook her head.

'Not a drinker?'

It was her turn to laugh, the flickering light from the TV making the merriment in her eyes shimmer. 'I've been known to indulge in my time but I've just brushed my teeth. Plus, someone clearly has to be the responsible party here tonight in case you decide to really let it rip and poor Pavarotti wakes up to a couple of Tonys in his cage as well.'

Oliver's lips twitched at the idea – a real Hollywood bro hang out – but he dismissed it as physically impossible. 'And that's you, huh? The responsible party?'

'Apparently,' she quipped but the shimmer dimmed a little and Oliver was reminded of that moment at the WI hall today when Doris had been pushing for a picture and Paige's shutters had come down.

Curious and curiouser.

'Sounds boring,' he said with a tease, hoping to lighten the mood. Hoping if he gave her enough space she might elaborate.

'That's me.' A really big, really fake smile pushed up the corners of her mouth. 'The boring one.'

Oliver's gaze dropped to the zipper in her cleavage. *Not from where he was sitting.* 'I have a tiger onesie that begs to differ.'

She shrugged. 'Another sibling purchase.'

'I think I'm going to have to meet this brother and sister of yours. They seem fun.'

'Yeah,' she murmured, the carnival clown smile softening into something much more natural. 'They are. Now' – her voice turned brisk – 'I'm off to Bedfordshire.'

Levering forward at the hips, she looked over her shoulder at him. For a moment he thought she was going to warn him to go easy or something boring but instead she shot him a wry smile. 'Do you think I can trust you not to put up your father's awards on eBay or something equally as impulsive?'

'Ooh...' Now that *would* be kinda awesome. 'Probably not.' He wasn't sure this strange mood he was in could be trusted with anything. Picking up his glass, he downed the last finger of cognac, sucking in the velvety kick on an indrawn breath. 'Better hit the sack too, just in cases.'

'*Love Actually*?'

'Ha!' He pointed at her. Or at least in her general direction anyway. 'You got it.'

'I'm not a complete heathen,' she said, rolling her eyes as she stood.

Oliver also pushed to his feet, flicking the TV off with the remote, plunging the room into darkness apart from the muted light spilling over the awards on the top shelf. Casper had already disappeared up the stairs by the time Oliver was following behind Paige, her tiger stripes swaying from side to side with all the natural grace of the animal itself which was really quite hypnotising.

She took the first two stairs and he dragged his eyes off her ass as he realised he really hadn't thanked her for today. 'Thanks,' he said. Her foot faltered on the third step. 'For today. Seriously. I know I made a fuss about going but it's given me a much deeper insight into my father. It was something I truly hadn't expected.'

Slowly, she turned, her elevation equalising their heights and putting her far closer to him than was good for his sanity right now. Her full lips were a ripe, red rouge as her familiar zestiness tickled his nostrils. The lush rise and fall of her cleavage was right there in his peripheral vision, daring him to look. To touch.

To prove that it was indeed as soft as it looked.

Oliver's mouth turned dry as the shavings in Pavarotti's cage and the air in his lungs followed suit. The low, slow thud of his pulse beat loud in his ears as the air around them seemed to bloom, thick with possibility.

'Even if you were roped into taking Oscar in for young Stevie's show and tell?'

Despite the intimacy encroaching around them, Oliver laughed, 'Yes.'

She laughed too and they were both laughing and it felt damn good. But it didn't ruin the intimacy; if anything, it intensified as his gaze zeroed in on her mouth. It was close – so close he could smell the minty note of her toothpaste on her breath.

Would she taste minty? Would the mix of cognac and Colgate be as heady in actuality as it was just thinking about it? The thick surge of blood beating through every pulse point in his body demanded he find out.

'You've been a real godsend, Paige Barker, you know that?'

He hadn't planned on saying that – hell, none of this was planned – but it was true. Except it appeared to not be the right thing to say as she seemed to flinch and the shutters slowly came down on her laughing eyes.

Which was more than Oliver could bear. So, he leaned in and kissed her, sliding in before they shut for good.

Also *not* planned. And, for a second, they both just stood there in the startling moment, bodies tense, joined only by two sets of stiff, unmoving lips, Oliver unsure about his next move.

Smooth, dude. Real smooth.

Should he withdraw and apologise? Brace for a kick to his balls? Or slide his hand into her hair and deepen the damn thing like every cell in his body was demanding? The moment stretched, one beat, two. A couple of seconds suspended in time, the fate of the kiss hanging in the balance, his heart not beating at all right now, also suspended as if the very next beat depended on how the moment played out.

Then she made a little noise at the back of her throat, the kind of noise that came from deep primitive places and her entire body relaxed, the tension holding her rigid oozing away, her lips softening on a sigh that Oliver felt right down in his own primitive places.

His heart kickstarted and he breathed her in as his lips moved gently, opening a little, brushing across her mouth, probing, coaxing, growing a little bolder as she responded to the deepening, kissing him back a little.

Chaste and tentative for sure but definitely reciprocal.

A hot, giddy rush of triumph and pleasure surged straight to Oliver's head and buzzed through every cell of his body. He'd had a lot of first kisses in his life. Many had been way more X-rated than this but none of them had been with this giddying woman who had confounded him from the start and was confounding him even now. The taste of her lips like the taste of his father's cognac – ripe, full-bodied, off-limits.

Addicting.

Alas, it did not last long, her abrupt withdrawal a confusing moment for both of them if the way she stared at him was any indication. Her breathing was as ragged as his as her tongue absently touched her bottom lip like she couldn't quite believe what had happened.

Clearing the thickness from his throat, Oliver broke the burgeoning silence. 'Paige—'

But she shook her head vigorously, cutting him off, which wasn't a bad thing given he had no idea what he was going to say next.

'Don't,' she whispered.

Oliver wasn't sure what she meant by 'don't'. Don't talk. Don't look at me. Don't try and make this better? So he just said,

'Okay,' because he'd say anything right now to ease the torment from her features.

'Don't do that again.'

He faltered at the edict but didn't hesitate in his response. 'Okay.'

'I mean it, Olly. It *can't* happen again.'

It was the first time she'd ever called him Olly and somehow amongst all the fucked-up confusion of the moment, it felt... *significant*. 'I understand.' If that's what she wanted, he'd of course respect it.

Even though he seriously fucking wanted to kiss her again.

One more long look was followed by a stiff little nod before she turned away and bolted up the stairs, two at a time.

Oliver stood on the spot long after Paige had disappeared from sight, his brain turning around and around like a washing machine on a spin cycle. Easing himself down on the step, he was conscious of not only the ache in his balls but the tightness in his chest. He'd just had the best damn *chaste* kiss of his life with his *ex's* friend.

Jesus.

Casper found him at that moment and sat his ass on the step beside Oliver, snuggling in for a pat which Oliver absently doled out. 'I think I fucked up, buddy.'

The dog thumped its tail as if in agreement and Oliver gave a mirthless half laugh. Yeah... that was pretty much par for the course for him.

9

Shit. Shit. Shit.

Paige's internal condemnation prattled along in time to the erratic thump of her pulse and the vicious swipe of the toothbrush as she *re-brushed* her teeth. She was no doubt taking off years of enamel right now but all she could taste was cognac and runaway groom and she *couldn't* go to bed with the taste of Oliver bloody Prendergast taunting her all night long.

God... *What had she done?* Why had she let him kiss her?

She knew why Oliver had done it – he'd been several cognacs the worse for wear. But what in hell was her excuse? Because she'd known he was going to kiss her in those weird, still moments just prior. Hell, her breath had evaporated as she'd waited for his move, her lips had tingled in anticipation.

Which was ridiculous. She should have been screaming at him to back off. She should have kneed him in the testicles. She should have turned her ass around and walked away. But it'd been the strangest thing – she hadn't been able to move. No, *worse* than that, she hadn't *wanted* to.

Oh, God...

Spitting and rinsing, she eyed herself in the mirror as she wiped her mouth. Her face was paler than usual, her freckles standing out like the Hobnob crumbs she took great delight in leaving everywhere in the house.

'Paige Barker, how could you?' she hiss-whispered. 'You are a... traitor to your sex. To the sisterhood.'

Her gaze zeroed in on her mouth. The mouth which Oliver had kissed so damn perfectly – soft, gentle, coaxing – her entire insides had dissolved. The mouth that had betrayed her newest friend, who thought she was in Oliver's house getting payback, not kissing up to the guy who'd left her standing in her twenty-thousand-dollar Vera Wang dress on their wedding day.

She was a horrible, *horrible* person.

Unable to look at herself, Paige curled her hands into fists and spread them wide on top of the vanity, dropping her head, until it was hanging between her shoulder blades. Staring at, but not seeing the dark marble grain, she scrambled for what to do next. She *should* leave. Go home. Get out now.

And not just because of how badly she'd betrayed Bella but because, how could she even face Oliver again?

It was tempting to hope that Oliver's alcohol consumption might result in a case of amnesia. But, there was a big difference in imbibing enough to loosen inhibitions and imbibing enough to be black-hole hungover the next day and he'd definitely not been *that* drunk. He'd certainly seemed *very* sober at the end.

So she was going to have to face him tomorrow. And the next day. And the next day. The memory of the kiss making things awkward AF between them.

Ugh. *Pass.*

But... up and leaving with another month of her payback plan left unfulfilled would lead to a lot of questions from her Just Desserts gang. *A lot.* And there was no way she could tell any of them what had just happened. Bella would be furious – rightly so. Sienna and Astrid wouldn't be far behind.

They'd probably cut her from the group and never talk to her again and Paige couldn't bear the thought of these women she'd formed such a fast friendship with, *spurning* her – cutting her off. She hadn't really realised how lonely the past four years had been isolating herself from any kind of close relationship, until she'd sat down at that table in O'Hare and magically found herself three kindred spirits.

She didn't want to lose their friendship.

Not to mention how worried her parents would be if she upped and left early. She'd brought enough angst into their lives, thanks to Harvey and the last thing she wanted to do was exacerbate her father's chronic health issues. She'd worked hard to get her life back on track so they didn't have to worry about her, she wouldn't ruin that now.

Which meant, she was going to have to stay and suck it up. Redouble her commitment to the payback plan. What Oliver had done was worth more than one lousy month of irritating inconveniences. She needed to stick to the plan, see it through. *Then* she could walk away.

You've been a godsend. That's what he'd said. Well… she'd see about that.

Lifting her head, Paige stared at herself in the mirror again, her curls rustling as they settled around her face. 'You can do this,' she told her reflection. 'It was just a kiss.'

An alcohol induced one at that and tomorrow morning she'd shrug it off like it was nothing and they could put it behind them like two mature adults.

But first, she needed to brush her teeth one more time.

* * *

After a night of half-formed dreams involving Oliver kissing her in just about every nook and cranny in the house *and* every nook and cranny on her person, Paige woke not only feeling guilty but also horny. The taste she'd sampled last night had morphed into something far more erotic in her dreams, making her excruciatingly aware of her body.

Even the damn sheets tangled around her bare legs were weirdly stimulating.

Gritting her teeth, she grabbed her phone and navigated to the WhatsApp group as she did every morning. There was the usual overnight chatter full of plans and logistics. Bella was in the process of setting up a king blow to Chase that she was excited about and Astrid seemed to have the Aiden situation under control. Paige wanted to join in the conversation but guilt weighed heavily on her shoulders.

Bella was getting on with her part of the deal – getting even with Chase for Astrid. The other two were also making inroads, even if just in the planning stages. And what was she doing? Kissing Oliver bloody Prendergast. She was not only failing to uphold her end of the bargain, she was *consorting* with the freaking enemy.

Paige shut the app down and groaned into the pillow. She couldn't bring herself to join in, not when she'd done something so egregious. She felt like the worst kind of friend. But, even more than that, she felt like all three of them would be able to read between the lines and know something was up.

For now, avoidance seemed the best strategy. At least until she could get some distance and perspective from the kiss. Although God alone knew how she was going to do that when her body tingled at the very thought of it and she was living in close proximity to the guy who'd dished it out.

A guy who'd, yes, jilted her friend at the aisle but who'd also, without hesitation, opened his door to her. And a hamster. And a dog. And been very sweet with a bunch of old ladies. A guy who was still struggling with the loss of his father and unpacking a lifetime of baggage in what had been a complicated relationship.

A guy who, had she met independently, she probably would have liked – a lot. Hell, even Bella had said he wasn't a bad guy.

But he *had* done a bad thing and that should be her only focus.

* * *

Oliver finally appeared at ten in the morning. Paige knew he was on the approach before she heard him because Pavarotti stopped running on his wheel and rushed to the side of his cage like a groupie. Then, as if to confirm it, the fine hairs on her nape prickled the way her skin had been prickling all morning at the thought of him.

'Morning,' he said from behind her somewhere, the click of Casper's toenails audible as he got closer.

His greeting sounded pained, his voice a little husky and Paige smiled at the distinct lack of *good* in front of his rather stilted greeting. Excellent, he had a hangover. She hoped it was a doozy.

Sure, she may have kissed him back but he'd started it and she was *pissed*.

Closing down her browser window, she took a steadying breath and pushed the chair back hoping for a horrendous scaping noise but it glided with effortless Scandi efficiency and quiet – of course.

'Coffee?' she asked, sparing him a quick glance only as she

entered the kitchen where he'd leaned his ass against the edge of a counter top. Casper wagged his tail at her.

'God, yes please,' he muttered, shoving a hand through his sexily dishevelled bed hair.

Of course. When she was hungover she woke up looking like a scarecrow.

Turning her back on the way his Calvin Klein boxers rode high on thighs that would have been perfectly at home in an anatomy textbook, Paige clunked her mug on the counter as loudly as she could without breaking it. Pulling one off the nearby mug tree, she slapped it down too.

'Must you make so much noise?' he grouched.

Turning, she shot him a sweet smile. 'Hungover?'

He eyed her *Sorry for having great tits and correct opinions* T-shirt warily, choosing to grunt in response to her question and not comment on the slogan.

Grimacing, he said, 'Who knew vintage cognac had a kick like a mule?' Closing his eyes for a beat or two, he opened them again. 'I don't suppose you have anything for a headache, do you? I could have sworn there was a packet of pills in the main bathroom.'

There had been. She'd tossed them out this morning praying like hell they'd be needed. *Ask and you shall receive.* Clearly, she was doing God's work.

'Sorry, no,' she said chirpily before turning back to the coffee mugs and hitting the button on the grinder. The beans didn't need any more grinding but he didn't know that.

Fixing them both a coffee, she left his on the counter and took hers back to the table and her work which she'd been trying to concentrate on for hours now. It had been impossible of course, her mind completely preoccupied with how this *morning-after* moment would play out.

Maybe he would pretend last night hadn't happened. She would be perfectly fine with that. Some things were better left unsaid. Right? Or maybe, given his hangover, he wouldn't even remember that he'd kissed her. The end result would be the same for both – the incident wouldn't be mentioned.

But the second option squeezed like a hand around her throat.

'You want to talk about last night?'

His quiet question put an end to her speculation and took her straight back to those moments. The beginning where his move had startled her and the split second it had taken for a tsunami of lust to rise and drown any iota of common sense as she'd leaned into the kiss.

Even now, the echo of that flood shot a frisson of awareness across her nape, down her décolletage and straight to her nipples, tightening them shamelessly.

With a shuddery breath, Paige blew on her coffee. 'Nope.'

'We probably should.'

She shut her eyes. He was right, of course. It was the mature, responsible thing to do. But she was sick of doing the mature, responsible thing. For once she wanted to stick her fingers in her ears and chant *la la la not listening*.

When she opened them again, he was pulling a chair out at the end of the table, Casper settling at his feet. Pavarotti preened at the bars of the cage, nose twitching, hoping for some attention but unfortunately for him *and* for Paige, he was staring right at her.

'We kissed.'

Like she needed reminding. '*You* kissed me.'

Cocking an eyebrow, he stared her down with those blue Prendergast eyes. 'And *you* kissed me back.'

The rebuff was gentle but Paige could hardly dispute it.

'Look,' she huffed, 'it happened, okay? It had been a big day and there was the cognac and... I get it. It was a moment, a *strange* moment that shouldn't have happened.'

'It shouldn't have?'

'Bella is my friend, Oliver.' Her rebuke was almost as sharp as her glare. 'Friends don't... fool around with their friends' exes. It's not just *bros* that have codes, you know?'

He nodded. 'Right, of course.' He was obviously chastened by her instant rebuttal but he didn't look so sure and that was confusing.

Surely, he knew that rule, too?

'So, I say, let's just put it down to the cognac and move on. Or... I could move out.'

Paige brightened at the thought. *Her* leaving would be too suspicious but if *he* indicated that might be the correct course of action, then she could hardly stay in those circumstances, right? Sure, she'd have left before her mission was complete but it would be a lot easier to face the others in that scenario.

'It might take me a couple of days to find a temporary living situation but—'

'No.'

His vigorous head shake cut her off and the hope that he would hand her an easy out evaporated. It seemed she was destined to stay and do her worst.

'You don't have to go. I'm sure, as you say, we can move on from this.'

'Absolutely,' she murmured.

Staying meant she wouldn't have to arrange some bridging accommodation which was a bonus. And also, she'd get to keep working on his book which she'd been enjoying immensely.

'Look...' He placed his mug on the table and sought her gaze. 'I'm sorry. About the kiss. I... don't know what came over me but I should have resisted. The last thing I want is to put you in a compromising position with Bella. I've hurt her enough already.'

Paige felt the sincerity of his guilt deep in her bones. Clearly Oliver was still feeling bad about his disappearing act which begged the question, what the hell had he been thinking? Because being in such close confines with him, seeing him through *her* eyes, not Bella's, he seemed like a good guy.

Grappling with some serious demons.

Bloody hell. Like *that* was an excuse. God, was she in full Stockholm syndrome? What the hell would her co-conspirators think of her going soft on Oliver Prendergast?

On the flip side, maybe hearing some half-ass justification was just what she needed to keep the fiery rage burning? And maybe getting to the bottom of it all would help Bella.

Maybe it would help *her*.

Holding his gaze she asked the question she'd been grappling with since meeting Oliver a month ago. 'Why? Why did you run out on her like that? All dressed up on the most important day of her life? That's pretty damn unforgiveable.'

If he'd been acting like a total horndog since the jilting, freed from an obligation he no longer wanted, she might understand why he ran – well, she wouldn't but she could draw a line from one to the other – but the man was a damn recluse!

He sighed heavily as he stared into the depths of his coffee and, for a moment, Paige thought he might decline to answer but then those blue Prendergast eyes found her again.

'Because I didn't love her enough. And that just wasn't fair to her.'

Okay, well... there was nothing half-ass about that. But still, not forgivable. 'And you decide this on the *morning of your wedding*?'

'I'd been feeling... uneasy about it for a while but we spent so much time apart, her living on the East Coast, me on the West and I just put it down to that, kept telling myself once it was all official, I'd feel differently. But...'

He didn't say anything for long, *long* moments and Paige grew impatient, her eyebrow kicking up. 'But?' she demanded.

'It was D Day and I was there in my monkey suit getting ready and I realised I couldn't keep kicking this uneasy feeling down the road. The wedding was only a few hours away and I had to face it – I didn't love her enough.'

A bubble of rage rose in Paige's chest on Bella's behalf. 'Why in the hell did you propose to her if that was the case?'

He shrugged. 'My father had just died. It put me in a spin and she was there as always to steady the ship. And I was... grateful for that. For her. It felt like exactly the right thing to do at the time but...'

'You didn't love her enough,' Paige mimicked, her lip curling distastefully. What was he? Five years old? Love was serious business, not something from fairy tales.

'I realised I couldn't use her as some kind of emotional crutch. That wasn't fair to her. My father never loved my mother enough and it damaged her deep down for a very long time. Sure, she has a flashy life with a lot of friends and things to do to feel good about herself but I think she's *still* damaged by his inability to love her the way she craved.'

Paige remembered the things he'd written about his mother in the pages she'd already read. About her feeling passed over and too afraid to become emotionally dependent on a husband who only really loved himself. Especially at the expense of her own self-worth.

'My mother deserved better than that,' Oliver continued. 'So does Bella. She's amazing and she should be with someone who loves her with every fibre of his being. Whose entire existence is predicated on her happiness. Who wakes up every morning just to see her face. She should be loved to distraction.'

Paige cut off the sigh that rose in her throat. Bella *did* deserve that. So did every woman. So did *she*.

'And there is that person out there for her,' he continued, 'it's just not me. I loved Bella but not in the way she should be loved. Which is what I finally faced on the morning of our wedding and I'm sorrier than she will ever know that I didn't have the guts to face it earlier but standing there in my suit, I knew I couldn't go through with it. Stand at that altar and lie to her like my father had lied to my mother.'

Jesus...

Paige shook her head. Parents could really screw a kid up.

The bubble of rage slowly deflated but Paige clung to it anyway. She didn't want to be affected by the admission. Didn't want to see that while his timing had been terrible, his reasons had been sensible. Noble even. Didn't want to have this heavy ache for him in her heart right now.

But, *more than that*, she hated that he was comparing himself to his dad. 'You're not your father, Oliver.'

She said it gently and meant it and then felt guilty about meaning it but it was the truth. She might never have met the famous actor but she'd glimpsed enough in Oliver's writing to know that Roger Prendergast was a narcissist. A benign one, sure, but his singular love for himself still had consequences for others.

In opening his place to her and a hamster and a stray dog, Oliver had shown a selflessness his father had never possessed.

'No.' He nodded. 'I'm not. And had the wedding gone ahead I would have been a very good husband and I'm sure we'd have had a very *nice* life. But Bella's bloody smart and at some point, she'd have worked it out and I would never want to hurt her like that.'

'Why didn't you tell her any of this instead of running?'

'On the day, I was in a panic. I knew I had to get away or I'd chicken out and end up doing the' – his lips twisted as he performed air quotes – '*right thing*. Going through with it so we could all save face. So I texted her, switched off my phone and got the hell out of Dodge. It was not my finest moment.'

Paige blinked. 'Ya think?' She may be able to empathise with the quandary Oliver found himself in but text dumping her really was unforgiveable.

'When I switched my phone on later that day there were a dozen missed calls from her so I called her back but she didn't answer and she dodged my calls for two weeks and eventually texted to tell me to stop trying to contact her, she needed space. So I did. After all I'd done I had to respect that. And I left for the UK because the goddamn press was all over me. When she finally did call I tried to explain but she said it didn't matter, that it was all sorted now and she *never* wanted to discuss what had happened again.'

Yeah, that sounded like Bella. Efficiently cleaning up the mess, putting on a brave face and carrying on.

It also sounded like her right now, not wanting to talk about the kiss.

'I told her if she wanted to go to every media outlet in the world and trash me, I would understand but she was horrified that I would even think that she would splash our private life around and made me promise that I wouldn't do it either. She said she didn't want much but she was asking me to keep my mouth zipped so I assured her I would. I was already ducking paps every time I stuck my head out the door and I felt bad enough about the way things had gone down without keeping the story going.'

Ugh. Oliver's sincere remorse, etched into every one of his brow lines made it very hard to stay mad at him. Yes, he'd done a terrible thing but the situation – as was often the case – was more nuanced than that. And it was clear he felt genuine regret and had done all he could to make the fallout easier for Bella.

As he should have.

Which didn't make him a bad person. Yes, he'd done a bad thing but he'd acknowledged it and done all he could to alleviate the situation. Which surely made him a decent guy?

But that was not helping the morning after they'd kissed. Nor was it helping her payback plan. She was here to mess with him. Not see his side of things. Not rationalise his actions. Not question the validity of what she'd set out to do even though the nuance was giving her second thoughts.

His phone chose that moment to vibrate on the table and Paige could have kissed it for putting a stop to her conflicting emotions. He broke eye contact to pick it up and read the message, setting it down again without replying. 'I'm off to London for two days. I'll be back Sunday lunch time.'

Paige couldn't decide if she was miffed or relieved at his announcement. Was he giving them both some space? Or was he running away like he'd run from Redondo?

Or maybe, *you idiot*, he just had some business to attend to.

'Will you be okay by yourself?'

Taken aback, Paige nodded. It was surprisingly nice to have someone other than her mother ask that question. A man, even. Maybe it wasn't very feminist of her but she liked it. 'I'm used to being on my own.'

As soon as the words were out, she cringed internally,

hoping they hadn't come across as sad as they'd sounded. After all, he was used to being on his own, too.

'I have a car coming for me in half an hour.'

Of course he did. 'Okay.'

Their gazes fused for a beat or two and neither said anything but the echo of the kiss lived and breathed in those nanoseconds.

'Can I send through more pages if I get some done on the commute?'

Paige blinked. Okay, clearly it was not living and breathing for him... 'Sure.' She nodded like a freaking marionette – stiff and wooden. 'Send through whatever you have.'

'Thanks,' he murmured before standing. 'Better get ready.'

Casper trailed after him as he departed and Pavarotti followed his progress looking utterly bereft – who knew *that* was possible for a hamster?

Great, just what she needed for company the next couple of days – the Oliver bloody Prendergast fan club.

***

Oliver left, as scheduled, half an hour later and Paige was relieved. She was almost positive that's what the feeling was in the pit of her stomach, anyway. The animals, on the other hand, went into some kind of mourning. Casper sat in the hallway near the front door as if waiting for his master's return and Pavarotti was so despondent, his wheel neglected, that Paige considered giving him some caramel popcorn to pep him up. But, it wasn't right to get him hooked again when he'd come so far.

Ignoring the animals and thoughts of what had happened between her and Oliver, Paige took advantage of his absence to do some work she'd been neglecting in favour of her payback shenanigans. She threw a ball for Casper on the beach for over an hour and wondered if the gusty grey weather would ever stop. After lunch, Oliver's first pages came through and she switched to that.

In it he talked about the first time he'd realised his father was unfaithful to his mother and how her often brittle smile had suddenly made sense. He talked about his profound disappointment and how his mother had tried to keep Oliver's rose-coloured glasses firmly in place by assuring him it was okay and that it was normal for men like his father and that it was just what they did.

Damn it. Compassion for that bewildered eight-year-old boy flooded in. It seemed like having those blinkers ripped away had been gutting. She wanted to go back in time and hug him and tell him it wasn't okay, it wasn't normal. It wasn't what men did.

She wanted to tell *her* that as well.

The pages the next day were just as wrenching as she read them curled up on the couch in her comfy but clingy yoga pants and a T-shirt that had a Dorito with Danny DeVito's face on it and the phrase *Danny Dorito* underneath. The new writing focused on Oliver's decision to accept his father's invitation to live in California at the age of fifteen.

With his mother's encouragement, Oliver had agreed. Ostensibly because he'd decided he wanted to work in movies and he might as well exploit whatever cachet the son of Roger Prendergast afforded him. But also because, as a teenager, Oliver had started to realise that his father was only human, despite the pedestal he'd put him on.

And, if his mum could forgive him, then maybe he could cut him some slack, too?

But, his mother had cried when he'd left and backtracked,

begging him to just go for a holiday then return to the UK. Which had left him torn. She'd been pushing Oliver to have a relationship with his father and now he was on the cusp of that, her tears had made him feel guilty about the decision.

It had clearly been hard and horrible and Paige thought it was a bloody miracle Oliver Prendergast had turned out as normal as he had and thanked God he was away until tomorrow lest she do something dumb like *hug* him. She supposed the therapy he'd written about quite openly had helped put things into perspective and she was envious of that for a moment. Maybe she could do with talking to somebody about the trauma she'd been through four years ago?

Not that she could afford an expensive London shrink like Oliver.

But she *could* afford a bottle of red wine and sometimes that was as good a therapy as any. It'd do for a lonely Saturday night anyway.

By eight o'clock, ninety minutes after she'd opened the wine, she was on the last glass, the bottle sitting empty on the kitchen bench, her mixed playlist pumping out of her Bluetooth speaker as she danced and swayed to the music.

Both Casper and Pavarotti were in the media room with a movie on – *101 Dalmatians*. The 1961 animated version, of course, because Oliver was a purist. Neither of them had budged. It was like, in lieu of having Oliver home, they were commemorating their adoration by indulging in one of his favourite past times.

It would be sad if it wasn't so damn funny.

Paige on the other hand, who'd only had a handful of crackers with her bottle of wine, was now officially tipsy. Tipsy enough to pick up her phone and re-read the private message she'd received from Bella yesterday.

> Just wanted to check in and see how you're doing. Hope everything's okay.

The guilt she'd already been feeling multiplied. It was so nice of Bella to be concerned. She'd obviously noticed that Paige had been distinctly quiet in the main group for the last little while. The fact she was sensitive to that spoke volumes about Bella's character and why she liked her so much and why she was in Cornwall doing this deed for her.

Busy – that's the reason she'd given herself for not responding to the group messages. And she *was* busy. But the truth was – that wasn't the only reason. Getting to know Oliver through his relationship with his father had given her second thoughts about her mission here. She knew that he had hurt Bella dreadfully but things were seldom black and white, right?

Which didn't mean she'd abandoned the payback plan but... it had given her pause.

And then, of course, there was the kiss...

But that had been an aberration. *Not* happening again. And by avoiding the WhatsApp group all she was doing was sewing doubt and worry amongst her friends. They'd been noting her absence in their chatter and, damn it, she missed being part of them.

At the moment, just drunk enough, she missed it acutely. Her finger hovered over the group chat button and then she started to type.

10

> **PAIGE**
> Sorry I've been a bit quiet.

She wasn't sure who would answer because of the time difference but within a minute three little dots appeared, undulating away, indicating someone was typing. Bella. Ack – it *had* to be Bella! Crossing her fingers, she hoped that Astrid or Sienna would make an appearance.

> **BELLA**
> Are you okay? Is Olly being awful?

Paige didn't know what to say to that. He hadn't been awful at all. He'd been the opposite of that really. Even if he *had* kissed her and she *had* liked it a little too much. Which made *her* the awful one.

> **PAIGE**
> No, no. Really it's fine.

BELLA
I can call if you want?

Oh, bloody hell – nope! Paige needed to be 100 per cent sober for any actual conversation with Bella. Otherwise the second she heard her wonderfully no-nonsense voice she might end up confessing all and make a real hash of everything.

PAIGE
Would love that BUT Oliver's started yelling about Pavarotti escaping again and threatening to take him to the pound and Bunky will never forgive me. I should go help.

She felt bad about using Pavarotti as an excuse given he and Oliver were in some kind of bromance now. But she was thinking on her feet here.

BELLA
If you're sure you're okay?

PAIGE
Absolutely!

Please could they just stop talking about her being okay? But then a thought struck. Maybe Bella was asking because something was up her end and she was trying to establish an in to that conversation.

PAIGE
Are *you* okay?

The dots danced for a long time. Bella was either writing a long message, correcting her spelling errors or writing and deleting a lot. Was she okay? Paige breathed a sigh of relief when her message popped up.

> **BELLA**
> I'm good. I've finally set up that interview for the day after tomorrow.

Bella's idea to instigate a scathing newspaper article – a real hatchet job – about Astrid's ex was utterly brilliant and Paige had hooked Bella up with a client who owned a trendy bar in New York as a possible venue.

> **BELLA**
> And that will be the beginning of Chase's downfall.

Chase's downfall. Well that certainly sounded gleeful enough. *Ugh*. Guilt sliced through her middle like a hot knife. Bella was doing what she was supposed to be doing – getting even for Astrid. And here she was, supposedly getting some payback for Bella, not playing kissy-kissy with Oliver. Her fingers trembled a little as she tapped out her response.

> **PAIGE**
> Go Bella!! Astrid will be THRILLED.

And because shame was riding her hard *and* she was a big chicken, Paige didn't give Bella a chance to respond. She went straight back in again.

> **PAIGE**
> Oh God, sorry, gotta run. Oliver is threatening to make Pavarotti sleep in the garage. Talk soon xxx

Then she shut down the app and slugged back the rest of

the wine. She might be able to make excuses to justify what had happened but ultimately, she'd betrayed Bella – *her friend* – and that sat like a cold, wet, rotting fish in her gut.

Needing to get out of her head, lest she open a second bottle of wine to drown her sorrows this time, Paige scrolled her phone until she found a song to get lost in. 'The Devil Went Down to Georgia' leaped out at her and she smiled.

Yep, that would do it.

Ignoring the fact that Cornwall could be easily substituted for Georgia, she hit play and turned it up as she grabbed her violin. She'd learned all the fiddle sections years ago and it used to be her party trick when she was tipsy enough to get the crowd really pumping.

She was alone right now but she was certainly tipsy enough. And the intricate finger work would take her mind off *other* things.

Tapping her foot and singing raucously along, she watched her reflection in the glass doors to the patio as she played her violin during the fiddle parts, leaning into it with as much flair as a bottle of wine could give her, remembering the bow strokes and the notes as if she'd learned them only yesterday. It was an energetic song and, by the time it was drawing to a close she was slightly out of breath.

The song finished with a flourish, as did she, performing a bow to the room and then laughing at her theatrics.

The next song started to play and, conscious of not annoying the neighbours, Paige quickly turned it down. Crossing the room to return the violin to its case, she was pulled up short when the handle on the door that led from the garage into the hallway rattled.

Paige froze as she peered into the darkened recesses. There were no lights on down that end but she was sure it had rattled.

It rattled again.

Her pulse spiked on a hot surge of adrenaline. Was someone in the garage? Trying to get into the house? There were a lot of expensive things that would satisfy a would-be thief – like an Oscar for example.

Through her red-wine fog she tried to figure out the best move. She could call the cops but they would take several minutes to get to her and if the person on the other side of the door had ill intent then she probably didn't have minutes.

As the handle rattled again she realised she was going to have to defend herself.

Had she not had a red-wine brain, she'd have gone downstairs with the dog and the phone and gone out the doors to the beach. But she was in full wine fog and all of a sudden, the violin in her hand looked like an ideal weapon.

Grabbing her phone off the table she hit 999, shoving the phone between her ear and her shoulder so she could brandish the violin. As she crept towards the door in the darkened hallway, an efficient-sounding person on the other end asked her if she wanted police, ambulance or fire.

'*Police*,' she hiss-whispered, her heart rate picking up as the door finally swung open and she lifted the violin.

Fingers appeared, gripping around the door frame just as the person on the line said, 'Police, what is your emergency, please?'

Operating completely on instinct now, Paige rode an adrenaline surge, mustering all her strength and smashing the violin at the knuckles yelling, '*Heee-yah!*'

Given her alcohol-affected hand-eye co-ordination, it missed the knuckles entirely and smashed into the frame, splintering the instrument. The action dislodged her phone which flew

The Payback Plan

from its position, landing on the floor and sliding along the hallway.

The person – definitely a man – obviously startled by her stealthy, ninja-like attack, yelled, '*What the fuck?*' as he stepped into the hallway, a stack of file boxes in one arm.

It was Oliver.

Blinking, it was Paige's turn for, '*What the fuck?*' He wasn't supposed to be coming home until tomorrow.

But it went unanswered as Oliver stood on a tiny piece of shattered violin which slid out from under him on the floorboards. Wobbling to remain upright and *not* drop his boxes, he let out a whoop. Unfortunately, it didn't help. Overcorrecting, the boxes slipped, crashing to the ground, disgorging their contents.

In a last-ditch attempt to stay upright, his arms flailing in mid-air, he grabbed hold of the closest solid thing. Which just happened to be Paige.

Before she knew it, they were down.

Thankfully, Oliver broke her fall as they collapsed in a pile, the remnants of the violin flying from her hand as sheets of escaped paper fell around them like confetti. He let out a wrenching, '*Ophf!*' as he landed on his back and she landed on his front, her face in his neck, her hair spread over his face, her breasts squashed into his chest, her legs straddling his hips and his hands firmly on her ass.

Their groins shockingly aligned.

For a beat or two neither of them did anything, they just lay stock-still, breathing. Paige shut her eyes and inhaled his scent as she tried to harness the analytical centre of her brain to make it make sense but he smelled of old boxes which she didn't know until right this minute could be such a turn on.

As was the scratch of whiskers against her cheek. And the

thick bulge between his legs pressing intimately between *her* legs. Her wine brain was all well *hello, sailor* and she wanted nothing more than to purr and stretch a little.

Stupid wine brain.

Yanking herself back from the ridiculous urge to rub herself shamelessly against him, Paige slapped her palms on the floor either side of his head and levered herself upright, the frizz of her hair falling forward as she stared into his face. Their eyes met and she wondered idly how fair it was that his eyes were almost freaking luminous in the dark. Like a cat. A sleek jungle cat.

Oh, *shut up,* wine brain!

'You're not supposed to be home until tomorrow,' she accused, glaring at him but the breathiness of her voice softened the effect.

Really, being sprawled on him like this was quite discombobulating.

'I decided to come back early,' he replied crankily, also glaring.

'Why didn't you knock or use your key?' she demanded. 'Instead of rattling the bloody handle like you were trying to break in?'

'I did knock,' he griped. 'But there was some kind of racket going on in here and I *was* using my key but with my arms full of boxes it was difficult and it took a few attempts.'

Racket? Did the man have no appreciation for classic hits?

Paige glared some more, so did he, the chug of their breathing louder than the background music. But then Paige became aware of his big hands warm on her ass and her heart rate, still elevated from her ninja moves, changed tempo. It morphed to more of a hard thud than a desperate trip as she tried to figure out why in the hell she was suddenly so *hot* and why in God's name she wasn't attempting to get off him.

As if he knew where her mind was or maybe it was just a reflexive thing, his fingers dug in a little. Ordinarily, when a guy had his hands on her bum, Paige would fret about its fleshiness but that was the *furthest* thing from her thoughts as the intimacy of their position was making itself more and more known.

Her yoga pants allowed her to easily feel every damn contour of what he was packing behind his fly and it was a *lot*. Between the thinness of the stretch cotton and their position, nothing was left to the imagination. Perfect for a little downward dogging.

Paige shut her eyes. Oh dear God, *shut up*, wine brain.

'Paige.'

It was soft and low and she opened her eyes slowly, willing herself not to grind against him, not to move. Their eyes met briefly, his black pupils large, almost obliterating the blue of his irises. And then his gaze drifted to her mouth.

'Paige...'

It was softer this time, lower. A rumble of air that sounded as if it had come from the depths of the earth. And that's what did it. The raw ache in his voice pulsing between them. He seemed as lost in this moment as she was, her guilt from only ten minutes ago evaporating, disappearing into the ether. Lust fogged her head, replacing propriety with a roaring imperative to touch.

Her pulse a percussion section in her ears, Paige swooped down, her breasts flattening against his chest as she pressed her mouth to his.

This time neither of them were tentative. Neither of them froze at the audacity of the action. The kiss flared bright, right from the first touch of their lips and Paige moaned as the hands clutching her ass pulled her in tighter.

There was no Just Desserts. No payback plan. No Bella. Just him, solid and *good* between her legs.

Her breath caught in her throat as she pressed herself against him, trying to get closer to those contours that were thickening by the second. His low groan filled her head and the taste of coffee on his tongue was like a spoonful of Affogato. Sweet and bitter and absolutely no good for her but hell if she could resist *anything* Italian.

A hand shoved into her hair, a palm grazed her cheek and she leaned into it as their mouths moved and shifted, their tongues tangling, hunting relentlessly for the next gasp, the next moan.

'*Jesus*, Paige,' he muttered against her mouth, his breathing hot and ragged on her face before he shoved his other hand in her hair and went back for more.

One kiss, two. Deep. Hard. Then a throaty groan and suddenly, she was on her back, his mouth barely leaving hers as he performed the feat, his body half over hers, pressing her into the floor, his hand sliding to her hip, to her waist, under her shirt, trailing fire.

Trailing desire.

His hand found her bra and Paige moaned, her fingers twisting into the hair at his nape and tugging as he cupped her breast and squeezed, her nipple hardening in a second streaking pleasure in a line that went directly to the bullseye right between her legs.

It did not pass go, it did not collect two hundred pounds.

Then, suddenly, two loud thumps on the front door, shattered their clinch as decisively as a falling axe. 'Police,' a voice boomed from the other side as blue light slid under and bled around the door surrounds, turning the darkened hallway into some kind of macabre disco as it strobed across the wreckage of the violin. 'Open up.'

Startled, they sprang apart as if they were about to be arrested for... what? Making out. Betraying a friend. *Again*. Paige winced.

Damn you, wine brain.

'What the fuck?' Oliver scrambled to his feet, raking a hand through hair that between the fall and the fornication, was exceptionally mussy.

Also standing, Paige straightened her clothes. There was no hope for *her* hair.

Another bang on the door. 'If you do not open this door, pronto,' the voice boomed, 'we'll have to force it open.'

'Coming,' Oliver called before turning to her. 'Why in the hell,' he whispered, his brows forming a vexed V, 'are the police at the door?'

Paige's brain was not in a fit state to critically analyse anything right now. Between the wine and the hormonal buzz she could barely remember her own damn name. But he was looking at her like it was all her fault and that rankled because this time, *she* had kissed *him* and guilt needled her hard.

'I don't fucking know,' she hissed. Oh, but actually... '*Shit.*' She looked around for her phone. There it was a few metres away, the screen lit up, presumably the emergency call taker still on the line listening to the crashing and kerfuffle and then the utter silence while they were making out on the bloody floor.

Cringe.

'I'd called 999 just before I karate-chopped your hand.' Man, that had been fast. Surely, it'd been no more than ten minutes since she'd first dialled?

Oliver stared at her for moment and she thought he was

going to demand to know why but then, as if he'd suddenly realised why a lone woman thinking someone was breaking into her house *would* call the cops, his annoyance deflated and he huffed out a sigh. 'Well... this ought to be good.'

Taking the half dozen strides to the front door, Oliver opened it with a smile. Paige joined him as he said, 'Officer. Oh...' Behind the burly copper who was laden down with about a dozen things hanging off his belt and his vest, there was another similarly encumbered. 'Officers,' he corrected.

'We got a 999 call to this residence,' he said with no preamble in a broad northern accent, eying Oliver suspiciously. He had two huge, greying eyebrows that undulated like furry caterpillars on his forehead.

'Yes, sorry,' Paige said. 'That was me, I—'

'Are you okay, ma'am?'

Was she okay? Not really. She and Oliver had now kissed twice and she was pretty sure she was going to hell because she thought maybe she was starting to *feel* stuff and what the hell was that even about? But she didn't think Eyebrows was worried about her sexual or *moral* discombobulation.

'Yes. Absolutely.' She nodded vigorously, her eyes widening, trying desperately to convey everything was fine. Although she may have looked slightly manic and possibly not okay. *Because she was not okay.* 'I thought someone was trying to break in but it was just Oliver.' She pointed at him. 'It's his house.'

Clearly of a suspicious nature – excellent quality for a police officer she supposed – the officer glanced behind them into the hallway taking in the scattered pieces of her now very dead violin and the mess of paper.

'I see.' He eyeballed Oliver. 'Do you mind if we come in, sir?'

Oliver shook his head. 'Of course not.'

He fell back and gestured for the officer to enter which

he did, followed by the second cop who was younger and ginger. They stepped over the debris in the hallway garishly lit by the flashing blue light, looking at it then at each other as Oliver shut the door. 'And what happened here?'

'Well,' Paige began, 'as I said, I thought someone was breaking in because Oliver wasn't supposed to be home until tomorrow night.'

'It's true, I was supposed to come home tomorrow.'

'So when he opened the door,' Paige continued, 'I... attacked him with the violin.'

'And I was carrying some file boxes which I dropped when I slipped on a piece of broken violin and the paper flew out everywhere.'

'And I slipped too,' Paige added. 'And in the...' She cleared her voice. 'Confusion.' Slash *debauchery*. 'That followed, I forgot about having dialled the emergency number. I'm so, *so* sorry, I know how busy you are. The last thing you need are nuisance calls like this.'

'I see,' he repeated, pursing his lips, his eyebrows undulating once more.

They moved slowly down the hallway, entering the open-plan, well-lit area, their eyes continuously sweeping. They stopped in the kitchen. 'Have you been drinking, ma'am?'

Paige's gaze flicked to where the officer's attention was focused. The empty wine bottle stood on the counter, *judging her*. 'Um, yes?'

He nodded. 'How much?'

'The entire bottle.' Her gaze slid to Oliver whose expression was inscrutable. Mr Expensive Cognac had better not be judging her. 'But it was over a couple of hours.'

Okay, that was a slight fudge of the truth but as far as she knew there was no law against getting absolutely stonking drunk in your own home if you wanted to.

The copper nodded as they both turned, two sets of eyes thoroughly assessing her and Oliver in the full light. Both sets drifted to her Danny Dorito T-shirt at the same time and Paige swore she saw the lips of ginger copper, twitch.

'You two got some ID?' Eyebrows asked.

'Ah... sure.' Oliver reached into his back pocket and pulled out his wallet, furnishing his driver's licence.

Paige crossed to the table and grabbed hers from her bag and handed it over. He passed them both to ginger cop who wandered down the hallway, murmuring into the radio clipped to his shoulder.

'The address is my parents' house,' Paige added for clarity. 'I'm just staying here. As a guest.'

Eyebrows flicked a glance at Oliver. 'That right?'

He nodded. 'Until the end of February.'

'And how do you know each other?'

'I'm friends with his...' *Ex.* Paige almost stumbled over the word as the thought of Bella sucked the air from her lungs, forcing her to draw in another. 'With his ex.'

Ginger cop returned and handed the IDs back to Eyebrows with a nod. Clearly, they'd checked out. The older officer returned their IDs.

A couple more questions followed but they left shortly after with cheery goodbyes, obviously satisfied that nothing sinister had gone on tonight. As embarrassing as the incident had been, Paige assumed domestic callouts were relatively common for them and it was good to know they'd arrived promptly and hadn't been brushed off with hasty assurances.

'So.' Oliver, who had accompanied the officers to the door,

wandered back into the kitchen, his hands shoved into the front pockets of his jeans. 'That was a thing.'

'God, I'm so sorry.' She shook her head. 'I panicked. I was a little tipsy and well... look at it.' She gestured around her. 'This place is worth knocking over.'

His gaze shifted to the empty wine bottle but he didn't say anything and silence settled between them. She didn't like the silence, it made her nervous. There was too much space to fill and only one thing on her mind to fill it.

Their hallway snog-fest.

God, where would it have led had the police not crashed the party? Because she'd been all in, Judas that she was.

'H... how was London?' she asked, her voice husky.

He shrugged, looking cool, calm and collected. A far cry from the Oliver who had said her name with such heated intensity. 'The usual.'

'Why *did* you come back early?'

'My business was done.'

More silence. Bloody hell, this was awkward AF. She couldn't decide if he was waiting for her to say something or trying to formulate something himself. 'Well... I'll' – she pointed to the hallway over his shoulder – 'just clean up the mess.'

He shook his head. 'I can do it.'

'No.' Her voice was firm. 'I'm the reason you dropped it all in the first place, I'll fix it. What is all that paper anyway?'

'It's a bunch of research on my father that a friend of his had collated for his own book but he died before he could write it. It's been gathering dust in the London flat for years and I thought there might be some interesting nuggets amongst it all. It was' – he looked over his shoulder at the mess before returning his attention to her – 'supposedly in order.'

Paige blanched at the jumble of paper but hell, she liked a

challenge and untangling paper trails and setting up filing systems – bringing order from chaos – were right up her alley. Once she'd patiently Sellotaped a dozen pages of torn up letters back together again.

She loved a puzzle.

It would also give her the chance to enter each article into the spreadsheet she'd already set up for Oliver's book to keep track of all of the pieces and where they might fit in the timeline of the story of Roger Prendergast. There was a lot of paper – it'd probably take her a while which suited her just fine. A project was exactly what she needed right now.

Oliver had project healthy hamster. And she'd have this.

'Okay, well, I'll just put it all back in the boxes and start sorting it tomorrow.' Paige was proud that she'd managed to move this back onto a businesslike footing. 'If you're okay with that?'

'Ah... sure. Thank you.'

Although he didn't seem sure. He seemed like he wanted to say more and that was her sign to get moving. Forcing legs that had gone from jelly to lead in a rapid sequence of time, to move, took effort that she hoped he couldn't see as she passed him by, giving him a wide berth. No way did she trust the pull he seemed to emit so effortlessly.

'Paige.'

The gravel in his voice stopped her in her tracks, the hairs on her nape prickling as she froze. One word. Just one word in *that* voice and he had her. She didn't know whether it was meant to be a question or a plea but she was sorting his papers, damn it – she wasn't going *there*.

'No.'

Shaking her head, she sought his eyes which smouldered with blue flame, and she curled her hands into fists at the corresponding flare of heat deep and low. She was in no fit state to talk about what had just happened when she couldn't even bring herself to talk about the first time. She'd been hating on herself ever since and now she'd gone and compounded the situation.

He quirked an eyebrow. 'We're going to pretend the hallway didn't happen as well?'

'Yup.' She nodded emphatically. 'And we're *not* letting it happen again, okay?' Yes, she'd said that before but she *meant* it this time. 'You and I are going teetotal from now on.'

It had to be the booze, right? There was no other explanation for the lowering of their inhibitions. Alcohol *was* known for that, after all.

He nodded his head slowly, dropping his gaze to the floor. 'Fine by me.'

And Paige exhaled a long, steady breath.

11

Oliver lay in bed a week later listening to the howl of the wind outside, the grey light of morning filtered by the sun-blocking blind. Casper, sound asleep, lay draped across his feet having claimed that position about three days after he'd arrived. Oliver had tried to dissuade the animal but Casper had looked at him with those pathetic stray dog eyes and he hadn't the heart to kick him out.

He'd woken on the coat-tails of another erotic dream about Paige with *another* raging hard-on. Day times were difficult enough without the nights. Co-existing with her in an atmosphere so cordial, they could have been on the set of *Downton* freaking *Abbey*. Pretending he hadn't had her under him, hadn't kissed her and stroked her, hadn't swallowed down her moans and those tiny, desperate whimpery noises she'd made at the back of her throat, that guaranteed him a crippling fucking erection the second they snuck into his brain.

They'd reverted to their own corners, intersecting when necessary but keeping their distance behind polite smiles and inane conversation. At least she was less *full on* than when she'd first arrived. Sure, the T-shirts were still amusing and there were always crumbs in her wake and cold, squeezed-out tea bags in the sink – which made his eye twitch – but she'd given up all pretence of veganism.

Halle-fucking-lujah.

That combined with zero Hamster Facts texts this week and things had definitely improved on the home front.

And, she was still working with him on the book. Maybe not side by side but she'd been transcribing his daily ramblings diligently and dumping them into the master document, moving them around, piecing them together into something cohesive for when it came to wrangling the manuscript into some kind of coherent state. And she'd been steadily sorting through the jumble of paper from Saturday night, cataloguing and slotting it into the timeline of the master document, too.

Saturday night. He stifled a groan as his dick tightened even further. He hadn't been prepared for what had happened that night.

He'd gone to London to talk to a publisher and retrieve the boxes then meet up with some old friends the next day for the usual pub crawl starting at lunch and pushing well into the evening. But, as he'd read the messages flying around their WhatsApp group about getting hammered and picking up, nothing had appealed less.

Oliver hadn't wanted to sit around noisy bars drinking to excess with a bunch of low-rent celebrities possibly getting hassled by paps. He'd missed Cornwall. He'd missed Paige. Despite the chaos – the tea bags, the mug rings, the menagerie – it had been good having her in his life. She'd bullied and pushed and inspired him to stop feeling so fucking sorry for himself and *do something*.

Not dabble, not pretend. Stop doing what wasn't working. Change track.

He'd have *never* started this book without her. Not in the head space he'd been in anyway but her insistence that he *try* had poked a hole in his mindset, letting in the light and the memories – the good as well as the bad. And it was proving to be an entirely cathartic experience. Better than any therapy he'd ever had.

He had a renewed sense of purpose now and that was entirely down to Paige. Hell, just the exercise alone, walking on the beach with Casper every day had helped declutter his head. Helped him see clearer. And that in itself had been a revelation.

But that wasn't all. In a little over a month, Paige had worked herself under his skin. She was the first thing he thought of when he woke up and the last thing he thought about as he went to sleep. Not himself, not the fucked-up mess he'd created, not the aimless drift his life had become.

Paige. And that was as inconvenient as his hard-ons.

He was starting to think there was something way more serious going on than just intense physical attraction although, God help him, he was so fucking hot for her. She was nothing like his usual type and yet all her soft curves, her bountiful cleavage, her goddamn *freckles* were fast becoming an obsession.

But it was *more* than that.

Something he felt way north of his dick. Something more… cerebral. Something he felt down to the core of his being. He liked her. He just *really* fucking liked her – anarchy and all. Something he'd never felt about another woman. Not to this degree.

The closest he'd come had been Bella, who he'd liked enormously. Hell, he'd loved her in that way love grew from familiarity, admiration and respect. But this was different. His feelings for Paige had been much more visceral from the moment she'd landed on his doorstep, in all her frazzled ginger glory.

There'd been nothing bland about any of the things he'd felt since that day. They'd been acute and jumbled and intense, flickering from exasperation to outright laughter to frustration, buzzing around him like fireflies, irresistible to look at but damn hard to pin down.

And then there'd been Saturday night.

His dick twitched again at the memory of her soft and breathy under him, her hands in his hair, her tiny moans filling his head. Not their first kiss. But nothing like the one on the stairs, either. That had been more a first kiss kind of kiss. Tentative, cautious, exploratory. Good – *so* good – but not Saturday night's explosive fiesta of passion.

The very last thing he'd expected as he'd stepped into his own house. From the violin attack to the kiss to the cops, it had all been slightly bewildering. Although, he should have known to expect the unexpected with Paige. But it wasn't the other stuff that fed his dreams or the blood flow to his cock.

It had been the kiss.

Their second kiss. Nothing like the first. Hot and heady and charged from the second her mouth has mashed against his and run out of control. Knocking every thought from his brain, the world narrowing down to just the space between the two of them and God knew, there'd been precious little of that.

But, more importantly – *she* had kissed him.

Sure, she had blamed the booze. And the fact she'd been drinking before his arrival had been sobering in the aftermath. Had probably been the thing that had stopped him from pushing her more on the topic that night when she'd wanted to leave it alone. A kiss given under the influence was something entirely different to one given when fully in charge of one's faculties. He knew that from his own cognac-infused faux pas.

Would she have lunged at him like that had she not consumed a bottle of wine? Would *he* have kissed her on the stairs had *he* not been affected by alcohol?

Oliver had kissed women under the influence before. Hell, there'd been a few times he'd slept with women he barely knew when they'd both been three sheets to the wind and barely remembered it the next morning. But those times had been in the setting of dates where both parties had known where it was leading.

The impulse to kiss Paige had come out of nowhere. Just like the feelings he was both struggling to define and scrambling to deny.

Because *Bella*. His ex. Paige's friend. Seriously, how much more muck could he land himself in. He'd already hurt Bella once. Kissing her friend, feeling whatever the hell *this* was... he couldn't go there. He knew Paige felt bad about it and he pretty much felt as low as a slug too and yet, he couldn't stop thinking about her...

Idly he wondered if it was too early to start drinking? It was Saturday after all and there'd been a lot of days since he'd walked away from his wedding that beer for breakfast had been his go-to. But then he remembered he'd made a commitment to Paige not to drink.

Great. Just his luck to agree to being teetotal when the woman sleeping down the end of the corridor was driving him to drink with her lush curves and her soft cleavage and those damn freckles.

His morning wood, which had mostly deflated thanks to his convoluted thoughts and reminders of how badly he'd treated Bella, re-upped. *Literally*. Oliver sighed. Time to get out of bed because the other option was to masturbate and he was damned if he was doing that in front of an innocent dog.

As if Casper knew he was on Oliver's mind his tail thumped twice and Oliver levered himself up onto his elbows.

'You hungry?' he asked.

Casper's leap off the bed was answer enough.

* * *

Five minutes later they were both entering the kitchen. Paige was standing at the large sink window, her back to him, looking at her phone and he paused for a moment, a hand curling around his gut. Her hair was up in some kind of twisty knot thing exposing her nape, curly tendrils springing out haphazardly from her attempt to contain them. She was wearing yoga pants like she had been *that* night and an oversized white T-shirt, that completely covered her ass from his view. The neckline was wide, barely clinging to her shoulders and looked all stretched like it was well-worn.

As if to prove his observation, the left side slid down, revealing creamy flesh speckled with a fascinating constellation of ginger freckles and he wondered what it would be like to be the man who was allowed to snuggle up behind her, wrap his arms around her waist and put his lips to the part where her neck sloped to her shoulder. What it would be like to have her turn and smile then lean in and lay her head down and sigh into one of those long, unhurried Saturday morning cuddles.

Oliver blinked. Jesus, dude – *what the what?* What in the hell was the matter with him? He'd be making fucking daisy chains next.

Giving himself a severe mental ass-kicking, he said, 'Good morning,' with all the posh Brit boy politeness he could muster.

But that all fell apart as she turned, her freckles popping dramatically in her ashen face. Oliver's heart kicked hard at her stricken expression. 'What's wrong?'

Forgetting all his lectures about keeping his distance, he crossed to her, his hands sliding onto her upper arms as if he'd been doing it for a decade instead of for the first time ever.

She looked at him, her hazel eyes huge in her face. 'Casper's owner just contacted me.'

* * *

The knock on the door Oliver had been expecting was delivered promptly at 3 p.m. as arranged. 'That'll be her,' he said, glancing at Paige who was petting an unsuspecting Casper from her usual position at the dining table.

The phone call had been a shock this morning; Oliver didn't think he'd properly processed it yet. The damn dog had been in his life for a month – just one month – and yet, he'd become Oliver's shadow. Sleeping on his bed, claiming the spot on the couch next to him, wagging his tail vigorously the second Oliver pulled on his beanie.

A month ago he would have been just fine for the owner to turn up and relieve him of the responsibility and the endless fucking dog hair but now? Hell, the damn mutt had wormed his way into Oliver's heart and his skin itched at the thought of Casper not being there whenever he turned around.

But this had always been a possibility. The dog had an *owner*, that was the reality.

Gathering himself, Oliver walked down the hallway. Casper whined a little and he wondered whether the animal wasn't entirely unsuspecting. On their long beach walk this morning he'd stuck close rather than endlessly chasing the ball and barking at the waves and the gulls. And during his bath he hadn't tried to excitedly leap out or shake water every bloody where.

Even when Paige had pulled out the blow dryer which he usually tolerated with clear distrust, he had just shut his eyes and leaned into Oliver, standing patiently until it was done and he was all fluffed up and presentable for his reunion. It wouldn't do at all for the owner to think he'd been neglected here this past month.

Reaching for the door as another knock sounded, Oliver pulled it open, plastering a smile on his face. The middle-aged woman was short and stocky and leaning on a walking stick, her hair completely tucked into the beanie on her head. There was nothing fancy about her clothes or her muddy old Jeep in the driveway. The deep crow's feet around her eyes and ruts in her forehead hinted at a hard life but her eyes sparkled and her smile was warm.

Deep down he'd been hoping for bad vibes from the woman coming to claim Casper. Someone cold or mean or mirthless that would explain why Casper had run away. But everything about her exuded salt of the earth. Like she always had a batch of scones in the oven and a pot of clotted cream in the fridge.

She probably belonged to the bloody WI!

'Hello there, my lovely,' she said, in a thick West Country accent. 'You must be Oliver. I'm Sheila.'

She stuck out her hand and Oliver shook it, her skin dry and rough in his grasp. 'Yes,' he confirmed. 'Do come in.'

He winced at the formality of his voice but she didn't seem to notice.

'I couldn't believe it when Derek from the butcher shop showed me the social media post,' she said as she followed him in, a slight limp affecting her gait. 'We'd given up hope. Fancy

Doggo getting as far as St Ives. That's over sixty miles from home.'

Just then, Casper let out a bark and trotted towards them, his tail wagging vigorously.

'*Doggo!*' Sheila's face lit up as Casper greeted her, turning in excited circles, his tail flapping madly. Bending over, she petted his head and accepted his licks. Casper clearly knew Sheila. 'You look right 'ansum. You've been on a fine adventure, haven't you my bewty?'

Paige joined them and they both watched in silence as the two got reacquainted. 'He's been pining right terrible for my da since he passed a couple of months ago,' Sheila said as she straightened. 'Worked the sheep with him every day, he did.'

'He certainly loves to chase a ball,' Paige commented.

She chuckled. 'Oh aye, he's a bundle of energy this one. Hard for him to settle in town with me. Not fond of my cats I'm afraid but I promised Da I'd look after him. It was terrible when he went missing. But I'm right pleased you've been taking good care of him.'

'It was our pleasure.' Oliver nodded.

Of course, it had been an entirely mutual relationship Oliver realised. Casper had also been taking good care of him, getting him out of the house, out of his rut, out of his head. He stroked a soft floppy ear, a big grin splitting the dog's face, clearly lapping up all the attention from his people.

'Would you like a cuppa?' Paige asked. 'We also have a packet of Hobnobs?'

Oliver glanced at her sharply, Paige didn't share her Hobnobs with *anyone*. He'd learned that in the first few days of cohabitation. But he could tell by the way she was looking at Casper she was just trying to delay the inevitable.

'Well, I am partial to a Hobnob,' Sheila admitted with a grin, patting her belly, 'but I gotta get dreckly back. It's a long drive and I know those cats will be up to all kinds o' mischief. Thank you though, that's terrible nice of you.'

Paige's smile was wan as she said, 'Yes, you'll be wanting to get on the road before the weekend traffic gets too much.'

'Aye.' Sheila nodded. 'Right-o, Doggo.' Casper thumped his tail at Sheila. 'Let's get you home.'

Oliver drew in a steady breath. 'I'll walk you to the door.'

'Lovely,' she beamed.

He indicated that she should lead the way and Sheila turned, hobbling down the passage stick in hand, Casper trotting along beside her, his toenails clicking on the floor. Paige fell into step beside him and he glanced sideways at her. She looked exactly like he felt, like they were walking to their execution, not returning a stray animal to its rightful owner.

But this was a *good* thing. A *happy* day.

At the door, Oliver reached over Sheila's head and opened it. She stepped out with Casper then turned to face them. 'Well then, Doggo,' she said, 'time to say goodbye to these lovely people. You were so lucky to end up here.'

Casper looked up at Sheila, turning his head from side to side as if he was understanding for the first time what was happening. He looked at Oliver and Paige and gave a forlorn kind of whimper as he trotted to where they stood in the doorway, nudging between them, so they could both pet him at the same time.

And goddamn if the hot needle of tears didn't prick the backs of Oliver's eyes as his hand sifted through soft, fluffy fur. Kneeling, he nuzzled the top of Casper's head and whispered, 'Thanks for the beach walks. You're a good dog.'

Oliver stood, glancing at Paige whose eyes looked suspiciously misty before she leaned over and planted a kiss where Oliver had nuzzled.

'C'mon then, Doggo,' Sheila said cheerfully. 'The cats will be a'frettin'.'

If that was supposed to be a selling point, Casper wasn't buying it. He didn't move, giving a low whine as he looked up. Oliver cleared his throat. 'Good boy.' He nodded encouragingly. 'Time to go home, now.'

'I has yer favourite treat waiting for yer,' Sheila coaxed.

'It's okay,' Paige said to him. 'We'll be okay. Off you go.'

Oliver nodded again and repeated Paige's words. 'It's okay.'

'That'll do, Doggo.'

Casper's ears pricked up and he returned to Sheila's side, sitting at her feet. She chuckled. 'Classic sheepdog command, that one. My da used it all the time. Works like a treat.' She smiled at Casper affectionately and petted his head. 'Well... thanks again.'

She headed for her vehicle, Casper following faithfully beside his owner. When she opened the back door, he leaped in like he'd done it a thousand times, settling himself near the window which slid down as Sheila kicked the engine over.

Casper's big eyes watched them solemnly as the car reversed and, as Sheila tinkled a wave at them through the windscreen, Casper barked twice as if he was also saying goodbye. Oliver raised his hand to wave as did Paige and neither moved or spoke until the car and Casper's head which was turned firmly in their direction, disappeared from view.

'She seems lovely,' Paige murmured, breaking the silence, turning in the doorway to face him.

'Uh huh,' Oliver agreed, also turning. 'Casper... I mean Doggo, was pleased to see her.'

A noise that sounded very much like disapproval slipped from between her lips. 'What kind of name is Doggo?'

Oliver almost laughed but that seemed wrong right now. He shrugged. 'I guess the kind of name someone gives a working dog?'

'Yeah.'

She sounded utterly miserable, her rapid blinking confirming her emotional state which hit Oliver hard. She was obviously gutted at the development as was he and he knew they were supposed to be keeping their distance from each other but that didn't seem important at the moment.

'Hey,' he murmured, his eyes locking on hers that were two hazel puddles.

She shook her head, blinking some more. 'I'm alright.'

'Really?'

Sighing noisily, her head fell back against the door frame. 'No.'

'Neither am I,' he admitted.

And then he opened his arms because it just felt like the right thing to do. And when she walked straight into them, her arms lacing around his waist, her cheek pressing into his chest, he *knew* it was.

Neither of them spoke, they just held each other, his chin on top of her head. The spring of her hair was a whispery caress against his throat and curiously comforting even if he was suddenly aware of the slow, thick, thud of his pulse flowing like molasses through his veins. As they stood in the doorway not speaking, a duck waddled by the driveway, stopping halfway to look at them and quack.

'Aww.' Paige pulled out of his arms. 'How cute is that?'

Oliver shook his head at her. 'Don't even think about it.'

She laughed and after the heaviness of what had just

happened it was soothing at a visceral level. 'Oh come on,' she teased and that was soothing in places *less* visceral. 'Maybe it's a sign from the universe? Takes away our dog, gives us a duck.'

Our.

Us.

Oliver liked how that sounded a little too much. 'The only way that bird is coming in this house is if it's going in the oven and being served with hoisin sauce.'

'*Shh*, Oliver,' she scolded but a smile flirted with her mouth. 'It'll hear you.'

If the way the duck quickly waddled on was any indication, it *had* heard. He shook his head as he pushed away from the door frame and they moved inside. 'You're like bloody Cinderella. I'm surprised bluebirds don't follow you wherever you go.'

She laughed again and started to sing as she walked down the hallway. 'When you wish upon a star—'

'That's from *Pinocchio*,' he interrupted.

But instead of being horrified at her terrible lack of film knowledge, he laughed and damn if he didn't feel a little better.

12

Later that evening, with the wind blowing a gale outside, Paige and Oliver were sitting on the couch in the darkened media room watching *Pinocchio* – the original 1940 animated version. *What else?* She'd known the song she'd sung this afternoon wasn't from *Cinderella*. That had been the whole point. She'd been trying to lighten the mood or at least distract from Casper leaving and she knew her getting film facts wrong drove him bonkers.

But, she'd obviously tripped something in his head because he'd announced over an hour ago that he was going down to watch it and she'd found herself following, pleased for the distraction of a wooden puppet who wanted to be a real boy. Or maybe it had been because seeing him go downstairs without the dog at his heel had broken her heart a little and the house had seemed oppressively quiet without the white noise of doggy pants and toenails tapping on the floorboards.

For goodness' sake, the damn dog had been a *device*. A way to annoy Oliver – to create chaos in his pristine, controlled world. Sandy paws, daily baths, loud barking, slobber and *all* the dog hair. But he'd become so much more – to both of them.

He'd become a... member of the family. Such as they were.

Sheila had told Casper he'd been lucky to end up here but Paige was pretty sure they'd been the lucky ones. Oliver for sure. Walking Casper on the beach each day had given him a routine and a reason to get out there and also the perfect environment for creative flow. If it hadn't been for Casper, she doubted Oliver would have been anywhere near as productive these past weeks.

They were in their usual positions on the couch. Him, in his standard boxers and T that sat snug against his abs emphasising *everything* at one end and her, in her voluminous, bilious-green velour, yoga pants and her baggiest oversized shirt which covered her from neck to knees and left *everything* to the imagination, at the other.

She'd thrown them on as a defence against this taut thread of awareness that had vibrated like an invisible trip line between them since their hallway make-out sesh. They were the two most unflattering articles of clothing she'd brought with her and, combined, they were really something else. But she needed the barrier to keep a physical and mental distance from him.

Especially tonight. With a Casper-sized space – or maybe that was *hole* – between them, lowering defences she'd been shoring up all week.

It certainly felt like the elephant in the room right now and Paige was pleased for the distraction of a wooden puppet who wanted to be a real boy.

A blur of light in her peripheral vision drew her attention to Pavarotti who was doing laps on his wheel. It was good to see him active again. After Casper's departure, Oliver had peered into the hamster's cage and said, 'Looks like it's just you and me now, kid,' and Pavarotti had barely moved since.

Paige hadn't expected the rodent to understand such a cryptic phrase but clearly, he'd picked up what Oliver had put down and wasn't best happy with the situation. In fact, if it was at all possible for a hamster to look glum, Pavarotti had looked glum, his normally jaunty quiff droopy as he sat near the bars of his cage, his beady little eyes trained on the distant door as if he was expecting it to open at any moment and for Casper to bound in barking.

And she'd known exactly how he felt.

This week hadn't started well and it sure wasn't ending that way either. Between the teeth-aching politeness between her and Oliver since snog number two and the Bella and Chase fiasco which had unfolded with her Just Desserts peeps, Casper leaving had been the mouldy, rotting apple core on top of the mud pie that had been the week.

Oliver hugging her in the doorway had been nice – comforting nice, not a *prelude to something else* nice – to start with anyway. But it had quickly sent a buzz through her veins and a flood of heat pooling in her belly as it morphed into something decidedly not nice. Something which she was sure he'd also felt if the way his heartbeat had suddenly thrummed a little harder against the wall of his chest.

So, the arrival of the duck had given her the perfect opportunity to step away without either of them having to acknowledge the intimacy.

She'd give anything to be hugged again now as the yawning gap between them echoed the yawning hole inside her. Oliver was out of the question – she was just too damn *aware* of him – but she knew her co-conspirators, who she'd messaged earlier today about the Casper development, would be up for a huge group hug.

Sure, she'd be seeing them all soon in New York when her,

Sienna and Astrid planned to surprise Bella at the pre-opening party for Chase's gallery but she wanted to be wrapped up in their love now, damn it.

It was at times like this she was insanely jealous of the other three. All living in the States meant they were actually able to get together face to face. On a whim if they wanted. Hell, Bella and Astrid (thanks to her uncle's apartment) were both in New York! Sure, video calling was a good alternative but it wasn't the same as actually being with them.

Although, right at this moment, it was probably Bella that needed the group hug the most. There'd been much jubilation when the hatchet job article had appeared in print, thrusting Chase into a very hot spotlight but it hadn't lasted long. Bella had discovered some inconvenient truths about Chase that had set her in a real spin.

Mortified, they'd all put their heads together and come up with a plan to fix things. Paige had everything crossed that it would work because Bella's guilt was real. And hell, if she didn't she know all about that? It seemed like Paige wasn't the only one learning that things weren't always so black and white.

The strains of 'When You Wish Upon a Star' dragged her attention back to the movie although with Jiminy receiving his golden badge it was just about done now and she'd barely taken any of it in. Beside her, Oliver's hand slid to the empty couch cushion between them as it had done several times tonight.

She supposed given Casper had been there every night for the last month, it had been reflexive, his quick withdrawal each time, when his hand had found nothing but couch, squeezing at her ribcage. But, as the credits rolled on the screen, he didn't remove his hand, his fingers absently smoothing the cushion and *ugh*, now it was her heart being squeezed.

It was just so damn sad.

Without thinking, Paige slid her hand across and placed it over the top of his. She didn't know why, it just felt right. Like the hug in the doorway.

Solidarity.

But then his movement stilled and he looked from the screen to where her hand was laid over his before slowly lifting his gaze and, just like the doorway, the buzz was back. Paige's breath stilled in her throat as those blue eyes lingered on her mouth before they locked on her hazel ones and everything faded – the music, the flicker of the television, the lights from the hamster wheel.

Even the race of her pulse became a dull beat in her ears.

It was a strange moment. Something that started on impulse and had been meant for comfort but was already teetering on something else entirely. Her blood throbbed with awareness of him, each *lub-dub* of her heart pushing the throb to every nook and cranny, every cell, every millimetre of her skin.

Oh crap. This *wasn't* supposed to be happening again.

Paige forced a lacklustre smile across her mouth, all *friendly* like. All, *nothing to see here*. He returned it with equally lacklustre conviction. 'It'll take a while to get used to, I suppose...' Her voice was stupidly husky and she swallowed against the tightening in her throat.

'Yeah,' he murmured, his gaze not leaving hers, his voice rasping at just the right octave to stand every infinitesimal hair on her body to attention in one sweeping wave.

Her nipples followed suit and a brief thought about her sexually repellent, decade-old sports bra that would have looked perfectly at home on a sumo wrestler, flitted quickly away as Oliver turned his hand over beneath hers, his palm hot as his fingers slipped between hers and furled tight.

'Thank you,' he said.

Paige swallowed. 'What for?'

'For *Pinocchio*.'

Because she'd brought it up? Because it had been a distraction? Because she'd kept him company? But those questions faded to black as he slowly, *slowly* lifted their conjoined hands off the couch.

She supposed she could have stopped him. Pulled her hand back. He didn't exactly have her in a vice-like grip. She could have opened her mouth, used her words.

But she didn't do any of it. She *couldn't*.

She was transfixed by the slow ascension of their hands across the gap, the glow from the flickering TV strobing shadows along her arm. Anticipation crackled through her blood like an atmospheric charge just before a storm, *humming* through her veins. As he drew her hand nearer, her body automatically followed, his action nudging her a little closer.

Finally, their eyes still locked, her hand met his mouth and Paige watched helplessly and with great fascination as he brushed a lingering kiss to the back, breathing fire into the network of blue veins and injecting a slug of rocket fuel to her system.

Oh, dear lord, she wanted him beyond all reason. This feeling hadn't gone away merely because she'd insisted it be ignored. If anything, as she stared at him across a dog-sized space, her breath like static in her lungs all haphazard and disorganised, it had grown.

It was now an unholy behemoth demanding to be fed.

'Oliver,' she whispered.

She had no idea why she said his name, what thought she was going to express. Her need? Her desire? Her torment?

It certainly wasn't to tell him *no* or *stop*.

And it sure as hell didn't matter, anyway, as his eyes flared blue light and her blood pounded thick and slow through her temples, her neck, her belly. All flowing to the almighty ache growing between her legs.

'Paige.'

Her name hung between them. One beat. Two. And then suddenly, the TV screen went black as the movie ended, plunging the room into full darkness and it was like the universe had not only given them permission but the cover of night. All Paige's moral fibre, all the reasons for *not* fucking Oliver Prendergast, disintegrated under the cloak of darkness and the weight of her carnal urges.

They met halfway with a clash of mouths and a combined moan that echoed around the room, bouncing off the walls and hovering in the air, spiking it with a heady dose of lust. His hands slid either side of her neck as his tongue licked fire and brimstone into her mouth which she met with her own, her fingers tangling in his shirt as their heads twisted, their mouths roving restlessly as the kiss went deeper and deeper.

Not sampling but tasting, full and hearty, their breathing as loud and hungry as the winter wind howling at the door, as hungry as the howling banshee inside her commanding full and utter capitulation as lips ravaged and hunted.

Seeking, demanding. Giving, taking. Decadence and debauchery.

'Christ, Paige,' Oliver panted, his warm breath fanning her face as he pressed his forehead to hers. 'If you want this to stop, you better say now because I don't know how much control I've got over it.'

Well, that made two of them. But she understood, despite the sticky globules of lust clinging to synapses like dew to a spider's web, what he was doing. He was giving her an out. And had the lights been on and Casper lying between them, she might have considered it. Hell, who was she kidding? They wouldn't be here like this had that been the case.

But it wasn't the case and for sure she was going to hell for this but, after four lonely years eschewing any whiff of physical closeness with another human being, she needed this like she needed her next breath.

Tomorrow she'd deal with the inevitable fallout. Tonight, she needed this to keep *going on*. She kissed him then, hard and sure before pulling away. 'I don't want to stop,' she muttered.

Getting to her feet, Paige quickly pushed down her velour pants and stepped out of them as she lifted her baggy shirt over her head leaving her in just her mismatched underwear. Had she not been so lust addled, she probably wouldn't have been so bold. But she was completely drunk on pleasure and the shadows were her friend.

'Holy fuck,' he swore, his eyes roving her body, like she was wearing the finest Victoria's Secret lingerie instead of rainbow-striped knickers that sat too low to cover the soft rise of her stomach and her ancient sports bra.

And hell, if her heart didn't skip a beat.

Drinking in his patent admiration for her curves, she stepped between his legs, dropping a knee to the couch beside his thigh, reaching for his shoulders as she dropped her other knee, looming above him temporarily as she straddled his lap. She sucked in a breath as he strung kisses across the valley of her cleavage, the husky serration of his breath sending spirals of sensation straight to her nipples.

Their heights equalised as she lowered herself, settling her centre against his. But where she was wet and soft he was hot and hard. *Very freaking hard* and she shivered as she ground against all that heat and thickness, dragging a low groan from his lips as he nuzzled the hollow at the base of her throat. She ground again and his fingers sunk into her ass, clutching her tight against him.

'Shirt,' she gasped as a furnace roared to life between her legs and a ripple undulating along muscles deep and low told her things were escalating fast.

Falling back against the couch, Oliver yanked his shirt off his head, exposing his flat abdomen, his smooth, firm pecs and the broad spread of his shoulders. Pillows of muscle in his belly contracted as he tossed his shirt, his gaze drifting slowly up her body, licking heat with those smouldering blue eyes until they met hers.

'Bra.'

Awarding him mental points for not calling it *that depressingly functional contraption strapping your titties in*, Paige complied eagerly. Her nipples were painfully tight and aching to be free. It still didn't stop her hands from trembling though as she reached for the back clasp, his gaze intent on the show. Considering Paige had almost, on several occasions throughout her adult life, been strangled to death while trying to get out of a sports bra, the hooks and eyes cooperated first time and the bra straps slid down her arms, exposing her breasts to his full view.

'Christ, Paige,' he said on a reverent exhale as he leaned in and dropped a gentle kiss next to each taut nipple. 'You're so fucking beautiful.'

Every disparaging thought Paige had ever had about her body – and God knew, there'd been plenty of them – completely disappeared from her head because, right now, with him looking at her like *that* she felt like goddamn Eve.

The OG temptress.

His hands slid to her breasts and, on a groan, he sunk his face into them, his fingers stroking and kneading as his hot mouth found a pale pink bud and sucked.

Paige cried out it was so exquisite. Raw and base and perfect as his teeth scraped against the engorged tip. Her head fell back as Oliver switched from one nipple to the other in a never-ending loop, hot darts of sensation arrowing south from where his tongue flicked to where the slick heat at her centre met his steely girth.

Paige was riding a fugue of lust so strong, she didn't even notice she was tipping backwards until the couch cushions were beneath her and her head was semi propped on the arm as Oliver's big, hard body settled between her legs.

So. Freaking. Good.

She stretched, undulating her body, revelling in the full-length experience as he kissed her, deep and slow for long drugging moments before he was gone again, his mouth teasing a nipple, his hand sliding into her underwear.

Paige's eyes flew open as his fingers delved into the all the slick between her legs and deftly found the perfect spot. She gasped and clutched his shoulders at how damn good it felt.

'Right there?' he asked around her nipple, clearly not planning on relinquishing it.

'Yes,' she panted. '*Exactly* there.'

Her eyes fluttered closed on a surge of pleasure as his finger circled lazily, his tongue slowing to mimic the pace. But when she moaned and shoved her hand into his hair, he picked up the pace, flaying her nipples with attention, his fingers working her clit in simpatico as she panted and moaned and writhed beneath him, her pulse like a hammer through her head as she hurtled towards orgasm.

'*Oliver!*' she cried out as that low ripple became two, then three, then more pulling everything to an excruciating, concentrated pinpoint of pleasure until it broke on a powerful *whoosh* flooding every inch of her body, showering her in a kaleidoscope of colour and soaking her in warm, electric rain.

'*Olllliver.*'

It was a moan this time, low and sonorous, coming from somewhere *other*, somewhere she'd buried so deep for so long, it felt like the earth was cracking open as she let it go, writhing and panting, clutching his shoulders, holding tight to him as her body bucked through the rigours of her climax and all the time he was whispering in her ear, '*Yes, yes, Paige... just like that... Yes... I got you... yes.*'

And, as the ripples ebbed, his finger action gentled and he dropped butterfly kisses on her cheeks and eyes and mouth but a fever still had her in its hold, her blood thick with the beat of it and she was greedy for more. Greedy for the feel of him pushing into her, for the rise of him over her, for the moment he lost himself *because* of her.

Reaching for his boxers, she pushed them off his hips but the erratic thump of her pulse made her dizzy and her fingers next to useless. She gave a frustrated little growl as she met his gaze. 'Off,' she panted. 'I want you inside me.'

The blue of his irises flared at her guttural request. 'Fuck *yes*,' he muttered.

As he swooped in to kiss her, Paige got lost in the mastery of his lips, only vaguely aware of him tugging at clothes and cursing their recalcitrance against her mouth as he awkwardly fumbled them both out of their underwear *without* breaking the kiss.

And suddenly he was right there. No barrier between them. The thick, blunt prod of him so damn good as she wrapped her legs around his waist and whispered, 'Please.'

They *both* gasped as he slid inside her, thrusting to the hilt in one buck of his hips. '*Fuuuck*,' Oliver panted into her neck. 'I never want to be anywhere else.'

Paige concurred. *Utterly*. But if she thought about it too much she'd ruin the here and now. Future Paige could worry about such a potentially calamitous statement. The Paige on this couch, under this man, joined as intimately as was possible for two people to be joined?

She was in the moment.

Furrowing her fingers into his hair, she turned her face, her lips close to his ear as she whispered, '*More*.'

So he gave her more. And more. And more again. Pounding in and out until they were both breathing hard, each withdrawal a prelude to the next breathtaking penetration which only stoked her fever – *their* fever – higher and higher. And when he draped her leg over his shoulder and rose up over her, the angle changed and he went deeper and harder and her orgasm was upon her before she could even comprehend what was happening, crying out his name again as it spun her around and around and around.

He joined her moments later on a long low, '*Yeeeeesssss*,' the rhythm of his thrusts changing as he rode his own release. His arms trembling, their gazes locked as they weathered the storm of pleasure together.

The fever broke as abruptly as it had started, leaving them in a panting heap of arms and legs. Oliver's big body was pleasantly heavy slumped on top, the tickle of his breath on her neck pleasantly intimate as the afterglow hummed around them and their breathing slowly returned to normal.

A rattling noise stirred them from their stupor and they both looked over to identify the source to find Pavarotti running on his wheel.

'Bloody hell,' Oliver said, his voice still a little gravelly as he stared at the blur of lights. 'Do you think he saw that?'

Paige blinked. 'I don't see how he could have missed it.'

'Oh God.' Oliver looked at her, endearingly askance. 'What if we've *damaged* him? Is there a special place in hell for people who expose their animals to...' He paused as if he wasn't sure what to call what had just happened. 'Rumpy-pumpy?'

Paige hooted out a laugh. The man was naked and still semi hard inside her after nailing her to the couch like he did it for a *living* and yet still managed to sound delightfully posh. 'Animals don't seem particularly bothered exposing us to their *rumpy-pumpy*,' she reasoned.

'Ah. Yes.' He brightened. 'Good point.'

And then he laughed too, all warm and husky as he lowered his forehead to hers and it would have been easy to feel guilt and shame and recriminations right now but there was *laughter* and Paige's heart just about floated right out of her chest.

13

Oliver woke at ten thirty the following morning, Paige snuggled into his side, her head tucked into the crook of his neck, her curls tickling his face and he smiled. He'd half expected to find her gone and the fact she wasn't made him ridiculously happy.

He wasn't fool enough to think that there wouldn't be a reckoning over what had happened on the couch last night – and another two times in his bedroom. Paige might have given in to the vibe between them under the cover of darkness but he'd been privy to her guilt over a simple kiss. He figured her self-loathing over them *sleeping* together would be epic.

And he understood it. He didn't feel great about sleeping with a friend of Bella's either given how appallingly he'd already treated her.

But, conversely, it also didn't feel *wrong*.

Despite the tabloids' attempt to brand every woman he'd ever stood or sat beside since the non-wedding as a *new flame*, the very last thing on his mind had been *hooking up*. Given the Bella disaster, he was happy to swear off relationships for life.

Yet Paige, who had come out of nowhere and disordered his life, had somehow infiltrated his brain.

Which wasn't nothing. Nor was it just *hooking up*, either.

Apart from a conversation (they should have had prior) about contraception and sexual health – she had an implant and they'd both been abstinent for a protracted period – they hadn't talked much last night. She hadn't seemed to want to and, selfishly, he hadn't pushed. Frankly he'd expected her to immediately leap up in horror off the couch and the fact she hadn't and then followed him – stark naked – to his room afterwards, had sewn a little seed of hope.

Maybe whatever this was, didn't have to be a disaster. Maybe it had... legs? If they could just move past the Bella thing. If *he* could move past the Bella thing.

It *had* only been eight months since his dramatic split with her and, given it had been the most significant romantic relationship in his life, it was probably wise not to rush back in. Especially not when at the first whiff of a romance there'd be paps around every corner.

Which was why he'd always dated women who ran in the same circles and were used to that kind of normal – which was *not* Paige. Why would he subject the woman he had a bunch of *complicated feelings* for, to that?

His stomach growled, interrupting the spin of his thoughts and he suddenly realised he was hungry. He didn't know what Paige would do next or even what he *wanted* her to do but he did know how to feed her and, after their epic, sweaty, calorie-burning session last night, they both needed to eat.

Hell, Oliver would probably need to carb load for the next three days just to make up for the deficit.

Paige stirred a little as he eased his arm out from under her head and he held his breath until her head settled on the pillow in a cloud of reddy-gold curls. He wanted to lean in and kiss the freckle on the tip of her nose but he didn't want to wake her – not yet. Not without sustenance on offer. A hearty breakfast always made a person feel better about themselves and would hopefully spark a calm, civilised, morning-after conversation.

No one could have a calm, civilised conversation on an empty stomach, right?

Rolling out of bed, Oliver quickly pulled on a pair of sweats and tiptoed out of the room. Taking the stairs to the kitchen two at a time he was greeted by familiar grey skies and the pound of surf through the large window.

It made him shiver just looking at it. Surely winter was on its way out? It was going to be *March* in a few weeks. He'd seen a scattering of daffodils growing across the road yesterday for crying out loud.

Ignoring the weather, Oliver greeted Pavarotti who he'd rescued from downstairs sometime during the night when Paige had realised they'd left him in the media room in their rush to continue their sex-capades. His cage in its usual spot on the kitchen counter, the hamster scurried to the bars and Oliver ruffled his finger through his ginger quiff.

'You hungry?' he crooned. Which was a dumb question – Pavarotti, even the slimmer version, never said no to food.

After dealing with the hamster's gastronomic needs, Oliver got to work in the kitchen, scrambling eggs, smashing avocado, crumbling fetta, squeezing lemon and producing two steaming mugs of coffee. It was strange not having Casper at his feet, shadowing him, waiting for food scraps that fell to the floor.

Rationally, Oliver knew that Casper had a home and an owner who'd been looking for him and it was right to see them reunited but that didn't stop him wishing it hadn't happened. Casper had been by his side as Oliver had bared his soul – his

The Payback Plan

deepest, darkest secrets – and that bond went deep. No matter what he'd spoken out loud, Casper hadn't judged him and that meant a lot.

Arranging the plates on a tray, Oliver inspected the aesthetic, satisfied with what he saw. It not only smelled good but was pleasing to the eye. It was missing something though and he knew exactly what. Striding down the hallway, he opened the front door spying the yellow blooms across the way.

Hoping like hell there wasn't a stray pap lurking around, he sprinted across the road.

* * *

To his surprise, Paige was staring at the ceiling when he entered, both arms above her head. The fact she hadn't disappeared the second she'd opened her eyes was something, right? Maybe she *was* up for a conversation.

'Morning,' he said cheerfully, tray in hand. 'I made breakfast.'

Her eyes met his. 'So I see.'

'You hungry?'

She nodded. '*Starving.*'

'Good answer,' he said with a grin as he set the tray in the middle of the bed.

'Would you mind throwing me my nightshirt?'

Oliver had brought their clothes up when he'd rescued Pavarotti and they were now sitting in a pile on the dresser. He didn't know whether it was a good thing or a bad thing that Paige wanted to cover up but she was still here and that was all that mattered.

He tossed her the requested article and in one little shimmy it was over her head and down her body as she'd hauled herself into a sitting position, without even a nip slip. It was startlingly efficient which shouldn't be sexy but somehow was, as was the grin she levelled at him like she knew she'd just bamboozled him and Oliver was utterly freaking charmed.

'Smells good,' she said, adjusting the pillows behind her back to prop herself a little forward as she gathered the duvet around her waist and crossed her legs lotus-style beneath.

Turning her attention to the tray, she noticed the flower for the first time, her mouth softening into a smile. '*Oh.*' Reaching for it, she brought it to her nose. 'I love daffodils,' she murmured as she fingered the stem and brushed the petals under her nose, inhaling the floral essence. Lifting her gaze, she met his eyes. 'Thank you.'

Oliver shrugged. It had been an impulsive gesture but, seeing her genuine delight, one he was pleased he'd gone with. Handing her the coffee mug, he waited until she'd placed it and the daff on the bedside table before offering her a linen serviette. Dutifully, she spread it over her lap and plonked the plate he passed her on top.

Mimicking her position, Oliver climbed on top of the duvet, his back to the door, also balancing his plate while his mug sat on the tray between them.

'I don't know, Oliver,' she murmured as she glanced at the food, picking up a piece of extra toast he'd cut in half diagonally and put on her plate. 'There's going to be crumbs. How will you cope?'

Oliver laughed at her teasing. 'I think I'll cope this once.'

'But...' She shook her head. 'Bed crumbs are the worst crumbs.' Then she bit into the toast.

She was right, bed crumbs *were* the worst crumbs but the way her eyes shut as she savoured the buttery crunch had him suddenly rather fond of them.

'Mmm.' She sighed, her lashes fluttering open. 'Good.'

They tucked in and for a couple of minutes there was just the sound of cutlery scraping on crockery and contented sighs as coffee was sipped. Paige was an appreciative eater but not in some performative erotic consumption of food way. No staged lick lipping or finger sucking. Just pure hedonistic enthusiasm.

Who knew that was such a turn on?

The silence was companionable and Oliver was loathe to break it but with the mood this mellow, it also felt like an opening for that civilised discussion.

Picking up his mug, he sipped it as he watched her devour her plate, all fresh-faced and wild ginger hair. He could picture her with a wreath of vine leaves entwined in her curls surrounded by ripe fruit and exotic flowers like a painting he'd once seen of Pomona, Roman goddess of fruitful abundance.

And she was in his bed. And he really *liked* her. Sure, he'd liked all the women he'd had in his bed but *none* of them had felt like *this*.

She lifted her eyes from the plate and met his as she swallowed her mouthful. 'What?' A reddy-gold eyebrow kicked up. 'Have I got food on my face?' She brushed at her mouth.

'No.' He smiled. 'I was just thinking you're much more...' Oliver chose the next word carefully. He wanted to say calm, but, in his experience, it was a word that could have the *opposite* effect in a conversation. 'Chill than I thought you'd be this morning.'

A storm of emotions turned her eyes the milky jade of the ocean and for a moment he thought he'd blown it. That she might not answer. That she might change the subject. But then she sighed and her shoulders slumped a little. 'I'm not.' Her curls shifted as she shook her head. 'Not really. I'm just trying not to think about it.'

'About last night?'

'Yep.'

'Because denial is better than self-loathing?' he asked tentatively.

She laughed but there was no joy in it. 'Oh, I absolutely hate myself and I know the second I leave this room and face reality it will be *all* I think about.'

Luckily, Oliver had a solution for that. But it was hardly appropriate in the midst of *this* conversation to suggest she didn't even bother leaving the room. That she stay naked in his bed for as long as she needed to stop the loathing and he would administer all the sustenance she needed through a constant supply of scrambled eggs, coffee and cunnilingus.

'The bigger problem is how conflicted I feel about what happened.' She rubbed her forehead. 'It should be cut and dried, right? But it's not. On one hand I feel truly awful about sleeping with my friend's ex. Kissing you was bad enough but going all the way like that?' She grimaced, clearly disgusted. '*How could I do that?*'

The question was rhetorical he was pretty sure so Oliver didn't answer. Plus, she was actually talking about it this time, not running away with her fingers jammed metaphorically in her ears, so it would be idiotic to interrupt.

'But, also.' She shut her eyes. 'It was... good.'

He grinned. He couldn't help himself because *fuck,* yeah, it had been. It had been seriously superlative *rumpy-pumpy.*

She hummed as if reliving the more salacious details then opened her eyes. 'I hadn't thought it'd be that good.'

Oliver wasn't sure whether to be affronted or pleased but, as usual, her frankness was weirdly endearing and he couldn't help but laugh. 'Um, thank you? I think?'

'No.' She shook her head. 'That makes it worse.'

'Would you feel better if it had been terrible?'

'*Duh.*' She bugged her eyes at him. 'It would have been the ultimate... sexual justice.'

'Okay.' Oliver had no idea what to do with that information. 'Well... whatever. I'm *not* sorry about it being *not* terrible.'

She regarded him for a long moment as if she was trying to find the words to explain. 'It's just that it's been a long time for me. And the last guy I was with... well...' Her lips tightened and the hazel of her eyes deepened to a rusty brown. 'It was messy. And, for... *reasons...*'

Paige paused and swallowed and Oliver's nape prickled. Something *bad* had happened.

'I can't disassociate sex from him. So I told myself I didn't want it and I didn't need it. That abstinence was a perfectly legitimate choice people made every day.'

'Paige.' Oliver placed his coffee on the tray in a slow controlled movement he absolutely *did not* feel. His stomach roiled as a cold oily slick settled over the contents. He knew it wasn't any of his business but he asked anyway. 'What did he do to you?'

What had that asshole done?

She shook her head, her curls ruffling as she waved her hand dismissively. 'This isn't about him. It's about me. Letting go. I've held myself so tight, so contained for so long. I haven't let myself go in four freaking years.'

Oliver blinked at the statement. He'd never met a woman more spontaneous and impulsive in his entire life. She'd been the exact opposite of contained. But, he'd been around enough to know that people's sexual personality *could* be very different to the one on display to the outside world.

'It was such a... relief,' she continued. 'And part of me wants to feel great about that and wants to rejoice which makes me a terrible person because it shouldn't have happened. Not with you.' She sighed as she picked up her coffee and settled back against the bedhead. 'Why did it have to be you?'

Oliver shrugged. He didn't know the answer to what cosmic forces had been at work to land her on his doorstep. He was just fucking delighted they had. He understood her guilt because he felt it too, but what Bella didn't know, couldn't hurt her. What had happened last night was between him and Paige and, for sure, they'd have to reckon with it but nobody else had to know.

'So, I might seem chill in here' – she gestured around the room – 'eating breakfast with you because I can steadfastly refuse to think about any of those things too closely in this alternate reality bubble where it's just you and me.'

Just you and me. Oliver liked the sound of that. Maybe a little too much.

'But the moment I step through there' – she tipped her chin at the doorway – 'the real world is waiting for me and that'll be brutal.'

Brutal seemed a little excessive to Oliver and he wondered if there was more to Paige's guilt than just Bella? Was it also something to do with the asshole? His jaw tightened at the thought and he had to make a serious mental effort to shake the sudden grimness that had descended because it was *none of his business*.

'Okay, so, how about this.' Oliver forced a smile as he pushed off the bed, gathering his plate then hers and putting them on the tray. '*Don't* go through the door. Not yet.'

She gave a half laugh. 'Oliver Prendergast, my partner in denial.' She shook her head. 'I have work to do. Clients to manage.'

Oliver placed the tray on the dresser that sat against the wall opposite the bed. Affixed to the wall above, sat a large-screen TV. He turned to face her and his heart gave a little skip at the fluffy, freckly, flyaway nymph in his bed. His hand slid absently to his belly. 'When was the last time you took a weekend off?'

Her gaze dropped to where his hand was splayed and lingered for a few moments which vaporised the air in his lungs and caused his dick to twitch. He couldn't decide if he was relieved or disappointed when she dragged her attention back to his face.

'I *never* take the weekend off.'

Ooh boy, it was worse than he thought. 'Well *that* is just criminal. How about...' He climbed on the bed but didn't attempt to get under the covers. This was supposed to be about her. Not him. 'We just stay right here. In bed.' He sidled up to her, lying on his back beside her, his arm lightly touching hers, his legs stretched out in front. 'And just... do nothing? Read a book, scroll TikTok, sleep.' He gestured at the television. 'Maybe we could binge watch something on Netflix.'

She rolled her head to the side, her gaze finding his. 'Netflix and *chill* huh?'

He smiled. 'I don't mean sex.' He really didn't. Not that he'd say no, either. 'I'll stay above the covers, cross my heart.'

To prove it, he crossed his heart and she laughed although it petered out quickly as her gaze drifted to the doorway. Oliver watched the play of emotions across her face, transfixed by the fascinating pattern of her freckles. When she returned her attention to him, he could see something had shifted. 'I guess there's nothing urgent requiring my attention.'

Oliver grinned. 'Well okay then.'

She grinned back and he made a fist, presenting it to her for a sideways bump and she obliged. 'Here's to your first ever weekend off,' he said. 'No, hang on, wait.' Oliver leaned over and whisked his phone off the bedside table. Settling back beside her, he navigated to the camera. 'Something as momentous as this, needs to be memorialised.'

He held it up and away to centre them both in the frame but that was as far as he got.

'No.' She reached up and snatched the phone from his grasp. 'No pictures.'

It was so quick, it was almost comical and Oliver barely had time to process it before his phone was tossed on the end of the bed. It was quite the reaction and reminded him of how she'd dodged Doris's attempts to get her in a photograph.

And how she didn't have her picture on her website or any of her social media.

'Are you in witness protection or something?' he asked with a laugh.

But Paige wasn't laughing. 'I know you've been pretty much photographed your entire life but is it *so* hard to believe that someone wouldn't need to get a photo with you?'

He thought about it for a beat. 'Frankly yes.'

Every woman he'd ever been with had been keen to be in pics with him, Bella included. Unfortunately, some of those – not Bella's – had ended up in the tabloids which had been irritating but something he'd come to accept. He didn't blame anyone for wanting their fifteen seconds of fame. Thanks to his father, Oliver understood the lure of it. He just hoped they got the going rate for a candid snap of the son of a famous actor.

'Well I guess there's a first time for everything, right?'

Oliver thought back to that day at the WI. What had she said? That she took a hideous picture. That even her baby photos were awful. And she was the most unphotogenic person anyone could meet. Something like that.

Turning on his side, his arm and shoulder pressing into the soft padding of the bedhead, he inspected her profile. 'This isn't about some fucked-up body image thing is it, because that just breaks my heart.'

'It's not that.'

Her denial was so swift, Oliver thought that maybe it actually *was* that. Growing up in celebrity circles where image was everything, he understood how much that could skew people's sense of self. 'Okay.' He watched as she smoothed the duvet. 'But if it is I just want you to know' – he reached out and gently tugged her nearest curl – 'you are the most—'

'It's *not* that,' she said as she jerked her head away, forcing him to drop the curl.

'Okay.'

She shot him an irritated look. 'It's *not*,' she insisted.

'Well...' Oliver frowned. 'What then?' When she didn't reply, he leaned in a little and whispered. 'We're in the bubble, remember?'

Glancing away she went back to smoothing the duvet and for a moment, Oliver thought she wasn't going to open up about whatever the hell deeper was going on here. But then her hands suddenly stilled and she drew in an unsteady breath.

'My ex...' She cleared her throat before she continued. 'Harvey.'

So, the asshole had a name. *Harvey*. That cold, oily slick from earlier roiled through his gut again. He had a feeling he wasn't going to like this one little bit.

'We were together for a few months. It all happened kinda fast and he was... good looking and charismatic and I was... swept along. For a bit. But I had exams to study for and grades to make, things I took very seriously. But... he didn't. Mine or his. And I realised we... didn't have very much in common and so I... called it off.'

Her palms had resumed their duvet ironing as she talked

slowly, haltingly, like she was trying to pluck the right words from the air as she felt her way forward. Oliver shut up and let her even though he had a dozen questions about what she'd been studying and where.

'The break-up was reasonably amicable. Or so I thought, anyway. He didn't seem that cut up about it. Then a few days later he...' She took a shuddery breath. 'Sent nude photos and a video of me to every email address in the law faculty and posted them to online sites.'

Every atom of oxygen in Oliver's lungs vaporised in an instant. His heart banged like a gun going off. A red mist clouded his vision.

What. The. Fuck.

'He'd taken them without my consent or knowledge and it was...' She shook her head. '*Awful.*'

'Jesus... Paige.'

He reached for her without thinking that maybe he shouldn't in this moment but it was just too *heinous* not to offer comfort as his blood boiled and his brain conjured all the ways he could make Harvey *the fuckhead*, suffer.

She didn't object as his arm scooped around her shoulder, her head settling on his chest, her hand flattening on his sternum. 'I dropped out. I went home. I...' She whispered the next bit. 'Made myself small.' Her fingers curled into a ball briefly before relaxing again. 'But only for a while. Then I picked myself up, I started my business. I charted a new way forward.'

Oliver's gut *burned*. He couldn't believe she'd been hiding all this behind a veneer of quirky bravado. He was incensed and enraged on her behalf at such an intimate betrayal even if she had managed to resurrect herself in the aftermath. So many pictures had been taken of him without his knowledge and posted without his consent that he'd become kinda numb to it. But this *wasn't* that.

This was private and personal. It was *reprehensible*. And vindictive. It was the lowest act. And Harvey the fuckhead had better watch his goddamn back because Oliver had money and time and a shitload of patience.

Also, very fancy lawyers.

Questions stacked on questions inside his brain, all battling for supremacy but he didn't think he should ask for all the ghoulish details so he went with, 'Did you... go to the police?'

'Yes. And Oxford, the law faculty, was amazing. But it was hard to prove it was him. And it's like the freaking Wild West out there on the internet. You get one place to take it down and it's been shared to two more. It's like the fucking Hydra.'

Oliver had no words. None that didn't centre his own outrage and he couldn't make this about *his* anger. Not sitting right here beside her when it was *Paige* who had been wronged so profoundly.

'Anyway.' She gave a shaky laugh. 'That's why I don't like my picture being taken.'

Yeah. Little wonder. On impulse, Oliver removed his arm from her shoulder, turning to roll on top of her, the duvet preventing any skin to skin as he settled between her legs. Supporting his weight on the flats of his forearms, he gazed down at her intently.

'I'm sorry,' he murmured, dropping a soft, brief kiss on the side of her mouth. Not sexual, not as a prelude, not with any agenda. Just trying to convey the depth of his emotion. 'I know that's inadequate but I'm *so* sorry that happened to you.'

He wished he had better, fancier words but he was at a loss. How did *any* words make this better? And that probably cut the deepest because he *couldn't* make it better. He could only acknowledge her pain and injury.

Right now, anyway. His brain was already seething with ways he could fuck up that asshole Harvey.

She nodded, her hazel eyes misty. 'Thank you,' she murmured and raised her head to kiss him. It was brief too but it was *not* on the side of the mouth and she withdrew very slowly. By the time she'd settled back against the pillows, her eyes had changed hue. There was a heat to them, a smoulder and her gaze lingered on his mouth like what she really wanted right now *wasn't* words.

'You could, of course,' she said, a smile hovering on her mouth, 'take a mind picture.'

Oliver grinned, picking up what she was putting down. 'I could definitely do that.'

Slowly, he pushed away from her, sitting back on his haunches as he tugged the duvet from her unresisting fingers. Her nightshirt was bunched around her middle, the hem sitting at the very tops of her thighs just covering her modesty.

And he knew for a fact, she wasn't wearing any underwear.

'I could also,' he said, dragging his eyes off the tantalising galaxy of freckles that dappled her legs and disappeared from sight behind that hem. 'Make a mind map. I'd need to survey you very thoroughly, though.' His gaze travelled up her body where her nipples were two tight points tenting the fabric. 'All those hills and valleys and curves.'

She quirked an eyebrow. 'Is there some kind of... instrument you'd use for that?'

Oliver nodded. 'I was thinking my tongue would work quite well.'

'Oh, right.' Her pupils dilated. 'Yes. That would probably do the job.'

Oliver, his blood pounding thick and hot now as it rushed *south*, leaned in, planting one hand on the bed beside her hip and sliding the other to the hem of her shirt. 'Are you sure?'

She nodded. 'I don't want to think any more today.'

Her words were like a hit of cocaine to a system that was already supercharged. If it was some sexual amnesia she was after he was more than happy to provide. Clutching the hem, he slid his hand up her body, dragging her shirt with him, exposing the trimmed thatch of golden red hair between her legs, the soft rise of her belly, the indent of her navel, the flare of her hips, the cage of her ribs and lastly, the heavy fall of her breasts tipped with the tight pink ruche of her nipples.

Oliver sucked in a breath at her glory. He felt like he'd been let loose in a very adult playground with permission to ride.

'I think...' He cleared his throat of its thickness, his head *buzzing* with desire. 'I should start here,' he said, his chest settling into the cradle of her pelvis, his boner pressing into the mattress, his mouth hovering over a nipple.

'Yeah.' She swallowed. 'Whatever you think.'

He leaned in and licked, her breathy moans a mantra as he worked his way south to her sweet spot. She bucked when his tongue touched down on the engorged bundle of nerves sitting proud and aching for attention. Her back arched and she cried out as he flicked his tongue hard against the sensitive bud, pushing her legs wide.

He knew she was close when her hand clutched his head, her fingers twisting in his hair, her foot sliding from his shoulder to plant firmly in the centre of his back like she was afraid he might pull away.

But Oliver had no intention of going anywhere.

14

Paige was alone when she woke the next day – very late. The clock told her it was after one in the afternoon but she was hardly surprised. Another night of marathon sex might have been healing in a way she'd have never credited but it hadn't left a lot of time for sleep.

Rolling on her side, she stared at the doorway, a.k.a. the portal to the real world. It was tempting to stay in Oliver's room another day. He could bring her laptop up and she could work in between bouts of mind-blowing *rumpy-pumpy*.

She was pretty sure he would be happy to oblige.

And if Oliver had been here when she woke up, she may well have decided why the hell not? But he wasn't and putting things off was not who she was. Add to that a very timely notification on her phone from a client panicking about some urgent work and she reluctantly left the bed to face the music.

Twenty minutes later, freshly showered, she was standing in the kitchen near Pavarotti's cage, coffee in hand as she stared out the window. Oliver was on the beach and she tracked his path as he trudged towards the end in his standard coat and beanie to ward off the chill of yet another grey day.

Was he dictating his book or was he on the beach trying to digest what had gone down between them this weekend? Like she was.

She couldn't believe the events of the last thirty-six hours. Not the sex. Not the way she'd checked all her baggage and common sense at the door to his room and left it there. Not how she'd opened up to him yesterday about what Harvey had done to her.

Outside her family she'd only ever told three other people – Bella, Sienna and Astrid. They weren't the only ones who knew, of course. Several police officers, a couple of lawyers, *hundreds* of people at Oxford University and probably a *zillion* internet users were all privy to her secret shame.

Unfortunately, she had no control over that. Only over who *she* told. And she'd chosen to tell Oliver.

A flock of seagulls took flight in front of him and she wondered if he was missing Casper dashing around, chasing birds and waves and fetching the ball as many times as Oliver was willing to throw it. He looked over his shoulder for a moment and Paige could see his mouth moving. Dictating his book, she assumed.

It made her ridiculously happy that he was persevering with the book and that it was coming together so well. She smiled then caught herself, her mouth slackening.

She had *nothing* to smile about.

Okay yeah, she'd got herself laid six ways to Sunday. *With Bella's ex.* Who she was supposed to be *messing with*, not... going down on in the shower.

Oh God, *idiot* – do not think about the shower. They'd had

their tryst and now she'd stepped out of the room and was back into reality.

The guilt piled in like she'd known it would but the real problem was, she didn't know what happened next. From the time she'd pulled herself out of the pit of despair four years ago, determined to start from scratch, she'd always known what was next. She'd had a strategy to get her life back on track and she'd stuck to it, seen it through.

The same thing had happened with the payback plan. She'd had a strategy and all she'd had to do was stick to it. But, her heart was no longer in it, which meant not only had she betrayed Bella, she'd sent a wrecking ball through the group objective.

She'd broken the chain.

The weight of her guilt was oppressive as she followed Oliver's progress. It had all seemed so simple in the beginning – a spot of harmless karmic rebalancing of the universe. But now it felt like the universe was having the last laugh. Getting its own payback and maybe it was just what she deserved?

She'd not only wronged Bella but she'd also been lying to Oliver, coming into his house under false pretences. And while that had felt righteous – *noble* even – back at O'Hare in December, it felt plain deceitful right now.

Sighing heavily, she tried to think of a way forward but it felt impossible, her brain a quagmire of indecision. She contemplated ringing her sister and dumping this all in her lap but she didn't want to drag her into the mess, not when there were three women who were already involved.

She should be talking to *them*.

Well, not Bella. She couldn't even contemplate that right now, fresh out of Oliver's bed. But Astrid and Sienna? Yes, they'd know what to do, right? After all, a problem shared was a problem halved. Her pulse tripped a little as she picked up her phone.

> WHATSAPP. MONDAY 14.00 GMT.
> TO: SIENNA, ASTRID
> SUBJECT LINE: SOS!!!
>
> PAIGE
> I fucked up. Are you guys free for a call??

Paige waited, her eyes fixed on Oliver's back as he trudged ever closer to the end of the beach. Her heart was in her mouth, hoping her friends would be around. It was nine in the morning in both New York and Massachusetts so the timing wasn't bad and she didn't think she could sit with this any longer, having decided to get it off her chest. Also, if she didn't do it now she may well chicken out altogether.

Strike while the iron was hot. Or the guilt was hot anyway.

But, oh God, what if they didn't want to *be* her friend any more after revealing she'd betrayed Bella in the most heinous way a woman could betray a friend.

Three little dots appeared and Paige's throat constricted even further.

> SIENNA
> I can jump on a call.
> ASTRID
> Me too!

Paige never knew it was possible to be so utterly relieved and yet so full of dread at the same time. She didn't think she could bear it if they hated her which would, of course, be a perfectly natural reaction.

Fingers trembling, she hit the video call icon in the PM group.

Her face appeared on screen, her freckles popping in her pale complexion as if to broadcast her guilt even further. They'd always been a true barometer of her emotions. The phone's muted ring felt like the chimes of doom as she waited for the other two to pick up.

Sienna, who was driving her car, beat Astrid by a millisecond and Paige almost cried when their faces filled their third of the screen. Seeing them again took her right back to that day they'd first met and she was both grateful and even more wretched that she'd screwed it all up.

It seemed like this was the morning for contrasting emotions!

Astrid was the first to speak with no perfunctory hello. She looked more aglow than usual, her cheeks pink – she'd probably been to one of those hot yoga sessions she loved so much – and her eyes bright. And why wouldn't they be? She was on the righteous path, unlike Paige who had submitted to the bloody devil.

'What happened?' she demanded straight out of the gate. 'Are you okay?'

Paige shook her head. She was decidedly *not* okay. Which sucked considering she'd just had a weekend of debauchery that had completely rewired her damn brain. 'I did a bad, bad thing.'

'Uh oh,' Sienna said, her eyebrows beetling together. Even frowning she managed to look like the honey-blonde goddess from the airport. When Paige frowned she looked like her uncle Fred who resembled a giant ginger Santa Claus. 'You want to start at the beginning?'

The beginning? Paige wasn't even sure where the beginning

was. How had this happened? When she tried to parse the events of the last month or so, she couldn't really pinpoint a moment when she'd started to mellow towards Oliver.

'Something's happened... between Oliver and me.'

'Something?' Sienna pushed.

Paige nodded miserably, her eyes still on Oliver. C'mon woman, big girl pants... 'Promise me you'll let me get this out before either of you say anything or I might not be able to get through it?'

'Paige.' Sienna's frown deepened as she pressed her lips together. 'You're scaring me a little now.'

'Of course we promise,' Astrid agreed, a sudden intenseness in her eyes, like she was invested in every word. 'You know you can tell us anything This is a no-judgement zone.'

Yeah. *Until it wasn't.*

'Now, come on, deep breath,' Sienna coaxed. 'You'll feel better once you've told us.'

Okay, well, here went nothing. 'We... kissed.' Which was a massive understatement but she needed to start small.

Sienna blinked at the confession, her eyebrows conveying her surprise by leaping almost to her hairline.

Paige cleared her throat as the lump intensified. 'The first time—'

'The first time?' Sienna interrupted, her voice an octave higher at the end.

'Sissi,' Astrid chided softly, using her nickname for Sienna. 'We promised.'

'Oh God, sorry, you're right.' Sienna grimaced. 'Keep going.'

'The first time he was tipsy and he kissed me. The next time' – Paige shut her eyes briefly before opening them and looking straight at these women she'd grown to love in such a short period of time – 'I kissed him when I was a little tipsy. So we just' – she shrugged – 'put it down to alcohol.'

'Hell, we've all been there, babe,' Astrid said, quickly dismissing the episodes. 'Totally happens.'

Sienna side-eyed Astrid, her expression conveying that it didn't happen in her world but kept her lips zipped.

'The third time...' Her voice wobbled. 'We were both stone-cold sober. And I can make up a bunch of excuses about feeling sad about Casper leaving and comfort and blah blah blah but really, we were just totally fucking hot for each other.'

There it was. Right there. She had the hots for Oliver Prendergast.

There were several long moments of silence during which Paige braced for their condemnation. Astrid broke the silence. 'Are we still talking first base here?'

Paige couldn't even bring herself to say the words. She just shook her head, misery and condemnation like a yoke around her neck.

'Uh oh!' Sienna blinked at the screen.

Astrid ended another long pause. 'So, is it just sex?' she pressed. 'Or is it something more?'

'Oh God.' Paige rubbed her forehead, her gaze flicking to Oliver again before returning to the screen. 'I think I actually might... like him. Like, *really* like him.' She'd told him about Harvey. That had to mean something, right?

'Like have *feelings* for him, like him?' Astrid pushed.

Paige nodded. 'Maybe... yeah.' But what kind of feelings she didn't want to think about just yet. She was still processing how she could be sexually attracted to a guy who had hurt her friend so badly.

'Paige...' Sienna expelled a slow audible breath obviously

trying to temper her words. 'I'm not trying to make you feel worse. It's just... he jilted Bella.'

'I know,' she wailed. 'I know that.' God, didn't she know that. 'It's okay.' Paige squared her shoulders. 'You can tell me I'm a terrible person. You can cut me out. You can expel me from this group. In fact, I think I'd rather it.'

Before the phone call she'd been dreading them excommunicating her, but right now, facing these women, she'd take any punishment to take the edge off the guilt.

'Oh honey,' Astrid murmured, her voice rich with empathy. 'We're not going to do that.'

'Absolutely not,' Sienna added quickly despite obviously finding it harder to get her head around the turn of events. 'We have each other's back, no matter what.'

Their swift support meant a lot but Paige knew this was one helluva *no matter what*.

'I guess I'm just struggling with...' Sienna's expression was earnest as she stared into the camera and right into Paige's soul. 'How it happened?'

'I am too, if it's any consolation,' Paige admitted.

'Bella did say right at the beginning he wasn't a bad person,' Astrid said and hell, if Paige didn't want to kiss her.

'And she's right,' Paige agreed quickly. 'He's actually a really good person.'

Sienna jutted her chin. 'Who did a really shitty thing.'

Paige nodded. 'Yep.' There was no disputing that Oliver had blotted his copy book. But instead of feeling outrage over his disappearing act like she had when she'd first heard about it, Paige felt a pang of emotion for the guy who, in ultimately trying to do the right thing by Bella, had completely ballsed it up.

'But here's the thing,' Astrid reasoned, 'if we've learned

anything thus far, it's that there's more than one side to a story. Look at me, I jumped the gun because I was angry and hurt and yes, Chase should have explained himself but... maybe there's more behind what Oliver did than meets the eye? All I'm saying is that when we came up with this plan in Chicago fired up on booze and sugar and our swift ride-or-die bond, everything felt cut and dried but, maybe it's not?'

She sounded pensive again and Paige wondered if she was reflecting on her own journey with Aiden? Was Astrid having doubts too? Or was Paige reading too much into it?

'Except for Horrible Harvey,' Sienna muttered.

'Oh yeah.' Astrid's lip curled in distaste. 'Fuck him.'

Paige blinked back tears. She hadn't been sure how this call would go but she'd been fairly sure Astrid and Sienna would be super pissed. At the very least Sienna could have easily reneged on her commitment to cut Harvey off at the knees – fair was fair.

They'd been wonderful though and if that gleam in Sienna's eyes was any indication, she was more determined than ever to settle the score with Harvey.

'So,' Sienna continued. 'When are you going to tell Bella?'

The question hit right between the eyes. *Tell Bella...* Bloody hell, she hadn't even thought that far ahead. It had taken all her courage to tell these two. 'Oh.' She pulled her bottom lip between her teeth then released it. 'I... I wasn't... I don't know if...'

'You *have* to tell Bella.' Sienna's tone brooked no argument. 'You can't tell us and not her. It's not a secret either of us wants to keep, right?' She paused briefly to look at Astrid, who nodded slowly, before continuing in a softer tone, 'I know it will be hard, but it's way better to get this out in the open, hon.'

Ugh. Sienna was right of course. And maybe that was why

she'd told them. Because she knew, deep down, they'd make her do the right thing.

But *oh em gee*. Just the thought made her want to throw up.

'Sissi's right,' Astrid agreed gently if a little reluctantly.

'Yeah.' Paige nodded. 'I know. The last thing I want is to compromise you both.'

'Okay. So, you'll tell her?' Clearly, Sienna wasn't going to let Paige off the hook.

She sighed. 'Yes. Sometime today. After she's finished work.' Paige was aware today was Redemption Day for Chase. And for Bella. It would be adding insult to injury for Paige to drop her bombshell before the event. 'My night.'

'Good.' Sienna nodded approvingly. 'It's going to work out, Paige.'

Astrid narrowed her eyes a little. 'Are you going to be okay? Do you need us in on the call?'

Oh, *hellz* no. Absolutely bloody not. It was going to be hard enough to do without an audience but she knew Astrid's query was only born out of concern. 'No. All good.' At the far end of the beach, Oliver turned and headed back. 'I'd better go. Rehearse what to say.'

'You got this,' Sienna said, mouth turning up in a sympathetic half-smile.

Tears threatened again. 'Thank you so much for being so amazing about this. I don't know what I did to have two women like you in my life but I am so eternally grateful. Your support has been gobsmacking.'

'Of course, any time,' Astrid said, waving it away as if Paige had committed some trivial faux pas instead of sleeping with her friend's ex who she *was* supposed to be fucking with, but not like that!

Astrid was being super understanding which made Paige

wonder again if things weren't going according to plan with Aiden.

'Okay, well... I'll let you know how it goes.' Paige waved at the screen. 'Bye for now.'

'Bye,' Astrid and Sienna parroted together.

Paige laughed at their manic waving, feeling cheered just by their presence. As they hung up, their faces disappeared from the screen until it was just her looking at herself and she quickly hung up too. She didn't know how long it would be until she could look at herself again but it certainly wasn't now.

* * *

Paige was at her usual spot when Oliver got in from the beach half an hour later. She was working on the urgent files her client had sent and frankly grateful for the distraction of it. Not that there wasn't plenty of work to catch up on after her thirty-six-hour time out. But a deadline always helped focus the mind.

Mostly anyway. She was excruciatingly aware of the opening of the media room door and his footsteps as he ascended the stairs. The hairs on her nape stood to attention as he entered the open-plan living area and her fingers faltered on her keyboard as he said, 'Hey,' somewhere behind her.

Taking a deep steadying breath, she resumed typing as she repeated his greeting. 'Hey.' And then. 'Still kinda wild out there?'

'Ooh yeah,' he confirmed. 'You want another coffee?'

'Yes please.'

She tapped away, trying to ignore his presence as he moved around the kitchen but it was impossible to do when he delivered her mug then pulled a chair out at the end of the table and sat. Her gaze was drawn to him and even with hat hair, chapped lips and pink, wind-burned cheeks, her heart flipped.

'I have some more words to send.'

'Oh, excellent.' She nodded, relieved that his opening salvo wasn't *about last night*.

'Yeah.' He blew on his coffee. 'I reckon I'm about halfway now.'

'That's so good,' she enthused. 'You'll be done before you know it. When you're finished you should get some people close to you, who also knew your dad, to beta read it. People who were privy to your relationship but who can be objective, too. Point out inconsistencies or where you might have pulled your punches. Stuff like that is invaluable.'

He nodded. 'Great idea.'

'Your mother would probably be a good one.'

Laughing, Oliver shook his head. 'Ah, no. I don't think so. I love my mother but she's not the best person if you want objectivity. There's still a lot of complicated emotions causing her to excuse and defend him even though his behaviour ruined their marriage and almost ruined her.'

Paige felt sorry for Oliver's mother. It can't have been easy sharing her husband with the world. Being invisible. Even to him. Paige had never been in love – Harvey had ruined any chance of that happening – but maybe given its power to break a person, that wasn't such a bad thing?

Look how it had wrecked Bella, Astrid and Sienna.

'Plus.' He smiled, oblivious to her internal wrangling. 'She believes celebrity biographies are *classless, darling*.'

Paige laughed as he, she assumed, mimicked his mother. 'Okay, maybe not her then.'

He grinned. 'I have some people I can ask.'

'Excellent.'

He sipped his coffee, Paige hyper aware of his scrutiny as he peered at her over the rim of his mug. 'Are you okay?' he asked eventually.

Paige shrugged because, the truth was, she didn't *know* how she felt. Not really. Talking it over with Astrid and Sienna had helped but she wouldn't really know the extent of her feelings until she'd spoken to Bella. Which was going to be tough and she was already wishing she hadn't agreed.

Everything inside her wanted to run far away from it.

'I'm going to call Bella later and tell her.' She hadn't planned on sharing it with Oliver but she figured if she put it out there, spoke it out loud, she'd have to see it through. Plus, it was only fair she told him given he might experience some potential blow back.

Slowly, Oliver placed his mug on the table, his brows knitting together in a deep frown. '*Why* would you do that?'

Paige blinked. So much for hoping Oliver would give her some accountability. 'You expect me to keep this from her?'

'Um... yes?' His expression was incredulous. Like he couldn't believe they were having this conversation.

'I can't carry this around with me and pretend it didn't happen every time I see her or talk to her from now on.' They'd be coming face to face in New York soon and Paige knew she couldn't have this secret hanging around her neck on Bella's big night. 'She's my friend, Oliver.'

'Exactly.'

'You don't think she deserves to know that I slept with her ex? Who jilted her on the morning of her wedding via *text*.'

'Hell no.' It was followed with a very definite shake of his head. 'You ever heard that expression, ignorance is bliss?'

Paige frowned as realisation dawned. So, this was how some men could so easily do shitty things to women because they viewed issues through the lens of whether they could get away with it or not. She'd just thought, given all the insight she'd gleaned into him these past weeks, Oliver wouldn't be one of them.

Which made her mad. 'You're only worried about how this will make *you* look.' She glared at him. 'A little late for that, isn't it?'

His lips flattened. 'I'm a big boy, Paige. I can own my part in this but, as you pointed out, she already thinks I'm pond scum. I don't have much to lose.'

The inference being that Paige did. *And she did.*

'If you were truly team Bella you'd realise you weren't doing it for *her* benefit. You're doing it to alleviate *your* guilt. So *you'll* feel unburdened. But what about *her*? Have you thought about how badly this could hurt her?'

Paige swallowed, hating herself a little more. 'Yes.'

He nodded as if she'd just made his point. 'But it doesn't matter because *you'll* feel better, right? Even if she feels worse.'

Paige closed her eyes. She hadn't thought about it like that. Only how good it would feel after it was out and she didn't have to keep it some deep, dark secret. She was being selfish and he was calling her out on it.

'Is that what you really want, Paige?'

His direct appeal hit her straight in the feels. No, it was not what she wanted. She wanted to go back in time and not have kissed him, not have slept with him. But she had and the whole situation was *complicated*. Opening her eyes, she stared morosely at the table top. 'She'll feel a lot worse if she finds out another way.'

'How's she going to find out, Paige? Only you and I know and I'm sure as shit not going to tell her.'

But they weren't the only two, were they? She wasn't the only spider in this tangled web they'd weaved. Except, she couldn't tell *him* that. Not without the whole sorry saga coming out.

Lifting her gaze to his, she said, 'These things have a way of eventually coming out.'

He let out a slow breath, placing his palms flat on the table. 'Okay, look... do you know what's going on with us, Paige? What are we doing exactly? Are we a... thing?'

If Paige had been taking a sip of her coffee right now, she'd have choked on it for sure. What the hell? Where had that come from? Was he serious about having *this* conversation *now*? Or was he trying to make some point? Either way, his blue eyes didn't waver as he waited for her answer.

Panicked, her pulse skipping a little too fast, she blurted the first thing that came to her mind. 'Don't be ridiculous. We've known each other for *six* weeks. This situation has always been temporary.' Bedroom antics or not – their time together had always been set to expire. 'I'm... going to freaking *Edinburgh* next month.'

That was pretty much the complete opposite end of the country.

'And you're' – she waved her hand in his general direction – 'Oliver freaking Prendergast. Your father was so famous, the paparazzi follow *you a*round.'

She quaked at the thought. That alone was a red flag. Only last week Doris had shown her a pic of Oliver on an online scandal rag entering a posh restaurant that had been snapped during his visit to London the previous weekend.

'I live a quiet, small life. I run my own business. I *mind* my own business. I'm a *peach* emoji for crying out loud. There is no world where you and I are a thing.'

There – she'd said it. It had come out in a stream of consciousness but she'd meant every word. Whatever had gone down between them had involved some weird kind of synergy that, had they met in the outside world, would never have happened.

If her quick dismissal affected him, he didn't show it. He just nodded. 'Right. So what you're saying is, you're going to potentially blow up a friendship over some' – he stopped abruptly as if searching for the right words – 'hot, spontaneous, mutual, convenient, going-nowhere shagging?'

Paige flinched as he boiled their weekend together down to its most base elements. And, from the outside looking in, it was a fair assessment. But he'd been on the *inside* and it hadn't felt like that. Not to her, nor she thought, to him either.

Gathering herself, Paige took a mental step back from the emotion of the moment. Oliver was making salient points. And she may even have taken his counsel had she not promised Sienna and Astrid she'd talk to Bella.

But she had.

Sienna had asked her not to make them complicit and, salient points or not, she wouldn't put them in that position.

'Are you prepared for it if Bella decides to cut you out of her life like she did me?'

Yeah, but you *deserved* it, Oliver. That's what she wanted to say. But the truth was, if Bella cut her off, she'd deserve it too. Paige might not have visited some grand public humiliation on Bella as Oliver had but what she'd done, in many ways, was much more personal. And those often cut the deepest.

As if he knew he'd been too harsh, Oliver huffed out a sigh. 'Look...' His gaze searched hers. 'Just think about it, okay? That's all I'm saying.'

Like she was going to be able to think about *anything* else...

15

By the time Paige tapped on Bella's number several hours later, she'd gone back and forth and back and forth on the issue a hundred times. But she'd told the girls she'd do it and that was the end of it. Didn't stop her from feeling physically ill as she waited for Bella to pick up the audio call.

Confessing to Bella was going to be hard enough without having to look her in the eye while she did so.

She was sitting on a step halfway up the staircase that led from the living area to the bedrooms. Oliver was in the media room watching a movie which she could vaguely hear from here. Muted light from the kitchen below pushed through the slats of the balustrading revealing glimpses of the blonde floorboards as the phone rang and rang. Paige contemplated hanging up a dozen times and almost did just as Bella picked up.

'Hey, Paige,' she greeted, in her delightfully upstate New York accent.

'Hey.' Paige injected an enthusiasm that she knew, if it sounded as fake as it felt, wasn't going to fool Bella for a second. 'How'd it go today? Did it work?'

'Oh, it was *ah*-mazing,' she gushed and went on to regale Paige with all the details.

Well, great. Bella sounded buzzed and Paige was about to rain on her parade. Maybe she should wait? 'That's... awesome,' she said, her enthusiasm sounding more and more manufactured as she pulled her nightdress over her knees, yanking the fabric down to her ankles. 'I knew you'd be able to pull this off.'

Bella was making everything right while she'd made everything worse.

'You must be...' Paige cleared her throat of the lump that threatened to cut off her air. 'Thrilled.'

There was a beat of silence before Bella answered. 'Paige?' A note of apprehension had crept into her voice. 'Is everything okay?'

'Yes, yes,' she assured quickly but her voice wobbled right at the end.

'Paige...' Apprehension morphed to concern which only made Paige feel worse. 'What's wrong?'

'I don't... I can't... Oh *Bella*...' Paige squeezed her eyes shut to stop the spill of threatening tears.

'It's okay,' Bella soothed. 'Whatever it is, it's okay,' she assured.

God... her kindness was too, too much which only intensified Paige's guilt. A tiny, strangled sob slipped from her throat before she could smother it.

'Are you hurt?' The enquiry was suddenly more strident. 'Did Olly hurt you?'

'No, no.' Paige's eyes flew open as she dashed at the tears on her cheeks. 'He didn't. He's... he could *never*.' Not in the way Bella was implying anyway.

'Is *he* hurt? Did something go wrong with the payback plan?'

It sure did – the damn thing had blown up in her face. Paige quelled the urge to laugh hysterically at how badly it had backfired but hastened to reassure Bella instead. 'No. He's fine,' she confirmed and heard a sigh of relief in her ear. 'It is... about Oliver though.'

Time to stop screwing around and just do it already.

'I've, we've... I...' Paige's palms were actually sweaty now. Bloody hell, woman. *Just say it already.* 'About two weeks ago... God, I don't know how to say this...'

'How to say what?'

Bella's voice had gone very quiet but there was a note of something in it that made Paige think that Bella knew exactly what she was trying to say.

'Something happened. Between us. We kissed. A couple of times and then this weekend we...' Paige faltered. She didn't know if Bella wanted the gory details. 'And I'm so, *so* sorry. The last thing I would ever want to do is hurt you. I had no idea it was going to happen. I don't even know *how* it happened... well, I kind of do.'

Indiscretion, thy name is booze. Except if she was being honest the liquor had only accentuated a vibe that had already been brewing.

'But that's just... oh *fuck*.' Paige rubbed her hand across her face. 'I'm a terrible person and a shitty friend.'

'No. No, you're not,' Bella denied but it was too quick and robotic.

'I am,' Paige wailed, wiping her running nose on the back of her hand. 'You were going to *marry* him and he jilted you *via text* on your wedding day and I was supposed to be getting some payback for you and—'

'It's okay,' Bella interrupted, her tone dull but insistent. 'It's fine.'

Fine? God, that was *way* worse than if Bella had yelled

because it sounded like Bella was trying hard to keep it together and she'd done too much of that in her life already. Paige suddenly wished they *were* on video so she could see how Bella was really feeling.

'Are you...' Bella cleared her throat. 'Do you have feelings for him?'

Oh man. That was the million-pound question, right? 'Yes.' Paige winced at how bald it sounded but there was no point holding back now. 'No... I don't know... I'm so confused.'

There was a long pause as if Bella was processing the information. Or maybe just trying to stop herself from yelling which was nothing less than Paige deserved and something she'd honestly prefer to Bella's muted, contained reaction.

'And what about him? Does he feel the same way about you?'

'I honestly don't know, Bella. Sometimes I think he might but—'

'If he feels the same,' she interrupted, her tone stiff, 'then I'm happy for you both.'

What? No, that wasn't what this was. Regardless of however her jumbled feelings might shake out, a relationship wasn't on the cards. 'No... it's not like that. I just... I needed you to know—'

'Paige,' Bella interrupted again, her tone a little sharper this time. 'It's fine. If you both feel the same way then I am happy for you,' she repeated.

'Bella—'

'I have to go,' she interrupted a third time. 'But I'll talk to you soon, okay?'

The phone hung up in her ear and Paige stared at the screen for a moment before fresh tears rolled down her face and she buried her head in her knees.

Dear God, that was worse than she'd thought. Bella sounded

so bloody contained and that wasn't healthy, surely? This outcome can't have been on her bingo card for this whole bloody karma exercise they'd embarked upon. It sure as hell hadn't been on Paige's.

Dragging her head off her knees, she scrubbed a hand over her face as she PM'd Astrid and Sienna.

> WHATSAPP. MONDAY 21.17 GMT.
> TO: SIENNA, ASTRID
> SUBJECT LINE: SOS!!!
>
> PAIGE
> Well, that was about as awful as you'd expect.

Three little dots appeared straight away, indicting Sienna was answering. She'd obviously been right on top of her phone.

> SIENNA
> Oh God, I'm sorry. Was she really angry?
>
> PAIGE
> No, it was worse. She wasn't angry at all. She was understanding.
>
> ASTRID
> Well, fuck... that's very decent of her.
>
> SIENNA
> But that's Bella, isn't it?
>
> ASTRID
> How are you? You want to jump on a call?

Paige really did not. She was about as thought out and talked out tonight as possible.

> **PAIGE**
> Thanks, but not now. I'm okay, really. I think it's Bella we need to concentrate on. I'll message her in a bit but I'm not sure she'll want to talk to me. She'll probably appreciate hearing from both of you, though.

ASTRID
Of course, I'll get right on it.

SIENNA
Me too.

> **PAIGE**
> Thank you. You guys are the best.

ASTRID
We know.

Paige hooted out a laugh – the first one since her and Oliver's difference of opinion earlier – before signing off and heading downstairs to find him. She wasn't sure if he wanted to know the outcome of a conversation he'd urged her not to have but it only felt right to let him know given he was part of it all.

He glanced up when she entered the room and gave her a small smile and Paige felt ridiculously like crying again. They hadn't spoken since their disagreement and she wasn't sure if he was a sulker – Harvey had been a sulker – but apparently not.

Reaching for the remote, he paused the movie as she sat down beside him on the couch in Casper's spot. He was in his standard pyjamas of T-shirt and boxers, his hair pushed haphazardly back off his forehead and he looked so damn *good*.

'How'd it go?'

The room was lit only by the glow from the TV but it was enough to highlight his disgustingly chiselled cheekbones and ridiculously long eyelashes.

Paige sighed. 'She said it was *fine*.'

He sucked in air through his teeth as he grimaced. 'Sheesh. That's not good.'

'No,' she agreed glumly. It might not have been the loud bust up that Oliver had predicted but it could well be a quiet one.

'Hey.' He slid his arm around her and it was the most natural thing in the world to drop her head to his shoulder. 'I might not have agreed with your course of action but that took real guts, Paige. Kudos to you.'

His admiration was appreciated but it wasn't a magic wand either.

A tear welled in her eye and spilled over and she dashed it away as she lifted her head off his shoulder and shrugged his arm away. 'I'm going to head to bed. I'm knackered.' It wasn't like she'd done anything remotely physical for the majority of the day but emotional upheaval always left her wrecked.

He nodded, regarding her for long moments. 'You want some company tonight? I don't mean,' he hastened to add, 'sex. I just mean...' He cupped the side of her face and traced the damp path of her tear with his thumb. 'A shoulder to cry on.'

Paige couldn't think of anything she wanted more than to curl up with Oliver and feel sorry for herself. But she didn't get to do that in the comfort of his arms when she wasn't the injured party. And besides that, at some stage through the night, she may well seek something more than comfort from him and she'd already screwed up enough with Bella, she wouldn't compound her guilt any further by continuing to sleep with Oliver under false pretences.

Not when she may well be falling for him.

Declining his offer, Paige took herself to bed. Lying on her side in the dark, she fired off a quick PM to Bella.

> Bella, I just… I don't know what to say other than how sorry I am. Your friendship means so much to me. I hate that I've jeopardised that.

Then she turned off her phone and succumbed to a crying jag.

* * *

Oliver was in the media room continuing his trawl through the boxes he'd brought back from London the following afternoon. He hadn't realised how long it would take for him to sort through it all. But each document, each piece of paper from a restaurant receipt to a playbill to an old script with scribbles in the margins, was a potential footnote in his relationship with his father and he pored over each and every one.

He hadn't found the deeper answers he thought he might to his father's complete self-involvement, just more pieces of the puzzle that was Roger Prendergast. But it was fascinating nonetheless to discover pieces of his old man, one titbit at a time and if nothing else the information he'd gleaned had sparked memories and directed his next lot of dictation.

And, at least for now it was keeping his mind off Paige who had looked so utterly dejected last night and wasn't looking that much better today. But she was in *peach mode* as he'd come to think of it – scanning, electronically entering and cataloguing the papers he'd kept aside from the boxes – and he'd learned not to disturb her when she was in the zone.

Her laser focus and single-minded attention to detail was the exact opposite of the woman who had created such irritating disorder in his life for the last six weeks. It was such a jolting contrast but also somehow the norm now. All part of the delightfully exasperating conundrum of Paige.

Who was never far from his thoughts. Whose name resonated like a drum beat in his blood. Who he'd crossed a line with – and not just physically. But in other ways that overwhelmed him if he thought too much about it. For the first time ever there was a woman in his life who he couldn't define his feelings for, couldn't put into a neat box. A woman who had made it perfectly clear yesterday she'd never contemplated a future with him.

Don't be ridiculous... This situation has always been temporary.

At the time, it had slid right off his shoulders because he'd been in the midst of convincing her not to do something stupid and it hadn't seemed important. But the longer he'd sat with it, the more her quick dismissal tangled him in knots.

As if his thoughts weren't fevered enough, his phone rang.

Bella.

He'd tried to call her before he'd hit the sack last night because it had felt like the right thing to do. He owed her an apology – *another* apology. Except there'd been no answer and frankly, he'd been relieved. They'd spoken and messaged a few times since the non-wedding, all of which, apart from the first one had been painfully civil.

But he wasn't so sure that would be the case this time.

Oliver took a deep steadying breath as he tapped the screen. 'Hi.'

'Hi,' she replied.

Her voice broke a little and Oliver's guilt flared hot, tightening his ribs and making it hard to catch a breath. '*God*, B... I'm *so* sorry.'

'I know,' she murmured tremulously after several long beats.

'She didn't... we didn't...' Oliver trailed off unable to finish his sentence. What could he possibly say to justify what had happened.

'I know it wasn't intentional. I do. And... it's okay.'

He huffed out a breath wishing she'd just yell at him already and stop being so damn *fine* about things. 'Bella—'

'No. Really.' Her voice had firmed up and there was an unmistakable edge of conviction. 'It *is* okay. I can actually see how you two work *so* much better than we ever did.'

Oliver wanted to ask her what exactly she saw that led her to that conclusion but Bella wasn't his relationship counsellor for fuck's sake. He'd hurt her twice now, *that's* what this was about. 'It's okay to yell and scream, B. I can take it. I deserve it twice over. You don't have to be so damn *fine* all the time.'

To his surprise she gave a small laugh. 'Yes, I'm beginning to understand that.' But before Oliver could query her about the cryptic statement, she'd moved on. 'Do you love her, Olly?'

The question hit him square in the jaw. *Love.* He'd been mentally dancing around the subject, not daring to go there only to have Bella come straight out and sock him with it. 'I'm not sure,' he hedged. 'It's... complicated.'

'Yeah,' she agreed. 'In more ways than you know.'

Oliver frowned as he tried to decipher the cryptic comment. 'What?'

'It doesn't matter,' she dismissed, her tone changing. 'What matters is this. You can't hurt her, Olly. She's been *through* it. *Really* through it, you know?'

'I know.' He nodded. 'She told me about the revenge porn.'

'She did?'

The surprise in Bella's voice was palpable. 'Yes.'

'Oh. Well... that's good then. So you get it. You understand why you need to figure out how you feel. You understand why you need to *get* sure. Because you can't play with her, Olly. If you do, if you hurt her, I will track you down and do things you couldn't even imagine.'

Oliver blinked at the vehemence. Normally he'd laugh at such absurd threats coming from petite good-girl *Bella* who never even harmed a damn fly but she was deadly serious. 'Paige deserves the world and if you don't provide, I will make sure you regret it.'

He believed her. Frankly, Oliver was a little terrified of this Bella. But it was clear, when he cut through her rhetoric, that to be championing Paige like this, Bella must really be *fine* about him and Paige. 'I have absolutely no intention of hurting her.'

And he meant it. As Bella had pointed out, Paige had been through it and hurting her was the last thing he wanted to do. But he wasn't sure it was entirely up to him.

'Okay,' Bella replied, obviously satisfied with his level of sincerity. 'Now, can I speak to Paige?'

'Sure. Hang on a second.'

Navigating the stairs, he stepped into the living area. She was sitting in her usual chair at the dining table facing the view, her back to him, her ginger frizz contained in a single twisty knot pinned at her nape, her spine ramrod straight.

'Paige,' he said as he approached.

Her fingers faltered momentarily on the keyboard before resuming their pace. 'Yeah?' She didn't turn.

'Bella wants to talk to you.'

That definitely worked. She whipped around in her chair, her gaze flicking from the phone to him. He smiled and nodded encouragingly as he passed over the device.

'Bella?' Paige's voice was quiet, her spare hand flattening to press against her chest. 'Are you okay?'

Oliver wasn't privy to Bella's reply but he could tell from the instant relaxing of Paige's posture and the smile that tugged at her mouth, that things were going to be alright and he left them to it.

* * *

If Oliver thought that everything was suddenly going to be better between him and Paige after the phone call two days prior, he was wrong. She was definitely relieved that Bella had essentially given her blessing but Paige hadn't gone there at all. If anything, she'd regressed even further and he'd been relegated firmly to the position of *house mate*. It was like everything that had happened prior to her relationship with Bella getting back on track, had been left behind.

She was perfectly pleasant, smiling as she went about her business, keen as ever to help him with the book, happy to be a nightly TV companion as well as doing her share of cooking and cleaning in the kitchen. But... it all just felt wrong. Gone was the whirling dervish he'd been used to and in her place was an agreeable automaton who put her mugs down on coasters and the remote in its correct place.

Who even *was* this person wiping up crumbs in his kitchen and what the hell had they done with the Paige he'd come to know and...

Seriously fucking like.

But that all changed Thursday when the weather finally broke. It'd been promising to do it all day, Oliver's weather app predicting afternoon sunshine and, around three o'clock, it suddenly delivered. The sun broke through and the wind dropped but not before it has chased all the clouds away, leaving a perfect Cornish spring day, the flat sea a dazzling blue, the sand a glowing golden hue.

Halle-fucking-lujah.

Oliver opened the doors between the media room and the beach and inhaled the salty sunshine, the first trickle of warmth he'd felt in months caressing his face as he gazed upon the breathtaking vista. It was stunning and totally deserted.

A sight like that had to be shared.

'Paige!' Grinning, he strode to the stairs, taking them two at a time. He doubted she'd even noticed she'd been so engrossed in her work. '*Paige?*'

'What?' she asked, swivelling to face him, her forehead scrunching in alarm as he strode in her direction.

'The sun is out.' He pointed over her shoulder and she turned back to the view.

'Oh yeah.' She smiled but it didn't quite reach her eyes as he came to a stop next to her seat. 'So it is.'

'C'mon.' He tapped the back of the chair. 'Let's go to the beach.'

She glanced up startled. 'What?'

'The *sun* is out, Paige.' He grinned again at her nonplussed expression. 'We don't know how long that's going to last.'

'Um, no.' She shook her head. 'Red hair and a UV index aren't a good mix.'

He laughed. 'It's Cornwall, not the solar surface. Live a little.'

'I'm good, thanks, I don't need any sunshine.' She returned her attention to her work, her fingers back on the keyboard.

Oliver scoffed. Sunshine was *exactly* what Paige needed. She hadn't left the house since Monday and that just wasn't like her. Addressing the top of her head, he said, 'Everyone needs sunshine. Think of the vitamin D. Your bones will thank you for it.'

She couldn't leave here with rickets. Bella had threatened him with all kinds of dire consequences if he hurt her. What sort of pestilence would she bring down on him if Paige ended up with a serious skeletal deformity?

'I'm not exactly dressed for the beach,' she protested, glancing at her clothes.

What exactly she *was* dressed for was the bigger issue in Oliver's humble opinion. Plain blue jeans, plain grey T-shirt. Her hair contained in that wretched knot thing he was really coming to dislike. It was just... wrong.

Which made this trip outside even more urgent.

He needed to get the old Paige back. Not for him. *For her*. Underneath all that perfect pleasantness, she seemed... sad. And he was worried.

'Neither am I,' he said as he slid his hand under her elbow and urged her to her feet. She didn't resist. 'But it's just us so, let's gather our rose buds. Make hay while the sun shines. Strike while the iron is hot.'

She narrowed her eyes. 'If you say carpe diem next I'm calling your shrink.'

Oliver laughed. *That* was more like the old Paige. 'C'mon,' he whispered, 'take a break with me. Tomorrow the beach will be crowded if this weather holds as forecasted and it won't be the same.'

Pulling her elbow out of his grasp, she bugged her eyes at him. 'I'm working on your book. I'm trying to get as much sorted for you as possible before I leave in a couple of weeks. I can't just... dilly-dally on the beach.'

It wasn't the first time she'd mentioned leaving these past couple of days and Oliver was more than aware that she was off to Scotland next. But it made his brain itch just thinking about it. He'd thought the place had felt empty without Casper; he couldn't even begin to imagine how desolate it would feel with her gone.

Not that long ago, he'd come to Cornwall seeking solitude as some kind of penance but now he'd had Casper and there was Pavarotti and a bunch of fucking *WI women* he always seemed to run into whenever he was in town and Jiya at the café who Doris had introduced him to and who had never heard of his father but laughed at his jokes anyway.

And Paige, full of colour and life, who had constantly kept him on his toes.

Suddenly, his life was full. And not like it had been full before, doing a bunch of inane things with fair-weather friends to occupy all the hours in his day while all the time hoping his father noticed that Oliver lived under the same roof.

He was *bone* full. Deep in his marrow, full.

Maybe he could suggest he pay someone else to house-sit for her in Edinburgh which freed her up to stay here and commit all her time to the book? To work on whatever this thing was between them. He could sign over the £100k advance cheque the publisher had put in his hand when he'd met with them in London. God knew, he didn't need the money and if it hadn't been for Paige, he wouldn't have ever even started let alone be halfway through it and organised as fuck.

But looking at her now, this fierce woman who had created a business out of the ashes of a relationship that could have cut her off at the knees forever, he figured she might just kick him in the goolies.

'Exactly.' He bugged his eyes back. 'Time's a ticking and you haven't experienced the true beauty of Porthmeor until you've seen it in the sunshine.'

He gestured out of the window again and she followed his direction. The ocean, devoid of waves and white caps, sparkled

– *beckoned* – through the expanse of glass and she appeared to be actually contemplating it.

'Fine.' She huffed out a breath. 'But only for twenty minutes.'

Oliver grinned. 'Perfect.'

16

His bare feet hit the sand less than a minute later followed quickly by hers. The air was definitely still fresh but there was an undeniable note of warmth permeating the afternoon chill and Oliver heard her sigh. Looking over his shoulder, he found her face upturned to the sun as she pulled that stupid knot out of her hair.

Thank *fuck*.

Released from its prison, it immediately floated around her head in the slight breeze and it already felt like the old Paige was back. She should always let it do its thing.

'See, wasn't I right?' he told her closed lids.

Her eyes opened and she immediately rolled them. 'Yeah, yeah. No one likes a know-it-all, Olly.'

But she said it with a smile and Oliver felt instantly lighter. Instantly less worried. Plus, it was only the second time she'd ever called him Olly and he really liked it.

The beach was still deserted but he knew that wouldn't last. People in the apartments up and down the front would soon make their way out. There were a couple of cars in the parking area belonging, he presumed, to the people he could see walking along the south west coast path that traversed the headland but it would fill quickly the longer the sun shined.

They strolled to the shoreline where, since the beginning of the year, the waves had rolled relentlessly in, battering away at the sand in vicious dumps but where now, they gently lapped with just the tiniest little ruffle before they turned to foam and retracted again.

'Still looks cold,' she said as she slowed, stopping a few feet from the water's edge.

Oliver nodded as he halted beside her. 'It'll freeze your bollocks off for sure.'

To his surprise she laughed then crouched to roll up the legs of her jeans. 'Only one way to find out.'

Game for anything, Oliver followed suit, dragging the ankle cuffs of his track pants up to below his knees and following her across the short stretch of wet sand.

At the first wash of frigid Atlantic water over her foot she cursed loudly. 'Holy mother *f*—'

Cutting herself off didn't help. Oliver was already laughing hard at the profanity which probably shouldn't have been a turn on but was anyway. Not that his laughter lasted long when water swirled around his feet causing him to also curse as he hopped from one foot to the other. '*Son of a bitch.*'

It was her turn to laugh, then he joined her, their gazes locking. Paige's cheeks suddenly had some colour. Her freckles, accentuated by the sun, gave her skin a golden glow as the breeze blew a curl across her face.

As their laughter settled she sighed deeply and looked out to sea. 'Thank you for dragging me out of the house. It's really very beautiful out here.'

Oliver gazed at her profile. It was on the tip of his tongue to tell her the beach wasn't the only thing of beauty but he didn't want to scare her back to the house. 'Of course.'

Her eyes on the horizon, a smile crept across her face. 'My bones thank you, too.'

Hooting out another laugh, Oliver turned his attention to the becalmed ocean and they just stood there, not talking, staring out over the gently shifting mass, an occasional breeze ruffling their hair. But it didn't feel strained or weird or like he should rush in and fill it up with words. It felt comfortable. Like two people who'd known each other for a long time.

Suddenly, Paige let out a startled yelp, ruining the ambience as she leaped backwards. Momentarily confused, Oliver wasn't sure what had happened, all he knew was that Paige had lost her footing in the wet sand that had been constantly washing out from under their feet making traction impossible.

In a re-enactment of their hallway performance he lunged for Paige, only it was her careening backwards this time, falling in slow motion. Oliver just managed to catch her hand but, with the momentum on her side, she dragged them both down and within seconds he was sprawled on top of her in the wet sand.

Her gasp told him the sand was cold and her grunt that she'd landed hard. 'Are you okay?' He raised himself on the flats of his forearms so she could breathe.

Panting a little, she nodded. 'Sorry. Some seaweed scraped over my foot. Scared the crap out of me.'

For a moment, neither of them spoke, then they were laughing – *again* – at the absurdity of it all. Paige pressed a hand to her chest as their laughter settled. 'My heart is beating like a train,' she said.

Oliver's gaze meshed with hers. 'So's mine.'

But it had nothing to do with being startled and everything to do with the woman under him, as their husky breathing fell into sync. She was as soft as he remembered and her cheeks were flushed and her hair fanned out around her like a corona and her hazel eyes were glowing and damn it all, he was *in love* with her.

The kind of love he'd never felt before.

Deeper, inextricably linked to this woman, like a fingerprint on his heart and it seemed like the most natural thing in the world to dip his head, to kiss her. So, he did, not bothering to check the impulse, groaning deep as her mouth parted without resistance.

Unfortunately, common sense kicked in quickly and realising he shouldn't be taking advantage of their situation, Oliver reluctantly pulled away. 'God… sorry,' he muttered.

But she didn't let him get too far. 'No.' She slid her arms around his neck. 'Don't stop.' And she lifted her mouth to his.

Oliver's pulse rat-a-tatted inside his head at her unexpected encouragement and he followed the urging of her lips, taking the kiss deeper, as she widened her legs to accommodate his hips. Everything faded to black – the water not far from their toes, the wet sand, the seagulls calling nearby – there was just Paige, soft and moaning, one leg wrapping around his waist.

A dog barking and a child laughing did however punctuate the sexual haze and they broke apart as two little kids ran to the water not far from where they were making out, a woman shooting them a cheeky thumbs up.

'Do you want to take this inside?' she asked, panting a little.

Surprised the interruption hadn't made her withdraw from him again, he muttered, 'Hell yeah,' before quickly levering off her and pulling her to her feet.

Her mouth was cherry red and kiss-swollen and, when she was steady, he shoved his hands into her hair and kissed her again. Melting into him, she sighed against his mouth and the small noise of pleasure she made in the back of her throat was like a fist to his groin.

Pulling away long, drugging moments later, she gazed at him, her eyes satisfyingly glazed. 'I think we should hurry.'

Oliver couldn't agree more as he grabbed her hand and tugged her across the sand.

* * *

The shit hit the fan a week later.

Until that point, Paige had been back in the bubble. It had expanded way beyond his bedroom to include *all* the rooms. Hell, any surface in the house had been fair game. They'd even got amorous on the balcony one night, Oliver's hand over her mouth muffling her cries as the moonlight had poured down on their heads like a bloody great spotlight.

Anyone on the beach could have seen them. But, at midnight, the beach was deserted and every resident in sleepy little off-season St Ives, was tucked up in their beds.

Including their neighbours either side – thankfully.

Paige had been *stuck* for a couple of days after the call with Bella who had essentially given her blessing to her and Oliver. Because, blessing or not, she hadn't been able to see anything long term with him and, deep in her gut, Paige was a pragmatist. But then they'd landed in the sand together in a tangle of limbs and she'd stopped fighting it, stopped trying to be pragmatic and ceded to *desire*.

Fully this time. Really let go of everything and just indulged. It had been an age since she'd allowed herself to surrender to the sexual being she'd suppressed for so long that Paige had doubted she even existed any more. But she *did*. Paige the hedonist had come out of hiding and revelled in Oliver's attention.

She'd ignored the ticking clock and just lived in the moment, laid herself bare, opened herself up to him. She'd felt free for the first time in four years.

And then, a couple of hours before leaving to catch her flight to New York to meet up with the girls at the gallery pre-opening party, Doris texted her and everything came crashing down.

> I always knew you and Olly were going to be a thing 💍 💍 💍 All of us at the WI are so thrilled for you both 👋 Just so you know, we cater weddings 🍰 🥂 🎂

Paige frowned at the text which had a link attached and wondered for a moment if Doris had been hacked but the message was too personal for that and she *was* overly fond of an emoji since her great-granddaughter had given her a tutorial on the subject.

So, steaming coffee in one hand, she clicked on the link. And her entire world came crashing down. There on the front page of the world's most scurrilous gossip rag was a picture of her and Oliver, horizontal, kissing on the sand, her leg wrapped around the back of his thigh the headline leaping out like a striking rattlesnake.

Redondo's Runaway Groom Gets Sandy with Buxom Beach Babe

Oh, dear lord.

Beneath that was a second picture of their passionate cinch as they'd both stood and a third of them holding hands, her laughing as Oliver practically dragged her back to the house. Considering they had to have been taken from a distance, they were good, clear pictures, her face easily discernible.

Shit.

Trying not to slide into a black hole of flashbacks from four years ago, Paige placed her mug on the table, scrolling to read the copy, her hands shaking, her gut roiling.

> After photographs emerged of Oliver Prendergast, son of famed British actor Roger Prendergast (deceased), attending a local WI meeting in St Ives with a certain golden statue a few weeks ago, our photographer was in the right place at the right time to catch Redondo's runaway groom making out with a mystery woman on Porthmeor Beach where he's been holed away in his father's beach house since jilting his bride-to-be last year.
>
> Olly was set to marry Bella Carmichael of the wealthy Upstate New York Carmichael family at their country estate in the Hamptons but changed his mind on the morning of their wedding. Soon after he fled America for his country of birth, creating a massive scandal and leaving behind a huge mess for his distraught bride-to-be to clean up.
>
> No official statement outlining the reasons for the wedding being called off has ever been released but it was rumoured at the time that, like his father, Oliver Prendergast wasn't good at keeping his fly zipped and he'd been caught in flagrante the night before with the bride's maid-of-honour.
>
> Or maybe the buxom beach babe whose identity is unknown, had something to do with it? Did he leave because there was another woman? Is she next in line to be Mrs Oliver Prendergast? We'll let the pictures speak for themselves.

Paige scrolled to the pictures that were speaking very freaking loud.

Her brain scrambling, Paige put her phone on the table and tapped on the laptop keyboard to wake it up. She'd been just about to shut it down to pack it into her hand luggage for the flight. Minimising Oliver's book doc she'd been doing some last-minute work on, she opened a new window and typed *Oliver Prendergast, buxom beach babe* into the search bar.

Her gut sank as the screen filled with the images she'd already seen. It appeared as though every online publication on the planet had picked them up and were proudly displaying them on home pages. People had shared them on social media.

Hell, apparently #redondosrunawaygroom was a thing on TikTok and videos were already being posted with the latest development.

Oh God. Oh God. Oh God.

They were everywhere. Just like last time. Was she naked? No. But were they intimate and private? *Yes.* And had she given her permission for them to be taken and/or published? *Hell fucking no.*

Paige's head pounded and her breathing quickened as nausea threatened. How long would it take them? She was a *mystery* now but how long until someone somewhere recognised her from a random porn site or from images they'd saved and put in a file on their desktop labelled spank bank. Or until some publication used facial recognition software to identify her?

And then she would be exposed all over again – literally and figuratively.

But it would be worse this time because now her name was associated with a guy who the paparazzi followed around and was a fucking TikTok hashtag! Those photos could well go *viral* this time.

Snapping the screen of her laptop shut, she yelled, '*Oliver!*'

Wanting to be as far away from the pictures as possible, Paige stalked from the table and started to pace, her mind spinning a million miles a minute, her arms hugged around her middle. She should have known something like this was going to happen. That the universe hadn't stopped screwing with her yet.

What a fool she'd been this past week, floating around in this blissful little bubble. An occasional thought about sleeping with Oliver under false pretences had needled her brain but Bella's acceptance of their relationship had lulled her into a false sense of security. She'd started to think she could actually pull this off. That she could go to Scotland for the month then come back and confess her sins and they'd both laugh and everything would be okay.

But she should have known that wasn't the way it worked. Not only had days of amazing sex made her completely forget the reason her and Oliver couldn't be together in the first place – *photographers* followed him around – worse still, she only had herself to blame for this debacle. The first time she'd popped her head above the parapet had been to engage in a deception and now it was biting her on the ass.

Whoever said karma was a bitch sure as shit knew what they were on about. She'd set out to get some karmic payback for Bella and the tables had turned.

The payback was on her.

'You bellowed,' Oliver said, breaking into her self-flagellation as he stepped into the living room, his smile fading the second he saw her face. 'What's wrong?'

He strode towards her, his brow furrowed in consternation but Paige waved him back. Unable to articulate a sentence right now, she tipped her chin at the table. 'Laptop.'

Changing direction, Oliver crossed to the table, opened the

laptop lid and touched the mouse pad, instantly bringing up the screen with those photos. 'What the fuck?' Glancing quickly at her, Oliver returned his attention to the screen, sinking into the chair while Paige paced miserably.

'Those *assholes*,' he said eventually as he shut the lid down.

For a posh Brit he sounded very American when saying that word, giving it the right amount of sassy emphasis. Paige might have even laughed out loud had she not overwhelmingly wanted to cry.

'Don't worry.' He stood and faced her. 'I can fix this.'

Paige did laugh then, a harsh and bitter snort-laugh. 'It's too late now.' She knew it and she knew he knew it too. There'd been a lot of valuable lessons from her last brush with this kind of thing but the biggest one had been that things lived on *forever* on the internet.

She buried her hands in her face. 'God,' she groaned. 'This is a disaster.'

'No.' He took a step towards her but halted when she shook her head vigorously. 'I'm not going to lie to you, it might be kinda intense for a while. It'll be open season on me again and they'll be knocking at this door and every other door on the damn street every day hoping to find someone with a juicy bit of gossip about us.'

Yeah, but what happened when that juicy bit of gossip was about *her* and not *us*?

'You going away for a couple of days before the vultures descend is actually perfect timing,' he continued, oblivious to her inner turmoil. 'By then some other poor unfortunate celeb will do something they deem newsworthy and they'll go away.'

He felt terrible, it was obvious, which only intensified the squall of feelings battering the inside of her brain. He wasn't really to blame here. Sure, the payback plan wasn't directly responsible for them being papped either – that was just the reality of Oliver's life. But it *was* indirectly responsible for the predicament they were now in because of the photos.

It had been the catalyst. Without it she wouldn't be in this house with him. She wouldn't have been on that beach with him. She wouldn't be in those photos with him.

She wouldn't have fallen in love with him.

Shit. Shit. Shit. Not now. God, please, don't have this epiphany now. How she felt was irrelevant. She couldn't live her life like *this* with the threat of the ugliness from her past being relived again and again every time some pap or TikTok creator posted something about her and Oliver.

Paige swallowed. 'It's not going to go away.'

'It will.' He gave her one of those genuinely empathetic smiles that might have been condescending has she not known him. She knew he was trying to convey that he was an authority on the subject and she just had to trust him. 'I've been doing this for a lot of years and invariably interest fades if you don't feed it any fresh meat.'

'But it won't be about you, Oliver.' A sob rose in her throat, a wave of panic gripping her as all the ways this could blow out of control bombarded her brain. 'It'll be about me.'

He frowned now, looking genuinely confused this time.

'God, *Olly*,' she wailed. 'The photos. *My* photos.' She poked her chest as she blinked back a sudden well of tears. 'How long do you think it'll be before some bright young thing after a scoop, wanting to make a name for themselves, finds the naked pictures and video of me?'

It dawned on him then. Paige watched it happen, realisation smoothing out his brow. 'Jesus.' He stalked towards her, halting just outside the zone of her personal space, shoving his hands in his back pockets as if he was trying to stop himself from pulling her into his arms. 'I'm sorry.' He shook his head. 'I... didn't think about that...'

'Of course not,' she muttered, swiping under her nose as it started to run.

It sounded bitter and angry and she was neither of those things *at* him. Or maybe just a little. At his celebrity. She was mostly just pissed at the situation all over again. If only she hadn't let down her guard. If only she hadn't agreed to this hare-brained scheme.

'You don't have to, do you?' she continued.

Now she sounded accusatory which was irrational but a veritable witch's brew of emotions was broiling away in her stomach right now and none of them were rational.

'*I* can't think of anything else. I haven't been able to think of anything else for four bloody years.'

'Paige.' His voice was soft as he removed his hands from his pockets and reached out, sliding them onto her forearms that were still clutched around her middle, cinching like a steel hoop. He tugged gently and she held fast for only a moment before her resistance crumbled and she melted into his embrace.

And it felt so damn good in the circle of his arms, squeezing back the tears as he rocked slightly from side to side, his breath warm at her temple. He felt good, this man she loved. Solid and steadfast and real. A fledgling glow took root inside, yearning to burst free.

Worst. Timing. Ever.

'I have plenty of money for a good lawyer I can—'

'No!' Horrified, Paige pushed out of his embrace, taking a step back. She didn't mean to be *quite* so vehement in her rejection but, *absolutely* not. She didn't want the circle to be any wider than it was. She might not have a choice in it soon but while she did, she was keeping it small.

The way she *should* have kept herself.

Sniffling, Paige brushed past, heading for the table, her legs decidedly unsteady. *Woulda. Coulda. Shoulda*. If she let herself spiral into all the what-ifs, she'd miss her damn flight and, as Oliver had said, that was exceptionally fortuitous right now. She could fall apart on the plane. She did have eight hours to fill.

Determined to be businesslike, she stood behind the chair and opened the lid of her laptop. Quickly closing the tab on the screen displaying a close up of Oliver's mouth locked on hers, she methodically set about opening the dozen other tabs minimised along the top, saving what was needed before closing them down.

'I am so sorry about this,' he said, from somewhere behind.

'It's not your fault,' she dismissed, not looking up from her endeavour, numbness settling in her chest. 'You're right about not feeding them fresh meat.' It was the only way she *might* be able to pull this off, if she disappeared from the picture completely – not just for a few days. Maybe the story would die down and the *buxom beach babe* would forever remain a mystery. 'I'll just drop out of sight.'

'That's not what I meant.'

'Go straight to my parents after New York. Or my sister's. Hopefully they won't dig too deep.' That could be possible. Especially if there was something else to distract them. 'Maybe you could go to London and be seen with a few different women.'

The idea pushed to the forefront of her brain and was out before it could be properly vetted. And it made perfect sense. But her fingers faltered on the mouse pad as the implications slid sharp as a stiletto between her ribs and twisted. It *hurt*. To say nothing of how calculated it must sound but, in full pragmatist mode, no idea could be dismissed.

'Paige.'

His voice sounded reproachful but, with her emotions already careening around like atoms in a collider, Paige didn't really care what he thought right now. She'd brought this mess down on her own head and *she* would fix it.

'It's fine, Oliver.' The last tab was his book document which she'd backed up to the USB stick she'd been using specifically for this project just before she'd got the text from Doris. 'It's my own fault. I should have stayed in the box. I should have stayed small.'

Suddenly he was there beside her, *glowering*. 'That is utter bullshit.'

Paige startled. She'd never seen a truly angry Oliver. She's seen him irritated and annoyed and exasperated. Maybe even a little cranky. But not tight-lipped with thunder and lightning clashing in blue eyes that had suddenly come over all stormy.

Why was *he* angry? 'What?'

His brows pulled into a livid V. 'Why are you being so damn passive?'

Bloody hell – was he serious? Did he have *any* perception of what it was like to be violated the way Harvey had violated her? She'd done what she could without losing herself in a quagmire of rage. She'd been *pragmatic*. It might not be very Hollywood but she'd got control over her life again.

'Oh, you think I should be aggressive?' she asked testily, half turning to face him.

'No. But you shouldn't shy away from it, either. Maybe you should take a stand?'

If he was trying to rouse her fighting spirt, he was far too late for that, it had died a long time ago. But he'd sure as shit roused her ire. Her fingers furled convulsively around the back of the chair. 'What is *that* supposed to mean?'

Shoving a hand through his hair, he huffed out a breath, looking at her like he couldn't believe he had to explain it to her. 'Why should *you* stay small? *You didn't do anything wrong,* Paige. *He* wronged you. And yet here you are still punishing yourself for something *he* did to you while he's out there having a grand old time. Don't let that asshole take any more of your life from you than he already has.'

A giant, hot, seething bubble erupted in her gut. How freaking dare he stand there and pretend to know *anything* about what she'd been through and what she'd done to survive the shitshow. Her pulse was a roaring water hammer in her head as she snapped, 'You have *no* idea how it feels to be exploited like that.'

'I've been putting up with non-consensual pictures and stories being posted about me most of my life,' he snapped back. 'I think I might know a *little bit* about how you feel.'

No, he didn't. Not like this. Sure, he'd been in and out of the paparazzi glare which was no doubt inconvenient but he wasn't even in the ballpark of knowing what *this* felt like.

'Really? But you got to bag a buxom beach babe who, *surprise*, turns out to be a *secret porn star*. Go you. I'm sure all your guy friends will throw you a parade.'

He sucked in a breath as she landed her punch. But Paige was on a roll now, a red mist settling in her bones, cold and desolate. If he truly wanted to feel her pain, then she had the perfect demonstration.

'You want to really feel how I feel?'

Paige was completely possessed now, operating on raw fury. How dare this man who had been in her life for less than two months pretend he knew her. 'If we take this...'

She turned back to her laptop where his document sat on the screen. The document that contained everything she'd collated including all the words he'd dictated during his beach walks. Quickly she tapped in the command for select all and everything highlighted.

'Paige?'

Glaring at him for a beat, she hit the delete button. A prompt asked her if she was sure she wanted to delete.

'Paige,' he repeated, his voice a low growl.

But she was beyond listening as she clicked *yes* and watched it disappear from the screen. Quickly then she navigated to her trash bin and deleted it from there. When she glanced at him again, he was staring agape at the spot where his document had been.

'Paige.' His gaze flicked to her, his stormy eyes steely now. 'What did you just do?'

'That feeling?' she said, looking at his face etched with an expression that was equal parts incredulous and horrified. 'Take *that* feeling and multiply it by a *thousand* and you might just be in my ballpark.'

'Please tell me you have that backed up in a cloud somewhere?'

She snorted. 'You think I'm going to put important, private stuff about a famous Hollywood actor into a cloud that any amoral news organisation can hack into?' She swiped the USB device off the table containing Oliver's saved files. 'It's backed up here.'

He let out a slow, steady breath but Paige was damned if she was going to give him any relief from *that* feeling. Not just yet. Letting the thumb drive dangle from her fingers over her still steaming cup of coffee she dropped it in with a triumphant satisfying plop.

'*Paige*,' he seethed, as he stared at her aghast.

'How are you feeling now?' she asked as she snapped the lid of her laptop closed.

'What the fuck?' he demanded.

But Paige was done with this conversation. She always obsessively emailed everything to two separate email addresses every time she updated anything she was working on so she knew the information was safe as houses but she was dammed if she was going to let him know that right now.

He could stew for a bit.

Snatching up her laptop and phone, she said, 'I'm leaving.'

Clearly still too stunned by watching the last six weeks of his work disappear into the ether, Oliver didn't comment. He didn't yell or even try to stop her. He just watched her stony-faced, his hands shoved in his pockets, his jaw clenched tight.

He hated her right now – she was pretty sure. And that feeling of triumph had been remarkably short-lived. But she hadn't done it to make either of them feel good. She'd done it to make a point. And now it had been made, it was time to go.

With everything ready by the door, all she had to do was walk out which was exactly what she did, steel in her spine and fire in her blood.

Her heart crumbling into thousands of tiny pieces.

17

Paige messaged the WhatsApp group on the plane. Not that she said anything about being on a plane of course because Bella didn't know she was on her way to New York. She'd filled them in on the tabloid pictures and they'd all been suitably outraged at the scurrilous reporting and bandied about suggestions for possible solutions, but Paige insisted that doing nothing and flying under the radar was still her best option.

She'd also told them she and Oliver had fought although she hadn't gone into the nitty-gritty except for the deleting his book bit. Then, deciding if she was in for a penny, she might as well be in for a pound, she also fessed up to falling in love with him. She didn't want any more secrets – not with these women, anyway.

They'd *all* been very sympathetic which had been wonderful and which she'd needed but wasn't entirely sure she'd deserved given how badly she'd botched the payback plan by falling for the guy she was supposed to be taking down. It had helped that Bella had pointed out that she'd not exactly stuck to the script with her plans either but there wasn't any real equivalence here – only *Paige* had truly let the side down.

Astrid, normally the most outrageous of the lot of them, had been strangely quiet during that part of the messaging but Paige figured she was preoccupied with her disguise plans for the party tonight so Chase wouldn't know she was there.

As good as unburdening in the group had been, it had been even better to get to Astrid's uncle's ritzy apartment on Central Park West two hours before they were due at the party. Finally, for the first time – for Paige, anyway – since that fateful meeting in O'Hare in December, she had been able to sink into a group hug that meant more than Sienna and Astrid could ever know.

Yes, she'd screwed up. Yes, Oliver hated her. But these women had her back.

Which was exactly how she felt a little over two hours later striding fashionably late and pre-charged into the Nayak Gallery to have Bella's back. Even if she was slightly trepidatious about seeing her face to face. Talking via message and over the phone wasn't the same as having to look Bella – whose *bastard* ex she'd fallen in love with – in the eye.

But here went nothing...

The space buzzed with the mingle of dozens of voices, the art looking as spectacular on the walls as the glamorous crowd milling around to view it. They sipped on champagne as they pointed and conversed like they knew what they were looking at and it pleased them very much. Every single one of them was dressed with the kind of flair Paige had always thought of as very *New York*.

Which meant Astrid in her ginormous black hat and dark sunglasses, didn't look that out of place at all. Paige had queried whether the hat would have the opposite effect but she had to admit the floppy brim did hide Astrid's face most effectively even if it had nearly taken Paige's eye out several times in the cab on their trip to the gallery.

Sienna and her, both in sparkly cocktail numbers, certainly looked *less* New York in comparison although suddenly none of that mattered as a shocked Bella walking towards them, champagne glass in hand exclaimed, '*Oh my God*, what are you guys doing here?'

Paige felt a thunk to her chest seeing Bella again and a sudden shyness rendered it difficult to meet her friend's eye. Thankfully that was subsumed by Sienna's excitement as she announced, 'We came to surprise you!'

But it didn't last long as tears welled in Bella's eyes and an overpowering flood of concern swept away any awkwardness Paige was feeling.

'Bella?' Sienna's eyebrows rose. 'Are you okay?'

Bella nodded but it was far too vigorous to be believed. Astrid certainly didn't as she stepped in to gather Bella into a tight hug. Paige, who had rescued Bella's full champagne glass while swerving to avoid potential blinding-by-hat-brim, glanced at Sienna.

'I'm good, I'm good,' Bella promised as she shrugged out of the hug, no trace of moisture in her eyes now.

'Okay,' Paige murmured but wasn't so sure. Was it just the stress of the opening event or had something happened? With Chase? Or was Bella perhaps not as okay with the whole Oliver thing as she'd made out? Offering the champagne glass back, she said, 'You look like you could do with this.'

Hell, she could do with one herself.

'Oh Paige.' Bella ignored the drink and grabbed Paige into a hug. Sienna rescued the glass this time. 'It's *so* good to see you,' she whispered fiercely. 'And I'm so happy for you and Olly.' She released Paige and earnestly sought her gaze. 'We would have made a terrible mistake if we'd got married that day.'

Astrid, clearly aware of the private nature of the conversation between Paige and Bella, herded them all over to a quiet corner of the gallery.

'I think...' Bella continued, 'I was looking for the full stop on what I thought I should be doing. I think we both were, really. But he was always more a friend to me than anything else.'

'Are you sure?' Paige hadn't realised how much she'd needed this. To *hear* it as she looked Bella in the eye and *see* the truth.

'Absolutely. I promise. On red velvet cakes.' Bella grinned as she drew an X over her heart. 'And I think you all know how seriously I take red velvet cake.'

Everyone smiled. Bella certainly did have a thing for red velvet.

'Now tell me,' Bella said briskly, belying the huskiness in her voice. 'How are you all here?'

'I thought it would be nice to be here for you tonight,' Sienna explained.

'And we agreed,' Paige added. 'But it was going to be tricky because we needed invites and we couldn't just ask because you were the one in charge of that.'

'And I said, who needs invites, when we can simply crash the event.' Astrid grinned. 'But of course, I couldn't just rock up so – ta da! You like my disguise?'

Bella eyed the *disguise*. 'The hat?' She looked at it doubtfully. Then, 'The hat?' she repeated looking at each of them as if questioning their decision-making skills.

'And the glasses.' Astrid turned her face from to side, endangering lives once more. 'Although I may have perhaps overestimated their suitability as a disguise.'

She laughed then and suddenly they were all laughing and

for the first time since they'd walked into the gallery as a *surprise*. Paige thought it was going to be okay.

'But you can't stay,' Bella said, clearly miserable over the edict. 'If Chase finds you here, he'll—'

'He'll *what*?'

The very male enquiry caused a swift, collective indrawn breath from each of the women as all eyes flew to a rather surly, rather big guy standing behind Bella, rocking his screamingly expensive suit to perfection.

Paige had seen pictures of Chase Miller online, of course, but none of them did him justice. He was as Alpha badassery as his images had portrayed and he was looking at Bella with a mix of suspicion and something else she couldn't quite place.

'What will Chase do?' he asked, his gaze flicking dismissively over Paige and Sienna before peering under the brim of Astrid's hat, his eyes narrowing then quickly widening in disbelief. '*Astrid*?'

His strangled exclamation ricocheted around the tight circle but no one nearby looked up from their conversations. *Ooh boy*. This was not going to plan. One look at Bella's face, drained of colour, told Paige her friend knew she'd been caught out.

'Bella?' Chase demanded. 'What's going on?'

'It's not what it looks like,' Paige blurted, rising to her friend's defence. It was the least she could do for the woman who had shown her nothing but understanding. 'Bella didn't do anything wrong.'

Except a resigned Bella was having none of it. 'It *is* what it looks like, and I *did* do something wrong. But this isn't the time.'

She looked utterly wretched, gazing at Chase with both guilt and resignation and Paige's heart went out to her – she knew exactly what Bella was going through right now.

'The girls will go,' she continued. 'I'll make myself scarce and wait in the office until everyone's gone.'

The three of them protested but Bella just smiled and said, 'It's okay. I'll call you after.' Then she turned, her head bowed and walked away.

With one last withering look at them all, Chase also departed.

'We're not going anywhere,' Paige said vehemently, her gaze tracking Bella's progress through the gallery. 'There's a café over the road. We'll wait there for her.'

Nobody argued.

* * *

Over two hours later, Paige was on her third cup of coffee, her eyes fixed on the Nayak as it slowly emptied out. They'd found a window seat when they'd first entered the café and had been staked out ever since.

'So... what's next for you?' Sienna asked, swishing her honey-blonde hair behind her as she leaned in a little.

Until now the three of them had been mostly chatting about Bella's predicament with Chase. Astrid was fretting about how her presence at the gallery had really screwed things up for Bella which had led to an upset stomach. She'd been to the restroom three times already and was there again now.

'I don't know.' Paige blew out a breath, her curls ruffling as she dragged her attention from the window to Sienna. 'I guess I have to wait and see if the tabloids manage to identify me then manage to connect the rather lurid dots.' She stared at the lipstick mark on her coffee mug for a beat or two. She had no idea what she'd do if that happened.

House-sit in Antarctica maybe?

'I'll have to go back and pack up the rest of my stuff, although as most of it was recently acquired from charity shops and I'm not likely to wear it again, I guess I could just leave it. But I do need to pick up Pavarotti.'

She could of course arrange for him to be moved through a pet transport company but she'd grown too fond of the hamster to subject him to a long road trip with complete strangers. Her father would do it, as would either of her siblings but with them already concerned for her about the tabloid pictures she'd alerted them to before she got on the plane, she didn't want to give them any more cause to worry.

This was a mess of her making, she should be the one to tie off the loose ends.

Sienna rested her elbow on the table, propping her chin on her palm. 'How do you feel about seeing him again?'

Paige had been trying not to think about it but she couldn't avoid it forever. 'I don't know. It'll be hard I guess.' At least having Scotland to head to would be a good distraction.

'Because you love him?'

'Yeah.' Loving him and knowing that it didn't change anything was gutting. Wasn't love supposed to be transformational? 'But also because I need to apologise for the way I left things. I was in panic mode and lashing out and I acted impulsively when he was just trying to offer me an alternative way of dealing with it.'

'Alternative how?'

Paige shook her head, desolation an ache in her throat. 'It doesn't matter. If by some miracle Oliver wanted anything to do with me after today, it doesn't change our circumstances. He's someone still very much in the public eye. And I am still very much someone with a lot to hide.'

Sienna's mouth quirked. 'Humour me.'

Contemplating her friend for a long moment, Paige huffed out a breath. 'He said I was being passive and that I was punishing myself for something that wasn't my fault. That I hadn't done *anything* wrong. He said I should make a stand. That I shouldn't let Harvey take any more of my life than he already has.'

Sienna didn't say anything for long moments, just nodded slowly as if she was trying to compute all this new information. Or formulate the right response.

'Maybe he's right, Paige?' she said eventually, her voice gentle. 'You *didn't* do anything wrong. This terrible thing was done *to* you through no fault of your own and yet you're the one hiding away.' Removing her hand from under her chin, she slid it across the table to rest on Paige's forearm. 'I'm going to do my bit to call Harvey out but... maybe you *should* make a stand.'

Paige snorted derisively. Make a stand. How could something so *ill-defined* sound so bloody grandiose? Yet, having this same conversation with Sienna, without all the heat and confrontation, the message hit differently.

What if she was right? What if *he* was right?

'I don't even know what *make a stand* means.'

'Neither do I.' She patted Paige's arm and smiled softly. 'But maybe Olly does?'

Paige didn't know what to say to that but Sienna seemed so sure of herself she almost believed it. Not that they got to discuss it any more as Astrid's, 'Heads up ladies,' interrupted the discussion. Astrid looked pale but also resolute as she strode toward them, pointing at the window. 'The eagle has left the building.'

Tossing money on the table, they hotfooted it out of the café and across the road, dodging traffic to reach Bella as fast as they could. She seemed dazed and lost and was shivering when they finally reached her, standing in the frigid cold in nothing but her slinky, not-made-for-a-New-York-February dress and heels, her fingers clasped around a small fashionable clutch. In unison they wrapped their arms around her and held her tight.

'Where the heck is your coat?' Sienna demanded.

Astrid nudged Sienna. 'I don't think she's worried about her coat right now.'

'Let's get her into a cab,' Paige suggested, worried Bella was going to fall down if they didn't get her a seat soon. Spotting one across the street, she walked three paces to the edge of the sidewalk and hailed it and less than a minute later they had all piled in.

'Where to?' the cabbie asked.

'The apartment,' Bella whispered.

Sienna, in the front seat supplied the address as a tear rolled down Bella's cheek. Astrid, who looked even more guilt-ridden than she had in the café, shot a worrying look at Paige who put her arm around Bella's shoulder, surprised when Bella, *keep-calm-and-carry-on Bella*, curled into her like a child curling into their mother.

Nobody spoke during the trip, not even the driver and Bella didn't even stir until they were pulling up outside her apartment fifteen minutes later.

'I need my phone,' she said absently.

Sienna, who had taken charge of Bella's clutch said, 'Here you are,' as she passed it over then fixed up the driver.

Bella tapped on a preprogrammed number and after only a second or two said, 'Daddy?'

More looks were exchanged between Paige, Sienna and Astrid. Bella didn't talk much about her family but they knew things were strained. Or had been anyway.

'Can I come home?' Bella asked, her voice breaking.

Paige swallowed a lump and hugged Bella tighter as she

choked out a, 'Thank you,' hung up and started to cry. Not a tear or two, actual gut-wrenching *sobs*.

It had been a long time since Paige had felt this helpless. Maybe that first sickening day she'd opened one of a hundred early morning texts from friends and acquaintances alerting her to Harvey's horrible act of spite. She wasn't sure exactly what had gone down between her and Chase but she was pretty sure it was more than a work thing and on that, she could most certainly relate.

'C'mon, love,' Astrid murmured after long silent moments broken only by Bella's choked weeping. 'Let's get you inside.'

* * *

Thirty-six hours later, Paige stood on Oliver's doorstep, almost eight weeks to the day since she'd first arrived, steeling herself for what was to come. She'd hired a car from Bristol airport and was just about as tired as she could be after hardly any sleep on the red eye and no sleep in New York. They'd stayed up all night with Bella, being distractions when required – tequila shots and movies, grilled cheese sandwiches and 4 a.m. Chunky Monkey – and shoulders to cry on the other times.

Bella hadn't said much about what had gone down and nobody had pushed. It was too soon and she was too close to it but the night had been all about Bella. Supporting Bella. Which Paige had been totally on board with. Bella had occasionally wailed about being such a downer when Paige and Oliver snogging on Porthmeor was plastered across a dozen social media sites but Paige had summarily dismissed her concerns.

She'd been *pleased*, almost grateful, to be immersed in someone else's drama. In fact, when the Carmichael car had arrived for Bella in the morning to whisk her back to her family, it was a stark return to reality for Paige.

To her drama. To Oliver.

Oliver who had been on her mind constantly since Bella had left. On her trip to the airport. On the plane. On her drive from Bristol. Oliver who she loved and wanted to be able to spend the rest of her life with but carried far too much personal risk to even consider. Oliver who she had to say goodbye to and never see again so those photos and the *mystery* woman would be nothing but an insignificant blip in the timeline of his celebrity.

Sinking quickly from view. And scrutiny.

Sienna's calm, reasoned, *maybe you should take a stand* floated into her mind as Paige lifted her hand to knock on the door and she shut her eyes to ward it off. It was much easier for her *and* Oliver to say than for Paige to actually do.

Just get in and get out, Paige. Grab the hamster, apologise, tell him you *haven't* deleted his book then grab your stuff and *go*.

Rapping hard – twice – Paige waited for the door to open. She had a key she could have used but it didn't feel right given the way they'd left things. When there was no answer though, she seriously considered using it. It was lunch time; maybe he was on the beach?

She gave two more firm knocks in quick succession but still there was no answer. Not sure how she felt about a non-answer after psyching herself up to face him for hours, she fished through her bag for her key. But, to her surprise, the door opened abruptly to reveal Oliver in sweats and a T-shirt, his hair clearly finger combed to bird's nest intensity.

Her pulse leaped at the sight of him – dishevelled or not – but she had no chance to fully assess her reaction as he stuck his head out looking rapidly left and right before pulling her into the house. 'Jesus, Paige. You were lucky no paps were lurking.'

Paige blinked. Stupidly, she hadn't even considered the possibility but it had obviously been a harrowing couple of days. She supposed that was naïve of her but also – *not her life*. Still, his irritated frown was wonderfully familiar and her stupid heart softened.

'They must have all buggered off to get some lunch.'

The door shut and they were standing in the hallway. Close – so close. And he was looking at her and she was looking at him and it didn't seem possible that a mere two days' absence could make her want him more. *Love* him more. But her pulse was tapdancing and the deep yearning ache she'd been suppressing intensified so she supposed it *was* possible.

As if realising they were standing a little too close he huffed out, 'Come in.'

Paige followed him into the living room, the ocean view looming ahead through the double glass doors. It was overcast again, the waves thrashing, a perfect backdrop to the final scene of this tangled web of a relationship.

'I've just come to pick up my stuff and Pavarotti,' she told his back as the cage in its usual position on the kitchen bench came into view.

'Sure,' he said, as he stepped aside to allow her to overtake him.

Paige crossed straight to the cage, smiling when the hamster who was now officially *ripped*, leaped off his wheel mid spin like a freaking gazelle and rushed to the bars for some loving. 'Hey there, little guy,' she crooned, sticking her finger in to caress his quiff, her smile growing as Pavarotti practically shuddered in delight.

'How was the opening?'

Her shoulders tensing, Paige gave a stiff nod. Small talk – fun. *Not*. 'It was great,' she enthused without any real excitement. 'Bella did an amazing job.' Which she had but the fact she was also a complete mess because of this bloody bargain they'd all made, tempered Paige's response.

'I read the reviews online. It seemed well received.'

He'd *read* the reviews? 'Uh huh,' she remarked noncommittally before turning back to face him. His hands were on his hips, his eyes intense as they met hers. Too intense. She couldn't deal with that level of intensity. 'I'll just go and grab my stuff.'

'Okay.'

Paige practically ran up the stairs and packed her relatively meagre possessions in record time, tossing clothes haphazardly into the ridiculous mishmash of suitcases, not thinking – just doing. Just needing to be away.

'That was quick,' he said as she tramped down to the living room, balancing the cases in a precarious hold. His ass was sat against the table edge, his arms folded.

She placed the bags on the floor. 'Not a lot to pack.' The story of her life – don't stay anywhere too long. Don't put down roots.

'I bought some pellets for Pavarotti yesterday.' He indicted the bag of food sitting next to the cage.

'Thank you.'

'I think Bunky will be very surprised at the new Flower.'

Flower. God, it hadn't been that long but the name seemed totally foreign now. Completely *wrong* somehow. 'He may well think I switched him.'

'I took heaps of photos and videos of his transformation process that I can send you if he gives you any grief.'

Paige almost laughed at the revelation. Of course he had. Several long beats passed as they stared at each other before she blurted, 'I'm sorry. About your book. I was angry but more at myself than anything else and the situation. I have got a couple of back-ups, it's not gone. I'll send the file to you tomorrow.'

He nodded. 'I know.'

She blinked. 'You do?'

'Well... not positively no. And I grabbed that stick out of the coffee and shoved it in rice quicker than you could blink after the door closed behind you.'

'Oh. I... don't think that works with thumb drives.'

'It doesn't. As of this morning it's still fucked. But, after I'd shoved it in the rice and for about two hours following, I took it as a sign from the universe that I shouldn't be doing this writing a book thing. That it had all just been folly and I was set to throw the towel in until I realised that there was *no way* you wouldn't have some other back-up system. It just didn't seem like the efficient woman behind the peach emoji I'd come to know.'

Paige couldn't decide if it was a good thing or a bad thing that she was so damn predictable. In the end, she guessed it didn't matter. She was who she was.

'But, thanks to her,' he continued, 'I've realised that being an author is my calling. I've actually got an idea for my next book. Fiction. A madcap caper set in Tinseltown.'

That was the last thing Paige had been expecting and she forgot temporarily that she was leaving and they were doomed and she was just trying to hang on until she could get out of here as a ray of sunshine burst in her chest. 'Really? That's amazing.' Her smile was so big her damn face ached.

'Really,' he replied, grinning back.

Considering she was about as miserable as she could be, Paige felt inordinately happy right now. At least until he spoke anyway.

'Don't go, Paige.' He stood, taking a step towards her. 'I love you. I'm *in* love with you. And I think... you're in love with me too.'

Paige shut her eyes to ward off the flood of feelings. *He loved her.* The words any person in love with another person wanted to hear reciprocated. And she believed him. She'd *felt* it the week they'd spent together before she'd left. In the way he'd looked at her and touched her and spoken to her.

And yes, she loved him. She loved him so much it hurt. But it didn't matter. Because the tabloids had happened and she couldn't risk it.

She opened her eyes. 'I do. I do love you.'

The slow, lazy grin he gave her turned her insides to molasses. He'd clearly been *very* sure she was going to admit her love and it should have been irritating how cocky he was but man, triumphant Oliver *oozed* sex appeal.

'Except...' Paige steeled herself for what she had to do. How she had to push him away and make it *good*. Burn all the bridges. Make it worse than a thumb drive in a mug of steaming hot coffee.

This was a job for the truth, the whole truth and nothing but the truth.

'I'm not the person you think I am.'

18

Paige watched his eyebrow quirk upwards, clearly amused in his cockiness. 'Oh yeah?' He stepped back, nestling his butt on the edge of the dining table again as if waiting for some half-ass attempt at convincing him they could never be.

'Yeah.' She made sure she caught his gaze as she said the next words. She needed him to know this wasn't a joke or a ploy. That she was deadly serious. 'I met Bella in December at O'Hare. We were two of four women who got the last table at a dessert café during a snow storm that had grounded all flights.'

'Okay.' He was still smiling, *indulging* her.

'There was champagne and cake and we all got talking about our bastard exes.'

'Ah.' He wriggled his eyebrows. 'That's where I came in?'

'Yep.' Paige nodded. 'All four of us had felt trampled by men who had gone on living their lives quite merrily while we floundered around and after about two hours we'd hatched a plan. Each of us was going to get some revenge on someone else's ex. Bella got Astrid's ex. Astrid got Sienna's ex. Sienna got Harvey. And I got...'

Oliver finally wasn't smiling any more. 'Me.'

'Yes.' Paige swallowed. 'I'm not here because I had a last-minute gap in my living arrangements. I'm here for...'

His jaw tightened. 'Revenge?'

She shook her head. 'More like payback. Irritation by a thousand paper cuts.'

'Like what?' he asked, suddenly very, *very* still.

'Like...' She looked at the dark grey turtleneck she'd worn on the plane with her baggy black harem pants. 'My clothes. I don't wear bright, mismatched, charity shop clothes, I wear monochrome. Because it helps me blend into the background. And I'm not this scatty, hot mess who leaves coffee rings on furniture and loses the remote control every day. I mean, I'm *not* as anal as you,' she conceded, 'but I'm not kitchen chaos crumb girl either.'

Except maybe that was the true tragedy of all this. She'd felt more like herself this past couple of months than she had the last four years. A more exaggerated version for sure but truer to the woman she'd been *pre-Harvey*. That Paige had been fun and spontaneous. She'd been easy-going and quirky. And the last couple of months, she'd allowed herself to be that woman again. To be herself again.

Except now she had to go back.

'Not *ever* vegan either I'm assuming?'

'Nope.' She shook her head. 'Pavarotti was part of the charade. Casper too, although that happened organically, not deliberately. Same as the WI talk but I leaped on it because I knew it'd be the last thing you'd want to do. I know how to play violin really well and I don't think *Die Hard* is a Christmas movie. Hamster Facts? That was me.'

She could see things clicking into place behind the sudden wintery bleakness of his eyes. 'The second phone.'

'Uh huh.'

'So this is what Bella meant when I told her our relationship was complicated and she said *in more ways than you know*.'

'Yeah.'

He shook his head, his eyes locking with hers. 'Why?'

'You hurt her, Oliver.'

He gave a harsh laugh. 'You think I don't *know* that?'

'I think knowing it and truly understanding the *depth* of it, are two different things.'

He pushed off the table and stalked to the other side of the room before turning accusing eyes on her. 'So the four of you appointed yourselves judge and jury?'

Paige shut her eyes. She supposed they had, in a way. She could see how it would certainly feel like that being on the other end. Her eyelashes fluttered open. 'It seemed like a good idea at the time. Some harmless fun. Some... inconvenience for a while.'

He shook his head in disbelief. 'I don't know you at all, do I?'

His statement hit her like a cannon blast. Because the truth was, he *did* know her. She'd been more truthful and open with him than she'd been with anyone – even her three besties – in the last four years. And it was almost unbearable that he would think the opposite. Paige might not have been honest with Oliver about her reasons for being in his house, she may have adopted a different personality but those deeply personal things she'd told him had come from her deepest, darkest depths.

'All this time we spent together,' he continued, his voice taut with anger. 'All the talking and laughing and getting acquainted. Getting *naked*. And it was all just an *act*.'

Another blast hit its mark. Yes, her being in his life had been performative. But not all of it. Falling in love with him hadn't been an act. It didn't alter the circumstances, though. She swallowed. 'You weren't supposed to find out.'

'Right.' His lips twisted derisively. 'But you're wielding it now like a weapon because you're hoping it'll make me want nothing to do with you so you can run away and hide behind that peach emoji again. Unless... all that stuff was a lie too?'

Paige sucked in a breath as this shot almost cut her in two, the jagged edges raw and bleeding. 'I would *never*' – she faltered as her voice shook in a sudden spurt of outrage – 'lie about that.'

'Really?' he demanded. 'How would I know? I have no idea who the *real* Paige is.'

She deserved that but that didn't make it hurt any less. And she wanted nothing more than to persuade him to see it from her point of view. To beg his forgiveness. But he was right. This *was* what she'd wanted. To be able to walk away from here and all the potential of public exposure and go back to hiding *behind that peach emoji*.

So she needed to suck it up.

Lifting her chin, Paige looked him square in the eyes. She refused to trade any more blows with him or let him see just how affected she was by his words and the path she'd chosen to tread.

'Well, congratulations.' He clapped slow and hard for several beats. 'You got what you wanted. Now you can *leave*. I hope you're happy having a good laugh with your little karma club.'

Paige pressed her lips together to stop them from trembling as his disdain reached across the room. But he'd given her an out and she was taking it before she changed her mind. Legs shaking, she picked up Pavarotti's cage and, leaving everything else, she once again walked out of his house.

This time for good.

* * *

Two weeks. It took Oliver two weeks to simmer down. Two weeks of stewing and not walking and not writing. Hell, he barely ate or showered. He just lay on the couch in the media room, watching TV in the dark. Working his way through his alphabetised CD collection that Paige – *purposefully* and probably with *great relish* he realised now – had constantly messed with.

He didn't answer calls and didn't bother responding to messages, notifications or emails. He was far too pissed off to be pleasant to anybody. The only exception had been Doris who knocked on the beach-side door every day and refused to stop knocking until he answered that he was okay.

And then a text arrived from Paige.

Oliver glared at it for long moments, wanting to hurl his phone across the room but wanting to read it desperately. He suspected it would be her saying she was sorry because she sure as shit *hadn't* said it the day she'd told him the truth and despite telling himself he didn't care, a perverse part of him revelled in the idea of a grovelling apology.

His throat as dry as the three-day-old toast sitting on the crumb-covered coffee table, Oliver tapped on the text.

> Hi. Just emailed your document. I wasn't sure if you wanted anything to do with it straight away so I've left it til now.

She was right, the book had been the furthest thing from his mind as he'd wallowed in self-pity.

> It's good, Olly, you should keep going.

That was it. Three lousy sentences. Nothing remotely grovelling about it but it did have a weirdly soothing effect on the boiling acid that had been gurgling in his stomach for the past fortnight.

It's good, Olly, you should keep going.

It was the fourth time she'd called him Olly and he hated how much he liked it.

Rolling up into a sitting position, Oliver grabbed his laptop that hadn't been opened since Paige left. He winced at the bright light from the screen as he navigated to his inbox and located Paige's email. He opened the attachment straight away, a tiny hum of joy resonating deep inside at all the neatly ordered tabs Paige had set up.

He hadn't wanted to write in two weeks but looking at it now all laid out, ready to go, his mid buzzed with it again.

Minimising the document, he read the email.

Dear Oliver,

I'm writing this because I realise I never said sorry that day. About pretending to lose the document or about lying to you. That was remiss of me so I must now apologise twice. One the actual apology, the second time for not apologising in the first place.

So... sorry. And sorry.

I'm also sorry that I minimised your experiences over the years at the hands of tabloids and the paparazzi. That was particularly egregious and deserves special condemnation.

I've been thinking a lot these past couple of weeks about my passivity. And you're right. I have been punishing myself. So... if those images ever do come into the greater public domain I've decided I will make that stand. To turn them around in my favour and use them as a way to speak out against the crime of revenge porn. To become an advocate for people who have experienced it and lobby for meaningful change in the legal system. I don't expect it will be easy but things worth doing seldom are, right? And I might as well put that three quarters of a law degree to good use.

I don't know if I'd be brave enough to do it without my hand being forced – maybe one day. But the point is, I'm no longer terrified of what happens if it is. And I couldn't have got to this place without you giving me a push. So thank you for that.

I've also been thinking about what you said about our time together all being an act. I just want you to know that while a lot of what happened between us was manufactured, my feelings for you never were. I don't expect you to believe me, but it's the truth.

Lastly, I want to thank you for my time in Cornwall. I know I was there for all the wrong reasons but it was the first time in four years I actually got to be someone more closely resembling me again and for that I will forever be in your debt.

Love always,

Paige (the real one)

Oliver read the email over several times, feeling lighter and lighter each time. She was sorry. Her feelings *hadn't* been manufactured. And she'd signed it – love always.

Love always.

She'd told him she'd loved him the day she'd left but it had got lost in the avalanche of hurt that had followed her terrible revelations shortly after.

But she *had* said it. And so had he.

Something unlocked in his chest at the memory. And the

love he'd been denying, that he'd pushed away behind a wall of rage, rushed back in. He might have been angry at her and pissed off at what she'd done but love was hard to cancel out.

Apparently. He was just new to this thing.

Picking up his phone, he dialled a number that answered on the second ring. He didn't give the recipient a chance to get in a hello. 'I need Paige's address.'

'*Olly*, I've been calling you for days!'

'The address, Bella?'

She huffed into the phone. 'Why?'

'Because I love her and I know she loves me and I'm going to go and get her.'

'Good answer.'

* * *

Paige stared absently out of the window that looked out on the Royal Mile, a tiny sliver of the castle visible if she leaned right over in her chair and cocked her head to the side. As far as house-sitting gigs went, she'd had worse. Not that she'd been particularly appreciative of the view, preoccupied as she was with thoughts of Oliver and how badly it had all ended.

She'd finally given in to the urge to make contact with him two days ago but there'd been no reply. She knew he was okay because Doris had kept her UTD with her daily check-ins but part of her had hoped he might respond.

It was futile she knew after everything she'd done but hope sprang eternal, right?

Her phone vibrated at her elbow and Paige picked it up, absently opening the text from an unknown number. It was probably just a new client enquiry.

> Thank you for subscribing to LOVE FACTS! We'll be sending you regular updates about falling in love. To STOP, reply with STOP. To see more reply MORE. Standard messaging rates may apply.

Paige frowned at the screen, taking a second or two to compute the text. Love facts? A small, confused smile pulled at her lips. Was this... Oliver? She sat forward in her chair. Her finger hovered for a beat before she typed MORE and sent it off.

Ten seconds later, three little dots danced on the screen and she waited.

> Thank you for continuing LOVE FACTS! Did you know that love is addictive? When you fall in love your brain releases dopamine which is similar to a sugar rush, turning you into a love-junkie. To OPT OUT of these messages reply OPT OUT! To continue reply MORE. Standard messaging rates may apply.

Paige's smile grew bigger. If the fact was correct, she was in serious withdrawal mode right now. She tapped in MORE and sent it off.

> Thank you for continuing LOVE FACTS! Did you know that some people believe that Die Hard is a romance? And the other people are wrong? To agree press 1. Standard messaging rates may apply.

Paige laughed out loud and pressed 1. And waited again as the dots did their dance.

> Thank you for your response and continuing to engage with LOVE FACTS! Did you know a heart can actually break? Research shows that break-ups can cause real physical pains in the area of one's heart. This is known as Broken Heart Syndrome. Press 1 if you're experiencing something similar right now. Standard messaging rates may apply.

Did she know that? Paige sobered, she sure as hell did. She pressed 1 and sent it into the ether.

> Thank you for continuing to engage with LOVE FACTS! Did you know that some men will walk 500 miles to fall down at your door? To OPT OUT of these messages reply OPT OUT! To find out how many miles it is from Cornwall to Edinburgh reply MORE. Standard messaging rates may apply.

Paige blinked. Was he...? Her heart gave a funny little flutter in her chest as she dialled Oliver's number. He picked up on the first ring. 'Hi.'

There was a roughness to his tone like maybe he *had* just walked 500 miles and Paige's tummy also got the flutters. 'Where are you?'

'I told you,' he said, a smile in his voice. 'I'm at your door.'

For a second, Paige just stared in disbelief at the window then she leaped from her seat and ran. Across the room, down two flights of stairs, straight to the door, her breathing now as erratic as her heartbeat. Yanking it open, she found him standing there in jeans and a plaid jumper, smiling in the weak sunshine, looking ridiculously sexy.

'Hey.' He held up a zip lock bag containing her fridge magnets. 'I thought you might be missing these.'

Paige laughed. *Definitely not*. But she had missed him. She launched herself at him then and he laughed as he caught her, his hands under her ass, his mouth hot on hers as they kissed like no one was watching, instead of a significant number of people on the Royal Mile.

'I can't believe you're here,' Paige muttered, dragging her mouth off his, her hands cupping his face. He was real. He really was real.

'Believe it.'

She kissed him again until somebody passing by said in a thick Scottish brogue, 'Get a room, you two.'

They broke off, grinning at each other as Paige dragged him inside. 'I'm sorry,' she said as the door shut behind him and she stood on the first step to equalise their heights, sliding her arms around his neck. 'I'm so sorry.' She stared into his eyes. 'About the payback plan and lying to you and the whole bloody debacle.'

'I know.' He smiled. 'It's okay.'

'It's not.' Paige shook her head. 'But thank you. Mostly I just need you to know that I meant what I said in my email. I might have been faking a lot of things in Cornwall but my feelings, falling in love with you, were 100 per cent genuine.'

'I believe you.' He slid his arms around her waist. 'I've been thinking about it a lot the last couple of days and I can kinda understand the genesis of the whole payback thing. Who can blame you for wanting to get revenge on Harvey and how that might make a normally measured individual do something a little… out of the box.'

She laughed. 'That's one way of putting it.' She'd never underestimate the power of prosecco again, that was for sure.

'And, honestly, if you hadn't? We'd have never met. So I can hardly be mad about that.'

Looking into those blue Prendergast eyes, Paige couldn't fault his logic.

'All I care about right now,' he continued, 'is how much I've missed you and love you and don't ever want to be apart from you ever again. These last two weeks have been hell.'

Paige's system flooded with cool relief. She'd spent the fortnight convinced she'd blown it for good. 'I love you too,' she said, her chest filling up.

His arms tightened around her waist. 'Please say you'll come back to Cornwall with me when you finish here in a couple of weeks. Or if you don't want to live there, pick a place. As long as I'm with you, I don't care where we live. Wherever we are, I just want to love you to distraction.'

Paige wanted nothing more than to love him to distraction, too. Pressing her forehead lightly against his, she murmured, 'Cornwall is perfect.' She'd been reborn there in so many ways that it felt like her *spiritual* home.

'Cornwall it is,' he said with a smile.

They kissed then, long and deep. The distraction beginning in earnest.

EPILOGUE
FOUR MONTHS LATER...

Paige stared at the bound pages Olly had just passed over. He'd completed the biography two weeks ago and she hadn't read it yet. Not in its fully pieced-together form, anyway. And now it was in her hands, a wad of white paper containing months of his blood, sweat and tears, the bolded title in large font staring back at her on the top sheet.

A Complicated Man: Memories of My Father.

'You did it,' she said, smiling at him as he pulled out the chair at the end of the table and sat.

He smiled. 'Thanks to you.'

'Nope.' She shook her head. 'This is all you. I just—'

'Kicked my ass and told me to stop feeling sorry for myself.'

Laughing, Paige shook her head. 'Pushed you in the right direction.'

She glanced at the title again knowing how hard it had been for him to dig this deep and lay himself bare and loving him all the more for it. These past four months had been intense for them with the on-again, off-again scrutiny from paparazzi but it had only pushed them closer. Oliver's protection of her had been fierce and, as each day passed, she fell in love with him a little more.

'Well?' he demanded as she smoothed her hands over the title page. 'Are you going to read it?'

She nodded. 'It's a big moment.'

'Yep.'

As she flipped the page, the dedication jumped out at her.

To Bella, Sienna and Astrid – thank you. Without your scheming I never would have met the love of my life. And to Paige. I love you to distraction.

Silly tears pricked at her eyes as she smiled at him. 'I love you to distraction, too.'

A knock at the front door stopped her turning the page and they looked at each other. It had been a while since a pap had come calling but it was always the first thing either of them thought when a knock sounded.

Quickly, Oliver checked the app on his phone that linked to the camera he had installed at the front door the second they'd returned from Edinburgh. 'Not a photographer,' he said, turning his phone around to show Paige.

She frowned at the black-and-white image of a short, stocky woman, a very familiar-looking Border Collie by her side. They were both on their feet and haring down the hallway in seconds, Oliver yanking the door open as he reached it.

'Casper!' Paige exclaimed, crouching immediately as the dog pushed between them enthusiastically, yipping and wagging his tail, his butt squiggling in excitement.

The tears that had started at the table came back with a

vengeance as Paige hugged Casper's neck. She buried her face in the soft fur of his head on one side as Oliver buried his face in the other side.

She'd missed this sweet boy.

Belatedly realising they'd been neglecting their visitor, she stood. 'I'm so sorry, Sheila,' she said to the woman waiting patiently for the reunion to be over.

'It's okay, my lovely,' she assured as she pulled off her hat to reveal a fluff of magenta hair.

Paige blinked at it, a memory tweaking somewhere in her brain.

'I hope yer don't mind,' Sheila said. 'But he's been pining for yer, right terrible. I held on to him for as long as I could, trying to keep me promise to me da. But' – she gave Casper an affectionate pat – 'he really don't like those cats and he keeps escapin' and I find him trottin' along the road to St Ives and I reckon Da wouldn't mind me letting him go knowing how well you two took care of him.'

'We don't mind,' Paige assured quickly, joy in her heart. 'We'd love it.'

'Good then.' Sheila nodded. 'That's settled.'

They watched as Casper licked Oliver's face like he was made of Hobnob crumbs. 'Reckon he's found his next forever person,' Sheila said, her eyes on Paige. 'Don't you?'

Paige nodded and smiled. Casper had. And so had she.

*　*　*

MORE FROM THE KARMA CLUB

Another book in the Karma Club Series, *How to Get Even*, is available to order now here:

www.mybook.to/HowtoBackAd

ACKNOWLEDGEMENTS

As an author, you are occasionally gifted opportunities that have the potential to light up your world. If you're really lucky one or two might be projects that involve the ultimate combination – great writers and good friends.

I think it fair to say I got really lucky with this one and I have to thank, from the bottom of my heart, my fellow co-conspirators – Pippa Roscoe, Rachael Stewart and Clare Connelly. The synergy and excitement between us was buzzing from the get-go and although writing can often feel hard, working with these fabulous women was always easy. Even when this quartet of books went through a long and convoluted path to finding a home, none of us ever wavered in our belief in this series. We loved the concept from the start and were invested in our characters from the moment we dreamed them up. It's truly been an honour and a privilege.

We've been helped by many along the way, as is always the case when your book is published. And let me tell you, the panic that grips you at the thought you might leave someone out is real! Which is my way of saying, in advance, huge apologies if I miss anyone.

Thanks to all the team at Boldwood for their terrific work on this series. An interconnected, four-author series hasn't been done before but they embraced it with enthusiasm. For that I have to thank Megan Haslam who championed the series and eagerly ushered it into the Boldwood fold. Thanks also to the rest of the team – Amanda Ridout, Niamh Wallace, Clare Fenby, Wendy Neale and Ben Wilson. And, not forgetting Candida Bradford and Rachel Sargeant for their editing chops and the amazing people in production who went above and beyond!

Big thanks as ever to my agent, Jill Marsall.

Biggest thanks to my husband, Mark, who has also, by osmosis, lived the strange life of an author this past twenty years. It's been a bit of a bumpy ride from time to time but having him by my side supporting me through all the crazy has allowed me to reach for my goals and be the best writer I can be. I could probably have done it without him but I'm forever grateful that I don't have to.

ABOUT THE AUTHOR

Amy Andrews is an award-winning, USA Today best-selling, Australian author of over ninety contemporary romances.

Sign up to Amy Andrews' mailing list for news, competitions and updates on future books.

Follow Amy on social media here:

- facebook.com/AmyAndrewsAuthor
- x.com/AmyAndrewsbooks
- instagram.com/amyandrewsbooks
- tiktok.com/@amyandrewsbooks

ALSO BY AMY ANDREWS

Look What You Made Me Do

Breaking the Ice

Undercover Billionaire

The Karma Club Series

The Payback Plan by Amy Andrews

How to Get Even by Pippa Roscoe

The Puck Stops Here by Rachael Stewart

Settling the Score by Clare Connelly

Boldwood EVER AFTER
x♡x♡

JOIN BOLDWOOD'S **ROMANCE COMMUNITY** FOR SWEET AND SPICY BOOK RECS WITH ALL YOUR FAVOURITE TROPES!

SIGN UP TO OUR NEWSLETTER

HTTPS://BIT.LY/BOLDWOODEVERAFTER

Boldwood

Boldwood Books is an award-winning fiction publishing company seeking out the best stories from around the world.

Find out more at www.boldwoodbooks.com

Join our reader community for brilliant books, competitions and offers!

Follow us
@BoldwoodBooks
@TheBoldBookClub

Sign up to our weekly deals newsletter

https://bit.ly/BoldwoodBNewsletter